A Specter Is Haunting Texas

A Specter Is
Haunting Texas

by FRITZ LEIBER

WALKER AND COMPANY New York

First published as a book in the United States of America in 1969 by Walker and Company, a division of the Walker Publishing Company, Inc.

Published simultaneously in Canada by The Ryerson Press, Toronto.

First published in Galaxy Science Fiction in 1968.

Printed in the United States of America.

Table of Contents

1 / Terrible Terra

. . . fruitful plains, waving with amber grain, cattle-nurturing thornless cactus, the pseudopods of nutritious amoebas, and Lone Star flags.

Ever since Lyndon ousted Jack in the Early Atomic Age, the term of a President of Texas has been from inauguration to assassination. Murder is merely the continuation of politics by other means.

Power ennobles, but Petroleum Power ennobles absolutely.

The end of life is liberty. Texans are empowered to enjoy, exploit, and handle liberty, while Mexes, Injuns, and Nigras—all those having dark faces or a dark hole in their pocketbooks—have the privilege of serving liberty and keeping their hands off it.

Ego was made to be used. It rises from the dark unconscious, energizes awareness, and transforms society. It is the oilfields of the human personality.

Longhairs have less brains than longhorns, and less ability to stand on their own hind legs. Most Longhairs perished in the Atomic War, or were exiled to that sick-cow-corral, Circumluna, and her unspeakable udder, the Sack. Praise the Lord and puff the marijuana!

The Battles of the Alamo, San Jacinto, El Salvador, Sioux City, Schenectady, and Saskatchewan. . . .

—Random excerpt from *How to Stand and Understand Texans: Their Fantasies, Foibles, Folkways, and Fixed Ideas as Seen in Their Own Writings*, Nitty-Gritty Press, Watts-Angeles, Acificpay Ackblay Epublicray

"SON, YOU LOOK like a Texan what got the hormone, but been starved since birth. Like your Ma, Lyndon bless her, lifted a leg and dropped you into a big black bag, and after you nothing but a crust and a mini-carton of milk once a month."

"True enough, noble sir. I was raised in the Sack and I am a Thin," I answered the Portly Giant in a voice like distant thunder, which almost made me wet my tights, because up until this moment of my life I had been a high baritone.

My senses told me I was whirling at a punishing six lunagravs in a large cubical centrifuge. In fact, I could see the spinning and feel it in my inner ears until my senses gradually adjusted. On the same surface as I were two giants and a giantess in cowboy costumes and also three barefoot, hunchbacked, swarthy dwarfs in dirty shirts and pants. They were all poised expertly on their feet, riding the centrifuge with élan. While under my black hood and cloak I was doubled up like a large bone-and-titanium lazy tongs, trying to make the left knee motor of my exoskeleton behave, it either hunted wildly or wouldn't respond at all to the myoelectric impulses from the ghost muscles of my left leg.

I realized that the Portly Giant must have seen me without my cloak, which now might be hiding an erect short Fat as readily as a folded tall Thin.

I was hazy about how I'd debarked from the *Tsiolkovsky*. When the Longhairs dope you to take accelerations of twenty-four lunagravs, they don't use aspirin—even when you're sandwiched between water mattresses.

But I knew that outside the centrifuge lay the spaceport and city of Yellowknife, Canada, Terra.

The centrifuge's two ends and two adjoining sides (but which were which?) were covered with a child-simple mural of huge chalk-white cowboys on horses like elephants chasing tiny lipstick-red Indians on ponies like Chihuahua dogs across a cactus-studded landscape. This battle of cockroaches and behemoths was signed with a huge "Grandma Aaron." The figures and scene seemed as inappropriate for frosty Yellowknife as my companions' costumes, which should have been parkas and snowshoes.

But who is a greenhorn, who has lived all his life in free fall a few thousand miles from Mother Luna, to pronounce on the customs of Terrible Terra?

The opposite surface was crowded with dazzling sunbursts, like a star cluster going nova.

In one of the adjoining surfaces were two rectangular openings side by side. Each was three feet wide, but one was more than ten feet long, the other less than five. I peered into them in vain to see stars or sections of Terra whipping past, but the rectangles were only hatches leading into another part of the centrifuge. Why there were two, and so different in shape and size, where one would have done, I couldn't imagine.

As I tried to coax my knee motor properly alive and felt the six centrifugal lunagravs cruelly press the support bands of my exoskeleton into my skin and bones at armpits, thighs, crotch, et cetera, I asked myself: "If this is what they use to toughen you up for Terra, what will Terra's naked surface be like?"

Meanwhile, I spoke aloud in the same almost inaudibly deep voice-from-grave, which indeed fitted my appearance of a black-shrouded burial mound with the central bump of my hooded head. I asked, "Kindly direct me to the Yellowknife Registry of Mining Claims."

The Portly Giant regarded me with benign interest. That one really rode the centrifuge with serenity; I marveled at his ability to handle so casually a mass at least five times my own *with* exoskeleton. The three shoulder-bent dwarfs peered apprehensively from close behind him, fear frowns furrowing their low foreheads under their greasy black hair. The Square Giant—I called him that because he was all sharp shoulder and jaw angles, like William S. Hart of ancientest cinema—glanced up suspiciously from my open luggage.

The Giantess went into a tizzy.

"There you go again!" she whined. "I try to hostess you the best I can. After all, you're our first visitor from space in a hundred years. But you keep booming at me like all the rest of them fearful furry Russians and drumming Afric foreignors. And you keep booming mysteries. Where in the name of Jack is Yellowknife?"

She had long yellow hair outside and big tits, or their simulacra, inside her quasi-military, mini-skirted cowgirl costume, but her fluttery stupidity was flattening my libido as well as my sanity. I recalled my father telling me that drum majorettes had been one of the chief ruinations of Terra, along with female-clad Communist athletes of whichever sex.

"Here!" I thunder-rumbled from my hood. "Right here, where the *Tsiolkovsky* debarked me on direct orbit from Circumluna. Incidentally, I'm not Russian, but of Anglo-Hispanic ancestry, though it's true there are as many Russians as Americans in Circumluna."

"The *Tchaikovsky* debarked you all right—in a stretcher, in case you've forgotten, and all wrapped up in that black blanket, like a candidate for a coffin. Say, what are Mericans? Ancient greasers? But what I mostly meant to ask you was: Where do you think *here* is?"

"*Tsiolkovsky!*" I thunder-corrected. My new double-base voice was making me nasty. "Great space pioneer, not gay composer of slurpy music. And Americans. A-m-e-r-i-c-a-n-s. While *here*," I thunder-crashed, "is Spaceport Yellowknife, Northwest Territory, Canada, Terra!"

"Name of Jack and Jackie!" she wailed, clapping her hands to her ears. "Where and what is Canada?"

The Square Giant looked up again and asked ominously, "Stranger, why does your luggage consist chiefly of forty-seven isotopic and lithium-gold batteries of the sort used in portable power weapons?"

"They're spares for my exoskeleton," I tossed him, while at the Giantess I rumbled scornfully, "Don't they teach you any geography on this planet? You a space hostess!"

"It's you don't know geography," she whimpered back at me, still holding her ears. "Up there in space, jumping from star to star and never caring which. Gun you, you're making me cry, you animated black laundry basket!" Whereupon very large tears did begin to plop from the inner corners of her blue eyes.

If only the centrifuge would stop, I thought. I could no longer see spin, but I was whirling inside.

"Stranger, what class of weapon is an X-O-Skeleton?" the Square Giant demanded, his mouth and eyes thinning to slits. "And watch your language when conversing with a cultured lady."

"You'll find out when you're kicked by one!" I snarled, meaning Faithful Old Titanium, not that female boob. "Cultured lady!" I continued zestfully. "Cultured in an algae vat! You yeast brain, how can you and that right-angle cowpoke mention culture when you confuse satellites with stellar furnaces, don't know where Canada is, don't understand the needs of a Thin visiting a solar-gravity satellite, and are unfamiliar with well-known prosthetic devices?"

The Giantess began to blubber. The fright frowns deepened and rose in the dwarfs' foreheads, their greasy hair stirred, and their flight muscles tightened.

The Square Giant whipped from his belt a lightning pistol I knew could numb or fry me, according to how much power he used. He took a step toward me and barked, "Hand over that X-O-Skeleton, stranger, without you cock it. And whatever other weapons you're hiding under that black sarape. Everything down to hatpins and penknives is confiscated at the Republic's borders—you'll get claim checks. But don't make any sudden movements!"

The tension sizzled. I stayed squat-crouched under my cloak and prepared to spit more insults from my hood. In fact, something violent might well have happened, most likely to me, if the Portly Giant hadn't intervened.

That one said in resonant, relaxed tones that muffed not a word (I'd been suspecting he was a fellow actor), "Simmer down, all of you, for Lyndon's sake, that secular saint of peace. There's been some natural mistakes made and some natural tempers roused. Bill, go easy with that shock-spitter, and Suzy, sweetheart, dry your tears and unsnuffle that cute little nose of yours.

"Scully," he addressed me, "Scully—for that's what you look like from what I can glimpse of your face, a sort of sensitive-featured skull. No offense intended! My own handle's Elmo and I'm as fat as and got a face like a hog cross-bred with a hyena. But well, Scully, I'm afraid that they truly didn't teach you quite all of modern geography up there in the sky. Yep, there's a few things that been happening here and there on this little old planet during the century you been sailing around the moon in your ivory tower with its attendant soap bubbles.

"Because there *is* a Yellowknife, you see, Scully, but now we call it Amarillo Cuchillo, and it's situated in Northern Texas. While Canada is a gone land, like Sumeria or Burgundy or Vietnam."

A cold and dizzy feeling—as if I hadn't been centrifuged dizzy enough—touched me. A feeling of history altering like the colors in a kaleidoscope and no patch of reality sure. I already knew, you see, that my father, who taught me everything, was weak on recent Terran geography and history, though expert in historical dramas and overall theory; he would wave at Spengler's dog-eared accordion-opened *Decline of the West* floating by our bookrack, then through the curving wall of the Sack at Terra splendid against the stars, and say, "They are all fellahin down there, Christopher, all of them. Fellahin swarming like moths over the embers of dead cultures. Ah, tomorrow and tomorrow and tomorrow creeps in this petty pace from day to day." (What is moths?) A picturesque and even ego-inflating generality, especially to one living a quarter of a million miles or so from Earth, but admittedly weak on details.

And now at last I was learning just *how* weak.

I looked up apprehensively at Elmo as the Portly Giant continued, "And I'm afraid, Scully, that the Russo-Yankee officers of the *Tsiolkovsky* are a little feeble on modern politico-geography too, because where they landed you—namely, here—is some two thousand miles south of Amarillo Cuchillo. Scully, my friend, you have the honor of being in Dallas, Texas, Texas—the heart of the human universe and the golden laurel crown of her culture."

"Texas includes Canada?" I asked in a quavering bass. "Is an independent nation?"

"Scully, I hate to voice the least criticism of a man's educational background—shucks, there's been notable brains 'mongst refugees from New York City College and Berkeley —but I do believe your heavenly geography instructors have been notably remiss and maybe—no offense meant here neither—touched with black or Slavic bias.

"Scully, son, ever since the Great Texasward Industrial Migration and World War Three, Texas has extended from the Nicaraguan Canal to the North Pole, including most of Central America, all of Mexico, nearly all of Canada, and all that matters of the Flibberty-gibbet Forty-seven—I mean, the former United States of America.

"That is, at present. We Texans might take a fancy to extend our boundaries any day. There's Cuba to be reconquered, and Indochina, and Ireland, and Hawaii, and Hither Siberia.

"But on the whole, we Texans are a peaceable, tolerant, shoot-and-let-shoot people. We whipped the Cherokees and the Mexicans and we tied the Russians and Chinese, and we're inclined to rest on our laurels—unless, of course, roused, when we get dynamic as an automated cotton-picking rig goosed by the program for an Irish jig.

"But as for being independent, let me tell you, Scully my boy, Texas is the goldurnedest independentest nation in the entire annals of political science. Nobody, bar some wise old Hellenes, really understood what individual freedom meant until Texas came along. But anyhow, welcome to Texas, Scully, welcome to God's Planet! Welcome down from the vastness of space, *amigo*—though you know, Scully, there's really more functional space in Texas than there is in the entire twiddling universe of free fall and galaxies and other foolishness. So, in Lyndon's name, lift yourself up from that black heap you're in, boy, and put her here!"

(Now I was sure he was an actor, though of ancient oratorical school.)

He advanced, followed closely, like timid children, by the swarthy dwarfs, and held out toward me a big open hand.

I did not respond, though truly touched by his hammy hospitality. (At heart all actors are hams and love it.)

I was simply too tired and dizzy.

For many minutes I had been balancing hunched-crouched in a souped-up crazy house of a centrifuge that was making my brain woozy as well as drowning my meager flesh in fatigue poisons. I had been fumbling futilely with tiring fingers at my balky knee motor. I had been forcing my aching diaphragm to drag into my burning lungs an atmosphere like yeast stew flavored with hydrogen sulfide. I had been putting up with rude nonsense from a dithery female and a fake-cowboy baggage inspector. I was still groggy from antigrav drugs and bone-crushing, organ-popping accelerations aboard the *Tsiolkovsky*.

I had become deadly sick of Terra while they were still getting me ready for her.

So now this news that I'd been stranded two thousand gravity-paved miles from my destination was the last weight, you might say, in my centrifuge training belt. (The centrifuge in Circumluna only builds up to two lunagravs and I'd weighted my exoskeleton to make it nearer earth-grav.)

"My unfolded handle is Elmo Oil-field Earp, lineal descendant of the noted gunslinger," the Portly Giant coaxed. "What's yours, Scully?"

At that instant a second female waltzed into our section of the centrifuge through the shorter of the two side-by-side hatches. At sight of her, my spirits skyrocketed as if I'd just got simultaneous shots of speed-euphorin in seven different veins or been invited by Idris McIllwraith into her cubicle to help her dress for Eve in Shaw's *Back to Methuselah* or Mary Sperling in Heinlein's *Children of Methuselah*. What is it that some girls have can turn me on, while the yellow-haired, tearful, sincere, big-tit Susies can extinguish me? I know—sex.

This new girl was dark, like the hunchbacked dwarfs, and she wasn't too much more than four feet tall, but she carried herself as if she were ten, her back flagstaff-straight with her glossy black hair for a banner. She had a form like a scaled-down Venus de Milo. She was shod with gleaming black slippers, heels almost as high as her dainty feet were long. A red skirt swirled around her black-netted dancer's legs, a yellow blouse bared her coffee-and-cream shoulders, while her dark eyes snapped bright black light as castanets do bright black sound.

I was so taken with her mere looks that I forgot to admire the skill with which she moved gracefully across areas having different acceleration vectors.

And then she gave it to me. The eye, I mean. Yes, she halted in midtwirl and she looked at me—yes, at miserable me, huddled under my cloak like a sick, giant spider monkey —and then her delicious eyes were fixed on my hooded, deep-socketed ones and glowing love into me, while her previously saucy lips were parted in a rapt smile of delight, as if I were the answer to some extremely private dream she'd been having ever since the first downy shiver of puberty.

My depression vanished like black magic routed by the White Goddess leading a train of nymphomaniac nymphs.

What were six lunagravs? Terra was mine! I was the Count of Monte Cristo—a part I have twice played.

Still operating wholly under my cloak, I untelescoped slim canes from my titanium exo-forearm-bones, and with them and my good leg pushed myself erect and then still more erect until my head was on a level with those of the giants. The dwarfs' eyes, steadily widening, followed me up. I noted that, although they were of different original heights, the dwarfs were all shoulder-bent to an equal four and a half feet—an odd detail.

Once fully erect—now I topped the giants by a half-head —I pushed down bolts to lock both knee joints of my exoskeleton and stood on my two feet only, my exolegs rigid rods from ankle to hip. Though teetery, it was practical; the taller the object, the easier it is to balance. I quickly retelescoped my canes—had Bill the Square Giant glimpsed them, he would have surely cried, "Concealed weapons!"

Meanwhile Elmo was calling to my vest-pocket Carmen, "Well, it's about time, Kookie. You better have those reefers or I'll turn you up and tan your Persian-rose-petal hide. Oh, Scully, this is La Cucaracha, one of my sociable secretaries. Kookie, this is my bosom friend, Scully, from outer space. Treat him as you would the President of Texas before he went crackers."

Ignoring these rude and boisterous, though apparently well-meant remarks, I stepped out swiftly and reached my dark lovely one in three long strides and bowed until my hooded face was level with hers. Considering I had no knees at the time, it was a remarkable performance, putting my black-shrouded butt a couple of feet higher than my head. My myoelectricity was tuning my stiff-kneed exoskeleton to perfection. It was truly a grand gesture, executed with ultimate poise and panache.

Thrusting a hand from my cloak, I plucked hold of her dainty one as if it were a dark orchid—and it was, ah, velvet-surfaced, manipulative multiwand!

"Señorita Cockroach *sublima*," I rumbled throatily (and

even the muted thunder of my rumble didn't faze her), "I am Christopher Crockett La Cruz, totally at your service!" And I drew the captured bloom into my hood and showered kisses on it.

She, in the intervals of a flattered laugh and with much rippling of long black eyelashes, whispered toward my ear in a voice very fast and businesslike, though tender, "At moonrise tonight, *amado.* At the bandstand corner of the cemetery, *querido mío.* Until then—*silencio!*"

It is the proper function of woman to attend to the practical details of affairs of the heart.

Assured by her words that I was not only loved but desired, I put into my obediently whispered "*Sí, sí, sí*" the hiss of a lovestruck micrometeorite whizzing through the self-sealing duraplast of one of the eggs forming the Sack.

Then I returned her hand to her with a flourish, unjack-knifed to normal height, and turned toward the others.

I felt as if I had just magnificently rendered one of Hamlet's soliloquies or Cyrano's tirades and the applause was about to break from the double curving walls of our free-fall theater-in-the-sphere in the largest bubble of the Sack. An inner voice said, "Stop your skulking masquerade, Scully-Christopher. Show yourself fully to these miserable earthlings and your dainty beloved."

With a Dracula batwing swirl, I threw back my black cloak and hood, flashing their scarlet linings, and waited for the gasps of admiration.

Suzy wailed, "Holy Halloween," vanished her large blue irises upward, and fainted. As he caught her, Bill yelled, "What'd I tell you? He's got power armor!" The three dwarfs jumped backward and I do believe would have dashed in terror from the room except that Elmo reached behind him and neatly collared them, meanwhile scowling at me incredulously. One of the captured dwarfs quavered, "La Muerte Alta!" Another gasped, "El Espectro!" The third stuttered, "El Esqueleto!"

Being called a tall death, a specter, and a skeleton irked

me greatly. To have people scared of one (unless the part calls for it) when one is a fine loving chap and, for lagniappe, a great actor, is most irritating.

But before saying anything cutting, anything with acid in it, I put myself in their places and rapidly looked at me.

They were looking, I discovered, at a handsome, shapely, dramatic-featured man, eight feet eight inches tall and massing 147 pounds with and ninety-seven pounds without his exoskeleton. Except for relaxed tiny bulges of muscle in forearms and calves (latter to work lengthy toes, useful in gripping), this man was composed of skin, bones, ligaments, fasciae, narrow arteries and veins, nerves, small-size assorted inner organs, ghost muscles, and a big-domed skull with two bumps of jaw muscle. He was wearing a skintight black suit that left bare only his sunken-cheeked, deep-eyed, beautiful tragic face and big, heavy-tendoned hands.

This truly magnificent, romantically handsome, rather lean man was standing on two corrugated-soled titanium footplates. From the outer edge of each rose a narrow titanium T-beam that followed the line of his leg, with a joint (locked now) at the knee, up to another joint with a titanium pelvic girdle and shallow belly support. From the back of this girdle a T-spine rose to support a shoulder yoke and rib cage, all of the same metal. The rib cage was artistically slotted to save weight, so that curving strips followed the line of each of his very prominent ribs.

A continuation of his T-spine up the back of his neck in turn supported a snug, gleaming head basket that rose behind to curve over his shaven cranium, but in front was little more than a jaw shelf and two inward-curving cheek-plates stopping just short of his somewhat rudimentary nose. (The nose is not needed in Circumluna to warm or cool air.)

Slightly lighter T-beams than those for his legs reinforced his arms and housed in their terminal inches his telescoping canes. Numerous black, foam-padded bands attached this whole framework to him.

A most beautiful prosthetic, one had to admit. While to expect a Thin, or even more a Fat, from a free-fall environment to function without a prosthetic on a gravity planet or in a centrifuge would be the ultimate in cornball ignorance.

Eight small electric motors at the principal joints worked the prosthetic framework by means of steel cables riding in the angles of the T-beams, much like antique dentist's drills were worked, I've read. The motors were controlled by myoelectric impulses from his ghost muscles transmitted by sensitive pickups buried in the foam-padded bands. They were powered by an assortment of isotopic and lithium-gold batteries nesting in his pelvic and pectoral girdles.

"Did this fine man look in the least like a walking skeleton?" I demanded of myself outragedly. "Well, yes, *very much so,*" I had to admit now that I had considered the matter from the viewpoint of strangers. A very handsome and stylish skeleton, all silver and black, but a skeleton nonetheless, and one eight feet eight inches tall, able to look down a little even at the giant Texans around him.

I realized now that my anger and my inability to see myself as others see me was because Father and Mother had found nothing morbid or eerie about me in my new, silvery antigrav prosthetic—nor had the Longhairs who had constructed it for me in return for free performances of *Hamlet,* *Macbeth,* and *Manhattan Project,* two jam sessions, and one "Dance of the Seven Veils" by Idris McIllwraith, the Sack's perennial sex-star, who is a Thin like me and looks like the ancient high-fashion model Teeny (Twilly? Twiggy?) drastically slimmed down, yet has much appeal. I ask her once a month to marry me, but although granting occasional favors, she refuses me on the silly grounds that she is thrice my age. Who dies in free fall?

I glanced down at my newer love, the sublime La Cucaracha, and she was gazing up at me and my exoskeleton with as fond approval as my parents, and with something spicy added. But when I made to bow to her again and perhaps hear more exciting whispers about our coming rendezvous, she twinkle-toed away, drawing from a fancy pack a long, very thin, pale-brownish cigarette.

"Scully Christopher Crockett La Cruz," Elmo meanwhile hailed me from where he stood talking with Bill, while still collaring the three dwarfs. Suzy had sat up from her faint and was looking at me with a thin-lipped disapproval that I connected with the attentions I had showered on La Cucaracha.

"That Crockett's a good Texas handle," Elmo continued. "Deepens my friendship for you, boy. Anyhow, Scully, I been considering your problems. There's a northbound cargo jet loading might lift you to Amarillo Cuchillo, but she mayn't take off for a week—we Texans conduct our commerce in a relaxed fashion. So Bill here has agreed to release you into my custody, and you and I are going to pay a little visit on the Governor of Texas, Texas—and what he can't expedite, nobody else can even budge.

"Besides, it ain't every day we get a spaceman. Governor bound to want to hear the gossip about the long-interdicted lands in the sky. Who can tell, they might turn out to be far-flung fragments of Texas.

"Scully, you can't refuse—you're going to experience Texas hospitality if I have to tie you up and have my greasers lug you.

"Now jump for his baggage, you black-hearted little *conquistadores*, or I'll sell you for cyborgs!" He released the three bent-backs, while to my darling he called, "Light me that stick now, Kookie, *pronto*, or I'll return your wardrobe to the theater man for refund, all but one medieval onion sack."

I hate to be pushed around, especially by big-brotherly shoves, nor did I care for the language Elmo directed at my new nymph, but his proposition seemed the best for me. Especially since I did not intend to leave Dallas before getting my gravity legs and—Eros ensure!—keeping my moon-cued rendezvous. For even now as the little one grasped Elmo's wide belt, nimbly vaulted onto his slightly bent huge thigh, and hung the smoldering slim cigarette on his long loose lip, she gave a quick conspiratorial smile and eyelash ripple telling of impending raptures.

Elmo took a long fluttering inhalation of marijuana vapor, his eyes going first glassy, then fever-bright as he called out, "Now forward hop, you greasers all! Come on, Scully, let's skedaddle."

The three dwarfs now each carried a black, silver-banded cushion case containing chiefly my food concentrates and spare batteries, my winter clothing and wigs. They still snatched fearful glances at me. As I followed Elmo toward the ten-foot door, they marched through the shorter door, each of the three barely missing bumping his head on the lintel, while my brunet darling scampered through behind them, her head held high.

Why their backs were variously bent, and hers not at all, was instantly clear to me.

The enormity of the revelation, plus my hunting for vector changes in the centrifuge's floor and still not finding them, must have caused me to take short, shuffling steps with my temporarily kneeless five-foot legs, for Elmo looked back and exclaimed, "Scully, son, you're walking like the first time on stilts or like you got paresis. Maybe our Mexican door sort of startled you. It's one of those charming, deeply mused Texan customs that make our glorious way of life possible. You see, Scully, a man can't feel really free unless he's got a lot of underfolk to boss around. That's one of the great paradoxes of liberty, first discovered by those proto-Texans, the ancient Greeks, who had slaves to burn, though I don't think they actually burned them much until Nero's day, or maybe the discovery of gasoline, which permitted Deep South lynching bees and Buddhist immolations alike.

"Incidentally, Scully, I'd appreciate it if you'd button up that cloak of yours and resume your hood. Mexes are superstitious little buggers. Even when cyborged, their odd primitive fears short-circuit through. I got my three boys calmed temporarily—and La Kook's a cool little bitch—but I wouldn't want you causing a riot in Dallas. History proves that the first time a man goes down the streets of Dallas, anything can happen to him, frequently bad."

I complied with his suggestion, but made no verbal retort, contenting myself with giving him a grim look, sucking in my cheeks to increase the skull-like appearance of my head, and stepping out after him recklessly.

"A vigorous paresis, I got to admit," he commented.

Ahead of him another pair of doors began to slide open, letting in sunny brightness and flashes of movement, and I braced myself for transition from centrifugal force to gravity.

2 / Dallas, Texas, Texas

When the scientific, engineering, and paramilitary communities of the international mega-satellite Circumluna were ordered to carry World War 3 into space, they refused, relying on their charters from the United Nations. In desperation and reprisal, the warring powers below repudiated the United Nations, clapped embargoes on all shipments of food, fuels, metals, medicines, and other supplies to Circumluna, and outlawed their rebellious nationals there. The Circumlunans, who effectually controlled the space fleets and were on the verge of achieving a self-sufficient economy based on raw materials from the Moon, declared their independence. This action of "the Longhairs" was enthusiastically received by the even longer-haired space-vagabonds—originally hippies, beatniks, mods, dropouts, stilyagi, actors, writers, pachucos, apaches, gypsies, and other quaintly styled rebels—parasitic on (or symbiotic with; accounts differ) the respectable Circumlunans and living in their hive of duraplastic bubble homes pendant on Circumluna and known as the Sack. For five generations there was no commerce and little communication between Terra and Circumluna, due to the latter's focus on survival and to the cultural upheavals and impoverished economy below after World War 3 killed its billion and fizzled out. When the Interdict, as it came to be called, was lifted one hundred years later, the first Circumlunans and "Sackabonds" to plumb the gravity well and visit Earth were a surprise to its inhabitants, but the centuries-alienated spacefolk found Terra a still greater shock.

—*Mother Earth, Father Space: A Short History of Circumluna,* by John Washington and Ivan Alapin

I TEETERED INTO blazing sunlight and a huge scene that was whirling around with me twenty times a minute, one full revolution every three seconds for the dozens of Texas giants I now saw, the hundreds of glass-and-metal living volumes, the thousands of rapidly moving Mexicans—most of these with massive metal collars from which rose small antennae—and even the blue sky, the marshmallow clouds, and the blinding disk of the sun.

The entire universe had become a vast centrifuge and I one mote spinning near its center, an axis a dozen yards above my head. I staggered and reeled on my stilt legs, waiting for the sky to burst and the cosmos to rip apart from the incredible centrifugal forces tearing at it.

Then I realized my error and the scene stopped spinning with a suddenness that almost knocked me down.

What I had been interpreting as centrifugal force back in the room muraled with Indians and Texans had been only normal Earth gravity.

I learned in that instant that you can endlessly *explain* to a person who's lived all his life in free fall that human senses cannot distinguish between the effects of acceleration, with which he's familiar, and gravity, of which he's had no experience. You can *tell* him that until your voice fails. No matter, he'll still go on believing that gravity will *feel* different, that it will grab him with invisible gluey fingers, that it will have in it the taint of unimaginable cubic miles of soil, rock, magma, incandescent core material, and other dirty planetary horrors.

No sooner had I been experience-educated out of one illusion than I became the victim of another: I felt I had returned to airless space.

When a man who has lived all his life in a nullgrav satellite, a large but limited homeland of many rooms, steps outdoors for the first time on a planet, one of his strongest immediate reactions is to hold his breath. Not from wonder and amazement, though they are there, but because the only comparable situation he knows is that of a man plunged into the vastness of space without an air supply. Ignoring the ground under his feet and the gravs pressing him to it, he will automatically see the unbounded sky as vacuum and any buildings around him as pressurized volumes to which he must win his way in seconds, or die.

I held my breath.

But I did not run, or—the actual impulse, to follow which would have resulted in my barking my nose on Texas—launch myself in an intended straight-line trajectory at the nearest window or door. Perhaps my first bit of experience-education made the second come quicker. Though still staggering about, I exhaled violently and forced myself to draw a lungful of the soupy air, stinkier now that we were outside. Besides discovering that I was in anything but vacuum, I also realized the explanation for my deep voice. All my life, even in the *Tsiolkovsky*, I had been breathing a light oxygen-helium mix with small amounts of carbon dioxide and water vapor. Now I was subsisting on a thick witch's brew of the same oxygen, but stewed in gravity's pressure cooker with nitrogen and assorted taints. A heavier atmosphere, a deeper voice. As obvious as that—but only after it's happened to you.

I looked around and down, to see that under La Cucaracha's directions Elmo's three servants had dropped my bags and were circling me as I reeled, ready to break my fall when I finally toppled.

Elmo called back cheerily, "You drunk, partner? Didn't know the super-refreshing open air of Texas was *that* intoxicating to the uninitiated. But I forget you're a Sackabond, reared on a little denatured oxygen and perfume."

As I steadied myself, a whole gaggle of new little Mexicans came scurrying all around me, a couple of the tiniest ones even tugging at my cloak, and most of them calling up to me, *"Bendiganos, padre!"* They were a raggedy, colorful lot, chiefly women and children, and none of them, praise Diana, wore those disgusting metal neck-and-shoulder pieces.

I'm enough of an actor to ad-lib any role I'm thrust into,
so I stuck two fingers out of my cloak, made a squiggle
with them, and rumbled benignly, *"Benedicite, mis niños y
niñas,"* adding for good measure, "Bless you, my children."

It seemed natural enough for them to mistake me, with
my robe and hood, for a tall priest or monk, maybe a Black
Franciscan.

My ready response to their request seemed to satisfy
them fully, for they were already scampering off when
Elmo boomed, "Get away from the god-man before you trip
him with your rosaries, you church-struck little greasers!
Scully, you're a card, but we got to make tracks for the
Governor's ranch house. Are you over your dizziness
enough to ride a horse?"

I was about to respond, "Yes, of course. You think I'm a
sissy, *hombre?"* when a feeling of dizziness and weakness
did strike me. A steady six lunagravs and assorted startle-
ments had been getting in their licks on my somewhat delicate physiology. My heart was pounding as it pumped
blood to my brain—no small job, considering my height and
the gravs. I was glad I was wearing an extra-snug Sack suit,
to help my leg veins from going varicose and maybe even
popping as they pushed blood up that weary distance from
my toes.

I tongued pep, instant glucose, and antigrav pills out of
their cheekplate container into my mouth. Even the tiny
dissolving pellets seemed heavy as osmium on my tongue,
and they dropped down my throat like bullets. I followed
them with a sip of truly heavy water from my other cheekplate, tilting my exoskulled head to do so. They quickly
helped. La Cucaracha beamed up at me her congratulations, as if she already knew my inner feelings as well as I
did.

By that time, however, Elmo had a twenty-foot whip
uncoiled and was cracking it over a low narrow vehicle
somewhat longer than I was. It rode on two caterpillar
treads moved by ten wheels. The wheels fascinated me;

except in pictures or employed as pulleys, one never sees wheels in Circumluna, where there is no gravity to put teeth in friction.

Off the vehicle were scrambling a couple of dozen Mexicans, including some of those who had received my benediction, while Elmo was shouting relaxedly, "Get off that cat wagon *pronto,* you fun-loving, irresponsible little monkeys! The Black Pope here needs it. I'll see it gets back to your *patrón.*" Then to me he said, "Climb aboard, Scully, and stretch out your weary exoskeleton. Ordinarily we don't let Mexes use power cars, but a cat wagon's no more than a toy. However, it's just what the metallurgical osteopath ordered for you. I can tell you're too frazzled to mount a steed yet, and come to think of it, I don't suppose they have too many cayuses in Circumluna, and those pretty spiritless."

Oddly, he was right about that. CL did have a few horses for old-style serum factories and on the Noah's Ark principle.

I started to tell him I was splendidly unfrazzled and eager to learn the art of horsemanship but my heart was still pounding a bit, so I decided to conserve energy and keep my attention free for the weird sights around me. I did another of my stiff-kneed bows, braced my hands on an end of the cat wagon, transferred my feet to the other end, let myself down on my face, and then rolled over with a minimum of exoskeletal clankings.

My heart quieted now that my circulatory system wasn't fighting gravity as hard. I felt better, except that I couldn't see much besides the sky. I raised my head and scanned.

Elmo had coiled his whip and was hooking it to his silver-studded leather belt, which also supported two lightning pistols. Otherwise he was dressed in what I took to be a conservative Terran business suit, complete with cuffs, buttons, lapel, collar, and great sky-colored tie depicting bluebonnet flowers, but on his feet were huge, high-heeled leather boots and on his head a six (twelve? factorial four?) -gallon hat.

He was astride a horse as huge, relatively, as he was. I marveled at the bone and muscle power of both—his to mount and the beast's to carry. In fact, for a moment I toyed with the notion that he had an exoskeleton under his suit, and the animal a surgically implanted steel one.

He noted my gaze and said, "Yep, Scully, we feed our mounts the hormone too. Next to Texans, they're God's noblest creation. And now you might punch the cat wagon's first go-button at your elbow. The lever next it steers her."

I complied and our small cavalcade started off at a pace brisk to me, a novice driver. Elmo merely walked his horse ahead of us, but its strides were long and smooth. Just behind him La Cucaracha jounced on a burro—now I understood those disproportionate murals better. My darling rode sidesaddle and regaled me with frequent smiles over-shoulder, while to the rear Elmo's three Mexicans jogged with my bags. There was a disproportion I could correct.

"Señor Elmo," I called, "tell your boys to throw my bags on the wagon and hop aboard themselves. There'll be no overload—despite my metal, I mass low."

"That's out, Scully," he boomed back. "Can't have greasers riding with anything Texas-tall, no mind how skinny or strange. Myself, I been around and tolerate indecencies, but 'twould shock Dallasians spitless."

"I want the bags for pillows," I explained, "so I can study Dallasian salivation, et cetera, besides scan the road."

"Then that's okay. But the other's out. Peel your eyes, partner. You got a lot more to see than Texas Adam's apples bobbing. Hey, you greasers, comfort my guest's cerebrum with his luggage!"

I was inclined to argue longer with him about them riding, but the three Mexicans gave me such apprehensive glances as they trembling-handed tucked my bags in a soft stack under my head, and seemed so eager to return to their rear-guard position, that I decided to postpone any equalitarian lecture. However, the frightened behavior of the three nagged at me.

There was indeed much to see, most of it crazy to me, like a 3-D motion montage with volumes moving at different camera speeds, and most of it jammed into a single plane—truly Terra is flatland. First there were the buildings, like cubical satellites crowded in disordered ranks, some many rooms long—no, high . . . on end—and made of metal and glass, reminding me of Circumluna. Between these went occasional gangways—streets—on one of which we traveled. Then there were the Texans, some on horses, others in slowly moving vehicles, others strolling afoot. The younger seemed even taller than the older—I wondered if the hormone had a cumulative effect.

Moving about thrice as fast and in numbers a decimal order greater were the Mexicans, all of identical bent-back height and almost all afoot. About sixty percent wore the metal collars and antennae, and these were all furiously busy at various construction and deconstruction jobs; half of our street was torn up, buildings were being dismantled, others assembled, great masts reared, great holes dug. I even thought at first the collared workers could walk up walls—no strange sight to a space-dweller—until I noted that those on vertical surfaces were supported by slim wires, which they swiftly climbed or down-climbed.

One might wonder at my being able to see so much while maneuvering a strange vehicle for the first time in a gravity field. But if one has a lifetime of experience moving in three dimensions, moving in two is child's play. I was soon driving the cat wagon with such easy competence that I was able to spare a hand to work at my balky knee motor and had it adjusted in a matter of seconds. I surely had been woozy on my first try!

I soon observed that I was attracting interest. The Texans' faces never turned toward me, but their eyeballs did, and they slowed down in passing. The collarless Mexicans goggled me frankly, but speeded up, making wide curves around our cavalcade. The collared ones, however, marched by with never a glance, like so many tiny, swift juggernauts, fortunately people-avoiding ones.

The speed of all the bent-backs surprised me. Father had told me all about Mexicans. A strict indoctrination in racial and national behavior had come very early in my education, because it is very important in the theater. Father had assured me that all Mexicans were short and wore sarapes and big hats, went barefoot, and spent their lives sitting against adobe walls, smoking hemp and sleeping, except for brief periods of firing off pistols.

These Mexicans were not at all like that, except for the short and barefoot parts.

In fact, there were many types. Just now some wee Mexican children, cute as dark kittens, came toddling up and scattered flowers over me, most likely thinking me a corpse bound for the boneyard, for when I lifted and turned my head to look at them, they ran away.

La Cucaracha had slowed her burro until she was jogging beside me. She observed, "Legends, or lies, from the black lands tell that flower power was once a great thing. But here at least it has died out."

Noting my special interest in the collared Mexicans, she explained disdainfully, "They are cyborgs, the *estúpidos*. Their collars feed them orders and happiness—straight into their veins and nerves. From a distance foremen control them—after a fashion." She added the last phrase when two files of cyborgs collided and instantly began a confused milling aimed at eventual disentanglement, like ants I had once watched in a flatland between grass.

"They live like this forever?" I asked with some horror.

"Ah, no," she assured me, "only during the working day. The other ten hours they exist as men, employing what fragments of pounded-adobe spirit they have left. Chiefly they feed, fornicate, and sleep. My countrymen!"

I recalled what had been nagging me. "Señorita K," I asked, "why is it that your countrymen regard me with a fear that is both more and less than fear? Explain that to me if you will, *mi amada bonita.*"

With a rapid frown and finger shake, she leaned down and whispered warningly, "No tendernesses until moonrise, as I first commanded you, you tall incompetent and undisciplined!" Then in an equally low, but most cool voice, she continued, "Señor La Cruz, my people are like children. They live by fairy tales, some sweet as sugar, some grisly as red bone. One of the latter tells of a Death tall as the sky who will one day come striding across Texas. He will have the form of a great skeleton—El Esqueleto, he's named oftenest. He will be tossing like *fritos* into his great naked jaws and grinding there human skulls—made of sugar candy, some say; of fresh-torn bloody bone and brains, say others. My people will flock to him. He will give them never a glance, any more than stars and clouds look down at men, but he will lead them to freedom."

I had become so engrossed in her small but colorful tale that I almost started when a large voice inquired, "Kookie been feeding you a sob story about cyborgs?" Elmo had gradually let his own mount drift backward until he too was beside me, on the opposite side of the wagon. "Don't you believe a single word comes out of her cute, lying, little postage-stamp lips. Scully, my pal, cyborgs live a lot happier than Texans. Their joy comes each day sure as Coca-Cola. Besides, they're essential to our liberty and freedom, as I've explained."

"Myself, I think they would all be trampled under the specter's bony feet—if they do not run like whipped dogs at the sight of him," La Cucaracha continued as coolly as if there had been no interruption at all. "Cyborged or not, my people are *estúpidos de estúpidos.*"

"Cynical little bitch, ain't she?" Elmo observed. "Kookie, you got an ice cube for a heart. Lucky for you your cold blood don't chill your skin and that it stays out of your tits and toes and tother place midway between 'em."

"My body, though small, is designed in more classic proportions than that, esteemed patron," she replied to him tartly. "It is midway between my head top and feet soles that my crotch has the privilege of being situated."

"Now, Kookie, you mind your modesty and keep your mind hidden," Elmo warned her. "Don't you go starting an intellectual striptease front of me and my guest. Tother kind's the only one a woman's fitted for, greaser or gringo."

"You wish me to mop and mow like a madwoman, master? Or grunt to Señor La Cruz, *no sabe?* Or discard my clothing perhaps?"

"Now, Kookie, I'm telling you that if you don't behave, I'll——"

The altercation might have become unpleasant, except that at that moment I involuntarily interrupted it. We were approaching a gold or gilded statue twenty feet high of a most muscular man in barbarian garb. From his helmet thrust very long and twisting horns. His right hand swung back a battle-ax, his left pointed a six-shooter.

"Who is *that?*" I demanded, pointing with a black-shrouded leg, because I was riding feet first and my hands were busy driving. "I did not know that Terra had regressed to full barbarianism during the Interdict."

"Scully, ain't you familiar with the discoverer of Texas, even, and its first decent-size *hombre?*" Elmo retorted in genially scandalized tones. "You mean to tell me you ain't ever heard of Leif Ericson, Paul Bunyan, Big Bill Thompson, John L. Sullivan, William Randolph Hearst, Abraham Lincoln, and such other great Texans?"

"No," I admitted, "though I have heard of Sam Houston, Jim Bowie, and my namesake Davy Crockett."

"Oh, yeah, they were Texans too," he admitted, "though on a more local plane, San Jacinto and Alamo boys. And old Raven Sam, though one of our early prexies, was pretty dubious in some ways—Indian lover and Yankee fellow traveler, it's said."

I thought of asking him about Julius Caesar and Jesus Christ, but refrained for fear of having an attack of history-epilepsy. I might learn that they too had been Texans.

Instead I said, steering the cat wagon around Leif Ericson, "I recognized some of the others you named, but thought them men of the United States and Canada."

La Cucaracha had jogged ahead again, though not without giving me a quick lip-pursed smile and eyelash ripple. Elmo leaned out of his saddle toward me and said, "Scully, I can see your heavenly instructors knew only the superficial version of Earth's history, the one pap-fed to the general public. Since you're going to be meeting some mighty sophisticated and influential men today, it's best you know a scrap or two of the truth. *Amigo mío*, the Lone Star Republic never *was* of the United States. In eighteen-forty-five she assumed *leadership* of them, because she could see they needed bolstering against foreign aggression and internal disorder, and that was a most accurate foresight, because she had to spend the next three years throwing back the attack of Mexico on them, and pretty soon she had the Civil War to run—both sides.

"Of course it was given out to the general public of the states, who never had no brains or guts nohow and flustered easy, that this assumption of leadership was annexation—but it was always known to the speaker of the House and the senators who counted in Washington that by secretest treaty Texas was boss. Thereafter the presidents in the White House were just figureheads for the Texas Establishment—Franklin D. Roosevelt, for instance, was the puppet of our Jack Garner, a mighty modest kingpin, just as later on Lyndon the Great bossed Jack Kennedy, though the latter was posthumously declared an honorary Texan and president thereof because of the grandeur and ritual importance of his demise. With the coming of the Third World War and the atomization of Washington, New York, San Francisco, and so forth, secrecy became unnecessary and Texas took over in name as well as in substance, includ-

ing for good measure the frosty top and hot, dry, jungly
bottom of the continent. We needed more greasers, anyhow,
for therapeutic reasons."

My mind was tossing like the cat wagon, which was
traversing a curving section of the street under repair and
trying to dodge Mexicans who were simultaneously dodg-
ing me. I wished now I had had other history instructors
besides my father, who would dispose of the conquest of a
continent with an offhand "Enter barbarians with battle-
axes," or of a civilization with "Exit voluptuaries, wringing
hands and screaming. Idris does quick naked dive-across."
I knew quite a bit of Greek, Roman, and English dynastic
history and the neurotic antics of twentieth-century man
from Ibsen and Bergman to Green Comedy and Inner-Space
Multistage, but our repertoire had no late plays set in Texas,
so Father had brushed past that land quickly. Oh, before
my down-orbit he'd briefed me on the Northwest Territory
and Yellowknife minutely and with great accuracy—I'd
thought (now I was not so sure).

"Well, I've had my say and it's your turn to talk, Scully,"
Elmo interrupted. "You were saying something back there
about the Yellowknife Registry of Mining Claims?" His
voice was suddenly so casual and his memory so precise that
for no other reasons I found myself getting suspicious. But
once again I was given opportunity to change the topic by
a golden sculpture, this one abstract.

Beside the street, about twenty meters up, hung a golden
rectangle, across the lower side of which there was affixed,
pointing acutely downward, what looked like a distance
weapon of some sort, all golden too. It was a few moments
before I saw the slim, transparent pylon supporting this part
of the abstraction, so near was the pylon's substance to
being invisible.

The distance weapon pointed at the other half of the
abstraction, a most complex structure of pipes, wires, rods,
springs, and boxes, all golden too, about as long as my cat
wagon but wider and thicker. This fantastic brick of golden

tracery was also supported by the near-invisible substance, but at a height of only half a meter.

Pointing, Elmo explained, "There's the window in the book depository from which Oswald fired the fatal shots, and that's the chassis of the car in which Jack got gunned down, providing by that one brave act of his an example to all future presidents of Texas to go their way courageously when their political bell tolled.

"Incidentally, Scully," he continued, leaning a little lower in his saddle and pitching his voice likewise, "what I'm going to tell you *now* is pretty high-security stuff, but the menfolk where we're going have got nothing else in their skulls—deep waters, Scully, deep waters—so it's only fair I give you a paddle or two to navigate with, and maybe an aqualung. And besides, we Texans don't care much for security; we like things loose as the reins by which we herd our second-class citizenry. Anyhow, what I was going to tell you is this: Our current president of Texas is hedging a bit when it comes to following Jack's great example. He's disliked, you see, but instead of standing forth and dying like a man, he's turned the President's Manse into a fort and —believe it and weep!—he's organized a corps of Mexican houseboys faithful to his person, and he's armed them! With laser guns at that! Which ain't playing fair at all to the political opposition. Why, he's even kicked out his Texas Ranger guards. Says he can't trust them not to kill him, which is true, of course, but uncouth to mention."

"It's him we're going to visit now?"

"No, you got it all wrong, Scully, though his Manse is here in Dallas, where all important things are. We're going to visit the Ranch of Cotton Bowie Lamar, Governor of Texas, Texas—that is, governor of the father state in the world's greatest nation. We're not going to have anything to do at all with that dastardly, Mexican-arming tyrant Longhorn Elijah Austin, current bossman of that same greatest nation, though it pains me to say so."

"You hope to defeat him at the next election?" I asked.

Elmo shook his head and sucked his lips with a plop. "Nope, Scully, in achieving real freedom we've long ago discarded the phantasms of democracy. For the immaterial, ignoble ballot we've resubstituted the material, ritually preferable, noble bullet, which is the item Longhorn E. A. most contumeliously refuses to face. Adverse ballots he'd let cascade off him like cottonwood balls."

Meanwhile the wheels of the cat wagon, the hooves of the burro and hormoned horse, and the rotting six horny soles of the Mexicans' feet were carrying us past a most interestingly different expanse. All metal, glass, and plastic were gone. In the distance was a veritable forest of tiny hutments bowered and lined by bursts of bright color—flowers, it occurred to me with pleased surprise. Between them and our street was a crowded city of pastel homes—pale violet, blue, and pink—but too tiny even for Mexicans. Then I realized that this was a graveyard.

Between the palely colorful homes of the dead was hobbling toward us, helped by long staff, a figure robed like myself, but in yellow and orange and about five feet tall, while his hood held only blackness. My exoskeleton suddenly felt cold to my Sack-suited skin. I stopped the cat wagon and sat up.

"Greasertown," Elmo explained succinctly.

With an effort I forced my eyes to scan away from the figure that disturbingly held them. Ahead, bordered on two sides by the cemetery and on one by our street, and backed by a structure of pastel arches I took for a church, was an even more colorful metal construction consisting of a large, round, empty floor ten feet off the ground, approached by several stairways and shaded by a rippling canopy supported by slim rainbow pillars ten meters tall.

A quick nod from La Cucaracha told me that my first thought was correct—it was the bandstand of our evening assignation.

But the romantic leaping in me was chilled as my gaze returned to the advancing robed one. I still could not discern a face inside the hood. I asked myself if it were only the bright sunshine making shadows blacker, or if——

"Here comes one of them consarned niggar Zen Buddhists from one of them consarned tidewater anarchies—California most like, which has been predominantly black ever since the assassination of Ronald the Third," Elmo observed. "Although their Zens are troublesome little locos, forever ranting and mooching and setting themselves afire, we let them wander freely through Texas out of the greatness of our tolerance and"—his voice dropped—"for diplomatic reasons."

Now I could see the slit-eyed, anger-contorted, almost inky-black face inside the hood. Because of intermarriage, such extreme skin colors have vanished from the Sack and even Circumluna.

Some of my apprehension disappeared, but only some.

He stopped two meters from me. Now that he limped no longer, but stood only, he gained a foot in height, or seemed to. His eyelids flew open wide, disclosing great orbs of madness, like bloodshot moons. An unseen power emanated from him and gripped me.

"O white dirt from the sky!" he cried gratingly at me. "Arise and shoulder your karma."

I nervously cleared my throat.

Grasping his staff two-handed by one end, he brought it straight down on my head before I could think to defend myself.

My titanium head basket rang with a muffled but sonorous *bong!* I wasn't hurt, but I was jarred, numbed, and startled.

"Arise, I command you, you miserable construct of flesh and metal, you abominable offspring of ofay and engine," he growled on. "Arise and accept the Great Destiny, of which you are totally unworthy!" And he swung back his staff for another bash. I felt powerless to defend myself.

La Cucaracha was kicking her burro toward him, but it was Elmo's whip that took him around the shoulders. There was a crackle and a faint bluish flash, and then he was writhing on his back in the dirt, shaking his fists and gurgling unintelligible words, presumably of anger.

With a most expert flick of the same whip, Elmo wound its tip around the staff, flipped it toward himself, caught it in a hamlike hand, and pitched it javelinwise far into the graveyard. Then the whip returned to strike sparks from the ground near the twisting figure.

"Vamoose, you nameless son of Nirvana, or I declare I'll grill you before you can get out your gasoline to do it for yourself!" he bellowed.

The Buddhist scrambled to his feet and hobbled off through the gravestones with great shoulder bobbings, using a fisted stiff arm for staff, but looking back across his sullied robes to glare and curse, or so it sounded.

"What was *he* talking about?" I asked in a voice driven by anxiety almost baritone-high.

Elmo shrugged. "Oh, those hash-blasted Zens always talk that way. With them, destinies and karmas and 'carnations are a penny a peck. Trouble is, they're always banging people over the skull—to emphasize their senseless statements, *they* say. Lucky you got that half-helmet, Scully. I'd run the maniac in, except we don't want to waste no time."

"A black bee bonnet, Señor La Cruz," my darling chimed in. "Filth beneath your feet. Think no more of him."

"But how did he know I was from space?"

Once more Elmo shrugged, screwing up his big face like a giant pepper. "Those niggars got odd ways of knowing things, now and again," he admitted.

"He also knew, despite my cloak and hood, that I combined metal and flesh."

"That's true. Maybe there's something here needs watching. Kookie, you take Gonzales and Company and find out what that black bugger's up to. But don't nervous him. He really might set himself afire, though he's black as a cinder already. Then report home."

"Ah-ha, I knew it would come!" my dear one cried, her dark eyes snapping with anger, real or assumed. "I knew you would once again find an excuse not to take me to the Governor's ranch. Is it that you fear my boldness will embarrass you?"

"Now, Kookie——"

"Or is it that you are afraid one of higher rank will demand me of you on a trade, and you lack spirit to refuse?"

"Kookie! You hop it now without no back talk, or I swear I'll ante you up first hand of my next poker game."

"Agreed! And they will have to send to the girl shops of Ciudad Mexico or New Orleans at least to match your bet. Pedro, Pablo, Pablito! *Vámonos!*"

As she spun her burro toward the graveyard, the three bent-backs trotting behind her, she spared me one more eye flash, and with three fingers she pitter-patted the pleasing bump on the left side of her chest, to indicate the feelings of the organ beneath.

Elmo said to me, "Scully, time's a-wasting. You must have got the hang of that cat wagon by now, so let's press a bit." And with that he removed his immense hat, swung it twice in a circle, cried, "Ki-yi-yipee!" and heeled his mount into a ponderous gallop.

Gritting my teeth, which I do with great power, I thumbed the last go-button at my elbow and sped after him, bouncing about a bit on my flatbed. As we raced by the bandstand neck and neck, the depression that had gripped me from first sight of the orange-yellow monk now lifted entirely. My spirits soared. I would fulfill my mission on Terra, yes!—but with even greater certainty, memorizing the route from now on, I would return to the romantically hued cemetery tonight at moonrise, even if I had to adapt jets to my exoskeleton and compute for the first time a gravity-atmosphere parabola!

A few brown-robed figures poured from the church as

we passed it. Perhaps they thought my vehicle was a run-away hearse, complete with shrouded corpse, and so their responsibility, since it fell within their traditional area of birth and baptism, confirmation, marriage, mortal illness, and death. But we soon outdistanced them.

3 / Governor's Ranch

Texas is a wandering and tattered ribbon of white
fascism, ineffectually separating the non-directive
black democracies and hip republics of Florida and
California, and occupying at most 2 percent of
North America. Two cents worth of bloated,
mentally bombed-out squaredom!

—*African America,* by Booker T. Nkrumah, Tuskegee
Institut de la Vudu et Technologie Librairie

Texas is a serene superstate stretching from the
Equator to Siberia. Bordered by the trivial
tumultuous black anarchies of the seaweed regions,
he inspires and tolerantly dominates the top half of
the New World, of the vast ranges of which he
occupies 99.9 percent, an area greater than that of
the King Ranch.

—*Lone Star Continent,* by Sam Houston Lipinsky,
University of Texas at Minneapolis Press

MY EXOSKELETON RESPONDING to its myoelectric orders with
purring efficiency, I speeded up at the last instant and entered the state-patio of the Governor's ranch, Beau Aston-
ishment, a long stride ahead of Elmo and the scuttling
bent-back houseboys in violet knee pants and lace-trimmed
violet jackets, but barefoot as Gonzales and Company.
These came in two converging clusters through the greaser
doors closely flanking the gringo door.

Then I stopped dead, standing perfectly erect, and let
them all pile up clumsily behind me. I had learned how to
steal an entrance before I ever played Tom Sawyer, Odd
John, Jommy Cross, or Little Lord Fauntleroy.

As Elmo began my introduction in suddenly subdued and almost faltering tones with a "Governor Cotton Bowie Lamar, Your Honor, and gentlemen . . . *other* gentlemen," I ceased listening carefully to him and rapidly scanned the scene without moving an exoskeletal link.

I was in a spacious area roofed by the sky, walled on three sides by metal walls four stories high and of many colors, and flagstoned by an even more rainbow jigsaw puzzle of polished minerals, marbles perhaps from many quarries, most of the pieces mosaic-small. In the flat distance were a few trees and many slender towers in the form of truncated cones. Two of these were five times the height of the rest, wider in proportion, and looked much newer. They all cast long, late-afternoon shadows.

Beginning in the middle distance and ending twenty meters away was a vast rippling rectangle reflecting the sky's blue. If it were water, there was, I decided, enough for a lake, far more even than in Circumluna's largest swimming volume. From a platform next to it, a large, long board extended, which made me think of pirate tales of "walking the plank."

But perhaps it was petroleum, I reminded myself, unrolling from my memory a map of Terra's resources, where areas rich in fossil animal fats were colored blue.

Nearer at hand, each occupying his own many-pillowed couchlike structure with low tables on either side, were a half-dozen male Texans more elegantly, or at least more neatly, clad than Elmo and all with noble craggy faces, as if they belonged in a quality western, circa 1950. (Circumluna's and the Sack's microfilmed and taped records of Earth's arts are said to be better than those of Terra herself.) Like Elmo's their legs were the heaviest part of them —it takes great columns indeed to support in six lunagravs the mass matching an eight-foot height. Their gleamingly polished boots were vast.

All held or had beside them glasses of amber fluid, while most puffed long reefers; there was a scent like plastics under heat treatment. Bent-backs scampered about noise-lessly, serving and erranding.

All the recumbent ones radiated an aura of power even greater than that of physical elegance, and all had one or more of the behavioral quirks that traditionally go with the possession of power. The nearest held in one half-closed hand a stack of gleamingly yellow rounds and clinked them in waltz time. Another had inserted three fingers under his gleaming white shirt and with them was scratching his solar plexus in another rhythm. A crop-haired one had a seven-second facial tic that with each convulsion threatened to dislodge, but never quite did, the large monocle occupying his left orbit. Yet, as I say, all had matinee-idol profiles, circa 1900.

I noted with approval that as they listened to Elmo, their gaze was on me.

Elmo wound up with ". . . and he has large mining interests in North Texas," which irked me considerably. The guesser and loose-mouth! (Yet it was truly I who had first been waggy-tongued when coming out of sedation.)

Without the least flourish I removed my hooded cloak and dropped it on the nearest houseboy. It covered him totally, but I did not pause to note how he handled this problem.

With the least bow, I slowly rotated my face like a pan-oramic camera from one end of the recumbent group to the other, meanwhile saying in my lowest audible voice, reso-nant with nerve-gripping subsonics, "Most potent, grave, and reverend signiors, my very noble and approved good masters, I come to you bearing greetings from the outside universe."

(Father had always advised me about vanity-mad hu-mans, which includes the entire species, terrestrial and spatial—even I have touches of conceit—"Lay the flattery on with a trowel, Christopher, and never hesitate to borrow from the Bard. He was himself the Prince of Borrowers.")

I could tell that my deep voice and slim, soldierly bearing impressed them. Sure stage sense had led me to use the lines of Venice's great captain, Othello.

Next I turned and bowed a trifle more—but only a trifle —to the man whom Elmo had first addressed.

"Governor Lamar, Your Excellency," I said, "I bring you the especial salutations of Circumluna and the Bubbles Congeries." (Sack seemed to lack sufficient dignity in this situation.) And then I eyed him commandingly.

Almost as if hypnotized (who knows my full powers?— not I), the Governor slowly got to his feet, meanwhile abstractedly picking from his dark coat two bits of invisible lint—that was *his* idiosyncrasy. He was the slenderest of the lot, which isn't saying a great deal, and by a shade the most distinguished-looking.

"Mister La Cruz," he said, "I'm grieved at the inconvenience your ill-informed pilot caused you—perhaps he understandably assumed Dallas the port of space entry for all points in our vast nation—but I'm pleased at the opportunity of welcoming you to Texas, Texas. We see few space-dwellers, sir, and—" He broke off to capture between finger and thumb something unseen on his left elbow.

"And I, sir," chimed in the clinker of gold pieces, copying Lamar in rising, "as Atoms Bill Burleson, mayor thereof, welcome you to Dallas." His gray-eyed gaze wandered up and down me. "Pardon me, sir, I mean no offense, but I've never seen a man slender as—no, pardon me further—as *emaciated* as yourself and still in the land of the living. We've heard of the terrible tortures practiced by the intellectuality-drunken autocrats of Circumluna, from whose tyranny I assume you're in flight, but I never guessed that simple starvation continued for years, nay, surely decades——"

I silenced him with a lifted hand and intoned, "Given energy and mass, even of the slightest, to manipulate, man can survive in any environment, including *internal* ones. Only a minimum of muscle and fat is required in sol-heated nullgrav or free fall. We become Thins or Fats, or maintain large muscles by nograv exercises, as suits our temperaments—asthenic, pyknic, or athletic. I, myself, sir, am fairly clearly a Thin. But I do not understand the mention of tyranny. Circumluna and the Bubbles Congeries are a technocratic democracy."

Another of the power men asked me, this one without getting up, "We've always understood that Circum and the Sack were inhabited solely by Longhairs. Now I'm a plain speaker. Are you one of those, Mister La Cruz?"

This one was the burliest and the most burly-legged of the lot and *his* eccentricity was squeezing lengthwise between thumb and forefinger a black column that lengthened to two decimeters or shortened to nothing without changing diameter—an odd toy, but I had his question to reply to.

"Let my shaven pate be your answer, Mister —?" I saw no point in mentioning the shoulder-length blonde wig in my baggage. I eyed him commandingly, but with him it didn't work—at least he didn't rise.

Another of the nonrisers broke in, the stomach-scratcher, with whom Elmo, I now noted, had been talking privately. "I gather you got mining investments in North Texas," he said, continuing to scratch, "but who are you with, stranger?"

"I am with myself," I instantly replied with a shrug. "And, to be sure, I am with Mister Earp there, who most kindly befriended me at the spaceport."

"That's right, that's right," Elmo put in hastily and also defensively. "That's the truth, simple as put-and-take poker."

I glared at him. He only stared back injuredly, but Lamar at least comprehended the meaning of my look.

"I'm sure that none of us intended to question Mister La Cruz's word," he said soberly. "By the by, I should have introduced—" But he broke off to flick suspiciously and several times with the backs of his fingernails at an apparently spotless area of his knife-pleated trousers.

"As for those mining investments," I seized the chance to say, "I have none. Mr. Earp misinterpreted one of my remarks. The matter I have to settle in Amarillo Cuchillo is purely an old family affair."

"Of honor?" Lamar resumed softly, a gleam coming into his eyes and also into those of the gold-chinking Burleson. But before I could answer, the Scratcher again broke in loudly.

"And you mistook one of my meanings, stranger. When I asked you who you was with, I didn't mean who you had around you, or anything complicated like that. I just meant *who are you with?*"

"I do not think I understand you," I said courteously. "When? Where?"

"Anywhere. Any time. But especially now. Who are you with?"

I looked around somewhat helplessly, yet with a bravely jesting small smile calculated to win the sympathy of any audience. "Is it a riddle, gentlemen?" I asked at last.

"It's no riddle and you're just making it more complicated," the Scratcher retorted almost angrily. Then he seemed to take himself in hand, and with such patience as one might bestow on a weak-witted child, he said, "Look, I'm asking it this way—like, before I became Sheriff of Dallas County, I was with Littleton and Lamar Lightning, and before that I was with Hunt Espionostics, and so on. Every male Texan who amounts to anything is with some company, unless he's a public official, in which case he's with the government."

"I comprehend," I said. "I am with—indeed, a featured player with—the La Cruz Theater-in-the-Sphere Stock Company."

"A thespian!" Lamar began warmly. "My daughter will be—"

"*Stock* company!" Burleson exclaimed at the same time, chinking his gold like the wild clash of cymbals. "Mean to say you issue shares, debentures, and—"

"*La Cruz* Company!" exclaimed the one with the black cylinder. "You *own* this business? I know for a fact that on Circumluna total communism—"

"Gentlemen!" I politely silenced them with my deepest voice, then rapidly explained, "I am indeed an actor, a free-fall Shakespearean. Our company is stock only in the old theatrical sense of employing stock characters, or types, though most of us are more versatile than that implies. While it is my father who owns the company, though it has cooperative features and—"

"Family business, eh?"

"Yes," I told Black Cylinder. "And we do have ownership, often private, in space. If objects and operations are not owned and valued, who will care for them, Mister —?"

Once again my hint that full introductions would be desirable was lost, this time because of the last recumbent, the one with the monocle. All this while he had been watching me with intensest interest, like a schoolboy impatient to recite or demonstrate, and constantly jiggling about on his couch working his features in addition to his tic, so that I expected it surely each time to dislodge the glass circle that magnified his left eye owlishly.

Now, as if obeying an impulse become irresistible, he sprang up and darted toward me, violet-clad houseboys altering their orbits to clear him a path. He stopped in front of me and, stooping and rearing, scanned my exoskeleton up and down. His fingers constantly fluttered over it without quite touching it, perhaps because I folded my arms and, staying most erect, gave him a slight frown.

"I am extremely interested—in *machinery*," he said in the enthusiastic but confidential tones of one who tells you, "I have a thing about flagellation." He continued, "In particular, prosthetic, waldoic, and robotic machinery. Oh, beautiful, beautiful! A strength-in-delicacy far beyond us. What lofting! Nature's own skeleton translated to T-beams—with a thousand improvements! Such tiny servomotors, yet so clearly powerful! What space-saving in battery housings! I take it that without this peerless device you would be—completely helpless here?"

"Yes, even in one lunagrav, let alone six," I admitted, somewhat taken off guard by his exclamations, "Mister —?"

He only continued his fantastical praises with "And how perfect a twin—or symbiote, rather—your own body is! As if bred to fit this one superb prosthetic and no other! Bone and metal in a perpetual exquisite embrace or communion—"

I began to feel too much like a starred slave girl stripped on the auction block, so that when he actually began to circle behind me, I turned so as to continue to face him. He speeded up, then suddenly reversed, without getting behind me. As this nonsensical ballet continued, I began a series of calisthenics, knee-bends chiefly and head-circlings and rapid arm-extensions that missed his hair-carpeted dome by fractional inches. He flinched not a whit, such was his ecstatic concentration. He was of German extraction, most likely, I decided, which would fit the cropped hair and monocle, standard stage indexes of the Teuton.

Governor Lamar, who had been totally absorbed in a most difficult episode of lint-picking, since it involved the left shoulder of his suit close to his neck, now put a stop to our ridiculous *pas de deux* with a "Professor Fanninowicz! Scientific curiosity can come later, if our visitor permits. Mister Christopher Crockett La Cruz, I wish to present to you Professor Cassius Krupp Fanninowicz, who heads the engineering school at UTD."

"Charmed!" the professor assured me, making the word hum. But his eyes continued to race over my exoskeleton as he very lightly pressed my hand, which extended bare of metallic or other support from my titanium wristplate. I felt mightily tempted, but controlled myself.

The Governor's gaze began to creep toward his right shoulder, but with a perceptible effort he looked up and continued, "I also wish to present to you, sir, Chaparral Houston Hunt, Commander-in-Chief of the Texas Rangers, and Big Foot Charlie Chase, Sheriff of Dallas," pointing in turn at Black Cylinder and the Scratcher. "But Mister—or do you prefer Señor—La Cruz, I've been remiss in my hospitalities. I've sent for my daughter, as I wished to present her too, but since she's delayed, would you care to recline" —he indicated an empty couch near at hand—"and partake of refreshment? Professor, perhaps you too would now be more comfortable on your own couch."

"Señor suits best," I said on one of my typical impulses, carefully letting myself down onto the couch indicated, while Fanninowicz heeded the Governor's suggestion, though obviously disappointed at not being able to witness more closely the new bendings of my exoskeleton.

"Thank you," I added to the Governor, meaning it. Twenty minutes on my titanium footplates had left me suddenly fatigued. I tongued in my three sorts of pills, then almost closed my eyes as relaxation hit me, except that I saw the Governor frowning a question at me. He looked toward Elmo, then faintly frowned at me again. I hesitated, then responded with a slight smile and nod.

"Mister Earp," the Governor said, "you take a couch too —that one," pointing at one outside the circle of the rest of us. Elmo somewhat shamefacedly gave me a quick smile of gratitude as he hastened to obey.

Meanwhile houseboys had placed on the table to my right a glass of amber fluid chinking with ice cubes and laid in a scalloped golden tray on the left-hand table a long reefer just set a-smolder with a hot point and a clever hand-suction device. But before taking either up, I once again scanned and sought to evaluate the Texans around me. The Mexicans could come later—there were more of them and in any case they seemed at first glance as alike as identical twins, psychically cyborged if not physically.

The Texans appeared to form two chief groups. Governor Lamar and Mayor Burleson were playing me up. Sheriff Chase and Ranger Hunt, despite curt nods and curter smiles when they'd been introduced to me by Lamar, were still putting me down. Why—in both cases—remained to be discovered.

Elmo's role at least was now altogether clear to me. He was the sort of minor political hanger-on who seeks to cadge small rewards, if only food, drinks, and moments with the great, by inventing favors to do them, such as bringing them a stranded space oddity, exactly as he might have brought them a wandering, halfwitted millionaire or good-looking showgirl. Yes, I had Elmo's number, all right, and my estimate was confirmed by the swiftness with which he latched on to a drink and reefer, also sending one of the houseboys for a large plate of appetizers. My feeling of growing friendliness toward him became mingled with a tolerant contempt.

Finally, there was the professor: seemingly all technical curiosity, which made him the easiest first object for the conversational attack I now mounted, with the intention of truly charming them all—the necessary first tactic of any traveler in a strange land.

"Sir," I said to him, "despite your Polish-sounding patronymic—pardon my familiarity—I take it you are of German extraction, an inheritor of the Teutonic scientific genius."

"I am indeed!" he responded, nodding so vigorously that I thought his monocle must surely go. "Only in Texas, sir, and the adjacent southwest could a Bavarian ever have found a spiritual home away from home. My great-great-great-grandfather came over with the first V-Two's."

"The Atomic War?" I asked politely.

"No, World War Two, not Three," he informed me. "The V-Two's lacked atomic warheads—my ancestor had a great sorrow about that—though they were the first true space vehicles."

"Tell me, gentlemen," I asked around. "How is it that Texas—or Texas, Texas, rather—escaped the atomization which I gather the rest of North America endured?"

"It was all due to the supreme foresight of Lyndon the

First and his immediate successors," Mayor Burleson took it on himself to explain. "Realizing that this was the true heartland of the continent, they walled it with anticontinental ballistic-missile missile defenses and drawing on the local excavation and drilling skill, and also taking advantage of its natural caverns, they filled it with nuclear shelters of the deepest and most strongly roofed variety, constructing what may be called the Texas Bunker, though it was then known as the Houston Carlsbad Caverns-Denver-Kansas City-Little Rock Pentagram, or maybe Pentagon. A step of profound wisdom, Señor La Cruz, for which we have reason to be eternally grateful."

"So that when the Atomic War finally came," Professor Fanninowicz took up with an excitement almost gleeful (now the monocle must surely go!), "Russia, China, France, England, Black Africa, my own tormented and divided nation, and the outworks of the Texas Bunker were shattered, mangled, tattered—while here snugly survived the virile spirit of Assyria, Macedon, Rome, Bavaria, and the brave Boers!" Now at last a tic coincided with a near screech and the monocle did pop out, though rather disappointingly he caught it deftly in his left hand and whipped it instantly back into its proper orbit, where it gleamed as brightly as his bared white teeth.

I meanwhile had taken the first of the three sips I allow myself of an alcoholic beverage—a small sip, for the drink was strong—and inhaled two puffs of marijuana vapor, a smoke I had never before sampled. It seemed mild stuff, but I soon began to feel a lofty well-being, despite the grisly things being told me, and the scene and sounds around and about me began to organize themselves symphonically, even the chinking of Mayor Burleson's coins fitting perfectly into the great rhythm. At first, I must admit, there was something sinister about the tiny tympanic tune of power men releasing tension—TIC . . . clink, clink . . . scratch-scratch . . . squeeze, squeeze . . . faintest plink of thumb and fingertip on captured lint speck . . . TIC—but swiftly even these noises became orchestrated into a blissful totality.

Mayor Burleson said, "Señor La Cruz, I don't doubt you come from space—in fact, I can't, seeing that handsome contraption you need to get around in gravity—but your middle name and height make me think you're originally a Texan who got the hormone. Now that hormone's a closely guarded secret, sir—the lower orders of society and the rest of the world haven't grown up enough yet to be trusted with bigness—and we wouldn't like to think of it being known to the Longhairs of Circumluna."

I said in words dreamy and poetic, yet perfectly enunciated and of course still very deep-pitched, "I may well indeed be of Texan ancestry. There can be no certainty about it, for my grandfather lifted to the Sack from Spanish Harlem in New York City, yet my middle name whispers its hint, and the lines of heredity are as mysteriously interwoven as the curves of the clouds now gathering above us to enchant our gaze. But as for your last fear, Mayor, set your mind at rest. In free fall, unconfined by gravity, human growth is freer and sometimes almost fantastical. My grandfather was tall and slender, my father more so, and I still more so. My mother too is of considerable length, though it is her pleasure to be a Fat."

The whole scene around me, though darkening toward sunset, presented itself to me with supernormal clarity, each detail a gem.

I took another small sip of my drink, but returned the reefer to its tray; a little of that stuff was enough for my attenuated physiology, as with most drugs. My feelings had reached a harmonious acme—why spoil it? I felt marvelously relaxed and at peace. I placed a titanium heel atop a titanium toe guard, in effect crossing my legs for comfort as I noted several of my companions had done, and continued, "Yet I feel greatly at home here, a Texan in spirit if not in fact. You are no longer my hosts, but my dear friends. Señor La Cruz is all very well, but I would be happier if you called me Chris—or perhaps Scully, the name Mr. Earp bestowed on me from my cadaverousness."

"That's fine, Scully, call me Atoms," Burleson responded. However, I noted the commander, the sheriff, and the professor bristled almost imperceptibly—my senses were vastly acute at the moment—and gave the Mayor slightly dark looks—a pale shade of gray—while the Governor was moodily absorbed watching a houseboy wipe his gleaming boots with a white pocket handkerchief he'd given him. I determined to charm them in spite of themselves and at that moment remembered an anecdote of my father's.

I took the third sip of my drink and firmly set it down. "Gentlemen," I said somewhat sharply, "whatever I am in fact, I feel myself a Texan at this moment, sharing your expansive relaxation, your wide wisdom, your tolerance, your homely but huge humor. May I tell you a story?"

I was pleased to note that it was the Governor who gave me the nod. It had been to rouse him that I'd spoken sharply.

"When time was young," I said, speaking softly, "God was sitting by a mud puddle, dabbling his fingers in the dirty water and playing with the mud. Because, you see, all things were young then and even God was a youth. Think of him as Ometecutli, the Papa-God of the Mexicans, but not yet a papa, only a young and stocky barefoot suntanned god in ragged pants, playing like the village loco in a universe of water and clay, of love and flowers.

"First he made balls of the clay and pitched them out and up so that they went spinning round and round, forever. So he created the sun, the moon, the planets, and the whole great universe.

"After a while he grew tired of this sport. Looking into the mud puddle, he saw for the first time his reflection. 'I will make something like that,' he said.

"So he made of clay the figure of a man, giving him a coat and shoes, for God was poor then and thought such things very fine, and making his hair very short, for at the

moment God was a novice sculptor and curls and such were
beyond him.

"Then he chanced to breathe on the figure as he was admiring it closely. To his amazement, the instant his breath
struck the figure, it stood up on the palm of his hand and
began to march about there, doing a goosestep."

Smiling gently at Professor Fanninowicz, I continued, "Seeing this, God said to himself, 'Ah-ha, a little German,' and
reached out and set down the figure in Germany.

"Next God made a woman. He gave her a long skirt and
long wavy hair—for God was gaining skill now—and he put
a high comb in her hair and high heels on her shoes. He
breathed upon her and she stood up and began to dance
most beautifully with much stamping of the feet. 'Ah-ha, a
little Spaniard,' he said to himself and he set her down in
Spain.

"Thus God made the Englishman, the Frenchman, the
Russian, the Negro, the Hindu, the heathen Chinese, and
almost all other breeds of Earth.

"God was growing somewhat tired now and his supply of
clay was getting low, so to speed things up he made two
male figures at once, giving them only his own simple garb.
When he breathed upon them, they sprang up instantly and
began to fight with each other. 'Two little Mexicans,' God
said, putting them down in Mexico.

"He had not quite enough clay left for two more figures,
so to finish his task—for although a loco, God was a con-
scientious worker and wasted nothing—he made and
dressed one great tall figure. This still left him with some
clay, so he made a great wide-brimmed hat for the figure,
and chaps for its legs, and fine boots. Two small dabs of
clay were left, so he used them to give the boots high heels.
Two more dabs of clay of the tiniest were still left, and so
that nothing might be lost, God made of them spurs for the
boots.

"He breathed on the figure. Nothing happened. God was
startled. Had he made a mistake? Perhaps the magic did

not work for large figures. Yet he breathed on the figure again, much harder.

"God thought he saw the figure stir a little. So he drew a deep breath and blew fiercely on the figure. His breath was like a gale or a tornado.

"The figure only pulled the brim of his great hat down over his eyes, and crossed his boots, and linking his hands behind his neck, began to snore there where he lay on God's palm.

"God became very angry. He drew in a tremendous breath, puffed out his cheeks, and breathed upon the figure a breath that was like a hurricane of hurricanes, like the shock wave of an atomic bomb!

"Without stirring otherwise at all, the figure pushed back his hat from his face and, looking God straight in the eye, demanded, 'Who the hell do you think you're spittin' at?'"

The laughter that greeted this tale gratified me. Even Chaparral Houston Hunt grinned and pounded his leg.

Before the applause had faded, I said loudly to them all, though I made a point of looking at Lamar, "So it was in the beginning, and so it still appears to be true of that great land stretching from Nicaragua to the Northwest Territory. Speaking of the latter, I trust I will have your aid in journeying to Amarillo Cuchillo tomorrow."

"Whatever you want, Scully!" To my surprise, it was Sheriff Chase who first answered. "Oh, that tale took us Texans off to perfection."

"Ask anything, Scully!" Again to my surprise, it was Commander Hunt who seconded. Elmo was standing beside him. "Sure you don't want to leave tonight—though we'll hate to lose you. Of course, we could have a round of partying first."

"Tomorrow would be best," I replied, thinking of La Cucaracha. "And as for partying, I thank you from heart's bottom, yet I fear this one will be all I can take. Although my exoskeleton is tireless even in Earth grav, my bone one and its envelope are not. It will be best for me if I spend the night in lonely quiet and rest." I was seeking to set up a situation in which it would be easy for me to make my sneak back to the cemetery.

And I didn't have too much time, come to think of it. The sun had already set and moonrise would come but two hours later. To one who lives in space near Luna, keeping track of Earth's phases is second nature. She is our month-clock.

"Not altogether lonely, I hope, Señor La Cruz—ho-ho, the German put down in Germany, very funny—" Professor Fanninowicz boomed at me heartily, "for I hope to spend the night at your side, studying your magnificent exoskeleton and perhaps experimenting——"

"Señor La Cruz shall spend his time as he sees fit," Governor Lamar cut in with authority. "The first demand of hospitality is consideration for—"

He broke off to get to his feet and turn toward the gringo door. The other men copied him. I could see without turning, but just the same I got up as rapidly as possible.

Since landing on Terra, I had experienced three great liftings of spirit. The first had been La Cucaracha. The second, marijuana. The third was the slender, statuesque female we now faced.

Oh, I didn't forget La Cucaracha in the least and I remained as firmly determined as before to be beside her at moonrise. But now, suddenly illumined by the sun's silvery afterglow from the clouds above, there was a gorgeous counterattraction.

She was nearly as tall as I and of Junoesque proportions, but, compared with the male Texans, she was slender. She wore Grecian robes of a pale-silvery silk that left an ample area of alabaster shoulders and bosom bare and fell in perfect folds to the floor. I had never seen the like, even on stage—one simply cannot achieve that wonderful classic draping without gravity to help.

Her face was at the moment grave and mystic, though

subtly seductive. A youthful Athene or Artemis, rather than Aphrodite. In one pale hand she held a scroll with silver knobs.

Her platinum-blond hair was piled high. Tiny lights winked in it. Under her arching brows, her pale-blue eyes were fixed on mine. For a second time on Terra I had lost my heart—something my father tells me a young man can't do too often, provided it doesn't interfere with rehearsals and he never misses an entrance or a cue.

"Señor Christopher La Cruz," Governor Lamar said, "I wish to introduce to you my dear daughter, the Honorable Rachel Vachel Lamar. Sugar, I've been waiting for you quite a while."

"Hush up, Daddy," the goddess said, wrinkling that delectable nose in a miffy grin. "To honor our guest properly I had to dart into my Diana costume—she's the Roman moon goddess, Daddy—and then I had to snatch time to dash off a poem of greeting. I'll read it now, if all you verse-scorning menfolk don't mind."

Then without pausing to note whether they did, she struck a pose that I had to admit was most amateurish (but the more delightful for that) and recited in an elocution-school voice that occasionally squeaked and/or went husky and invariably found the worst spots to suck in an over-obvious breath (yet how it all stole the heart!):

> Ho, traveler from outer space!
> How swell to see your sunk-cheek face,
> Your somber form that's flagstaff-trim,
> Your flashing eye and sword-slim limb.

She must have got an earlier glimpse of me, I realized, perhaps from an upstairs window, embowered like a Muslim maiden. The poem continued:

> We've gazed at your abode for years
> Serene o'er earthly joys and tears,
> It sails the sky without a sound
> A million miles above the ground.

We never thought we'd get a chance
To hold a moon man in our glance,
But here you've dropped out of the blue
And all of Texas welcomes you!

The other men applauded politely, Elmo Fortissimo. As she moved forward toward stage-center—a little too fast and coltish for a goddess, but just right for a girl—I swiftly intercepted her, caught hold of her hand, and bowed over it, pressing it briefly to my lips.

Then as I stood "flagstaff-trim" again, holding her hand a moment longer, I said, "Miss Lamar, I never have been so moved since when clutched in the arms of my mother, who was doubling as a member of the mob, I first heard my father give Antony's oration."

It was borderline truth, though I had been moved in different ways. My father had terrified me in that black toga.

"Go on, you flatterer, you," she giggled, giving me a playful shove that sat me back on my titanium heelplates.

Then her eyes got big. "Your pa's an *actor?*" They got bigger still. "*You're* an actor too—you stayed one?"

I shrugged. "Oh, an occasional Hamlet, Peer Gynt, Orestes, Cyrano . . ."

I could have sworn that for an instant she was going to hug me. Instead she looked me up and down, grinned, and said, "I bet you overlapped your ma to either side when she clutched you."

"Yes and she wrinkled her nose too," I countered. "I wet myself."

Governor Lamar said, "My colleagues and I have a bit of business to finish discussing before dinner. Señor La Cruz, I imagine you and my daughter can entertain each other for a while. You appear to have interests in common."

4 / Rachel Vachel

Lamar, Mirabeau Buonaparte, 1798–1859, first vice president (1836–38) and second president (1838–41) of Texas, a poetry-writing, history-bemused, personally charming Georgia newspaper editor who arrived in Texas sword in hand, inquired his way to Sam Houston's little army, and became one of the heroes of the battle of San Jacinto, April 21, 1836, where he commanded the cavalry. As president he ousted the Cherokees and Comanches from the infant nation (although Houston was a blood-member of the former tribe), secured Texas' recognition by Britain, France, the Lowlands, and the German States, guided her through the Pig War of 1840, created the piratical Texas Navy, set aside vast leagues of land for educational and cultural purposes, achieved for the Lone Star Republic even vaster, credit-building debts, and also conceived the goal of Big Texas, foreshadowing Lyndon Johnson's Great Society.

—*Thumbnail Texans*

"TELL ME SOME more, Captain Skull. But let me light you another reefer."

"Thank you, princess. But perhaps you will tell me something for a change. What is moths?"

"Furry butterflies."

"What is—are butterflies?"

"Butterflies is— Oh, they're like two tiny swatches of batik or embroidery flappin' along. And you'll likely be seeing a few moths in a few minutes for yourself. We even got lunar ones in honor of your homeland. Go on talkin' theater of space—that's what interests me."

"Very well, princess. Yes, acting in three dimensions in

free fall has its special techniques and requires its special conditions. For instance, upstage lies in all directions from stage-center, but so does downstage. You must learn to favor all sections of the audience by rotation in at least two planes, and that requires motivated or surreptitious contact with the other actors on stage. Also, to make an exit, you must take off from another actor or preferably several, and there should be a counterbalancing entrance—unless you use an air jet or are drawn off by fine wire, devices we try to avoid. Ideally, 3-D nullgrav acting becomes dramatic ballet with dialogue. Think of *Don Juan in Hell*, the actors afloat, or of Antony's oration again, with the mob a ragged sphere between the orator and the larger sphere of the audience."

"Oh, it all sounds so excitin'—makes our little theater here seem positively earthbound, even though Daddy insists on spending millions on lighting and special effects and sets, sometimes a heap too much of those. We wanted to do *Our Town* the right way but Daddy insisted on building us a real town with the smallest house big as the Petit Trianon. We actors were positively lost among those gingerbread skyscrapers. And I had to bust into tears seventeen times before he'd drop his plan to build us a life-size, practical, moving glacier for *Skin of Our Teeth*."

"The last time we put on *Our Town*, princess, we used only six kitchen chairs borrowed from the Circumluna Museum of Terran Domestic Artifacts—all floating, of course, as I mentally float now."

"Oh, spit! I might have known. But do go on, Captain Skull, please."

Our "interests in common" had indeed drawn the Honorable Rachel Vachel and me closer together, and in less than ten minutes. Our princess-Captain Skull personae derived from her conceit that I was Sir Francis Drake reporting the unknown lands of the Pacific to a youthful Queen Elizabeth. We were seated side by side in the gracious dusk on a large couch facing the dark horizon with its mysterious truncated cones across the very faintly shimmering ripples of the vast swimming pool (Rachel had identified that for me and assured me it was water), and we were quite alone. My companion had shooed out all the Mexican houseboys shortly after her father's departure.

I was still determined to keep my date with La Cucaracha—after all, she seemed the earthier and more easily had of the twain—but at the moment I was stealing my left arm along the top of the couch behind Rachel Vachel's ivory shoulders and also an occasional eye wander down her delicious frontal décolletage.

"Wilder is one of our minor favorites among the old playwrights," I meanwhile continued. "He rouses and satisfies simply and beautifully our nostalgia for Terra. Other old ones often in our repertory are Ibsen, Bergman (we live-stage his films), Shaw, Wycherly, Molière, Euripides, Gorky, Chekhov, Brecht, Shakespeare of course, and——"

"Hush, you're makin' me drool green with envy! Our group's forever tryin' to stage real serious plays like *Macbeth* or *Pillars of Society* or *The Gods of the Lightning* or *Waitin' for Lefty* or *Manhattan Project* or *Frisco After the Fallout* or *Uncle Tom's Cabin* or *Intolerance* (let Daddy use his hundred millions live-stagin' that, I say) or *Streetcar*, but (wouldn't you know it?) Daddy's forever insistin' on *another* revival of *Oklahoma!*, callin' it *Texiana!*, of course, and usin' Corpus Christi or Texarkana 'stead of Kansas City, to make it scan—and five times out of six Daddy gets his way. And even then he won't let me play Ado Annie, the cain't-say-no-girl—always got to have some little Mex whore on stilts for that part."

Edging my arm a little closer, I remarked, "Your father seemed to me a most courteous and mild gentleman."

"Mild? Huh! You should see him when—"

In turning to make her comment she had suddenly leaned back against my slithering arm. Now with a little scream she bent forward, quickly turning her head to remark, "My, that skeleton of yours is awfully chilly, Captain Skull. Can't you take it off even for a little while, while you're on Earth?"

"To my great regret, no," I informed her. "Without it, I literally could not move an arm or leg or lift my head, while a fall, especially without exoskeletal protection, might easily fracture a limb or my skull. I have just begun to realize that when one is eight feet or more tall, one has a lot farther to fall in gravity than——"

"Don't explain to me about that. I'm eight foot two myself and I know all about chipped and busted bones. Well, we can't have you fracturing yourself, that's for sure, you spacemen are too precious, so"—she gave a small sigh of resignation—"I guess I just got to endure the chilliness," and she flopped herself back against my arm before I could have withdrawn it, had I intended to.

She turned her face toward mine. Amid the mists of her platinum hair, her eyes were dark pools of wonder in which stars glimmered faintly.

"Anything for Texas—that's a joke," she said. "Go on, Captain Skull, tell me some more."

"But there are many things I would like *you* to tell *me*, chiefly about yourself," I countered, carelessly draping my free hand across my knee so that it happened lightly to touch one of hers. She did not move that leg. "I know you are a poet," I said. "Are you by any chance also a playwright?"

"Oh, I got a little old script or two in a secret compartment in my lingerie drawer," she admitted nonchalantly. "But don't for worlds whisper a word about them to Daddy. One of them's called *Houston's Afire* and another *Storm Over El Paso*."

"I also would guess that you are named for a poet," I continued. "Vachel Lindsay."

"My, you're brilliant, Captain Skull. I never dreamed anyone on earth, let alone in the sky, remembered anything about that little old 'Chinese Nightingale' or 'General Booth.'"

"Rachel Vachel," I said, leaning toward her, "the first

poem of any length my father ever taught me was 'The Congo.' That is, after Chesterton's 'Lepanto.'"

"Recite 'Lepanto'!" she commanded me, but before I could utter "White founts falling . . ." she countermanded that with, "No, don't! Daddy and his crew'll be back any minute and that poem's too long, much as I'd be ravished by it. Lemme think."

"Rachel Vachel," I asked, as my free fingers lightly walked up the silvery silk draping her thigh, "there is an aspect of the landscape puzzles me—the many conical towers."

"Oh those!" she said impatiently. "Those are just oil wells. Grandpa insisted on keeping the derricks for sentimental reasons, but Grandma thought they were unaesthetic and made him cover them up with those antimacassar lighthouses, I call 'em. Antimacassars were originally doilies to keep hair oil off chair backs, you know. I'd rather the naked derricks again—be honester."

"And the two very much larger and newer towers?" I continued. It is sometimes effective, I think, to talk of irrelevant matters while moving closer to a female. Besides, I have a curiosity that operates simultaneously on all levels, and when the sexual is awakened, all the others are too. "Only two much larger oil wells?"

"Fact is, I don't know the answer to that myself," Rachel Vachel said, anger in her voice. "When they built them six months ago, I asked Daddy, but he put me off with his standard lecture about how women shouldn't interest themselves in science and technology, but culture and religion only. I tried to ride out to them a couple times, but got turned back." Suddenly she sat up straight, though clapping a hand over my free one, which had reached her waist. Now her voice was entirely exasperated anger on the verge of tears. "Oh, Captain Skull, you don't know how Daddy strangulates me, hidin' a whim of patriarchal Texan iron under all that suffocatin' courtliness and courtesy. I'm supposed to get bowed to and stood up for and my feminine mystique done reverence, at the price of limitin' my activities to silly little poems and re-productions of *Oklahoma!* and *Babes in Toyland* and *The Wizard of Oz* with a Texas 'stead of a Kansas Dorothy—yes, and of bein' bossed around like a nine-year-old! Honest, some days I wish I could die!" That outburst over, she instantly flopped back against my left arm, this time throwing her own right arm over it to keep it from straying, as if it would, and leaning her lovely white-misted head against it so that she could dark-wonder me even more effectively with her glimmering eyes.

"Go on, tell me some more," she murmured meltingly. "Tell me some more about acting in the Sack." She sighed softly, at least for a young woman eight foot two, and added wistfully, "I suppose all you actors up there are stars, just like the ones twinklin' above us now."

"Far from it, princess," I told her, my left hand beginning to feather-stroke her bare shoulder and my right hand resuming its tiptoe journey. "Our situation is far more like that of any Shakespearean or later actors in puritanic Northern Europe and America before the twentieth century deification of entertainers. We are no better than strolling players—worse, because with vacuum outside we have nowhere to stroll when things get hot for us. We are given no special honor by our fellow Sackabonds and at times we are denounced and threatened by Circumluna's scientists, engineers, and technicians, on whose continuing ticket-buying, nonetheless, we depend for the essentials of life. In that sense we are much like the artists of the Renaissance, dependent on the patronage of their individual princes, our prince being the Circumlunan Establishment. Him we must please, or starve, and the former is as difficult as the latter is easy."

"Renaissance is just the word I was looking for to describe you!" Rachel interrupted. "You're like one of those tall, thin, somber-lookin', small-steppin' Spanish grandees, the kind that wear great cloaks and hats with black plumes and are deadly duelists. You fence and duel by any chance?"

"Those were among my first accomplishments," I contented myself with saying. I was tempted to give her a demonstration that might have surprised her, but it would have interrupted our passage toward togetherness, so I stifled my vanity.

"I might have known, you bein' an actor," she said. "Go on about those Longhairs you put on your plays for."

"The scientists, yes. Well, you see, princess, they began over a hundred years ago as—and have continued to be—quite rigid, atheistically puritanic types. They greatly need the catharsis we give them with our dramas—everything from high tragedy to low comedy—but there are always those among them whose violent, temporarily uncatharsized desires, masquerading as high scientific conscience, demand our muzzling and even our expulsion. They accuse us of great sexual laxity, thievery, political and social irresponsibility, corrupting the morals of the young, and dirty personal habits such as not sterilizing our night soil before returning it into the ecologic cycle—in short, all the things actors have been accused of since Egg-oh the Exhibitionistic Cave Man first cavorted in front of the nightly fire."

"Scuse me, Captain, but your left-arm skeleton bone's cuttin' into my neck," Rachel Vachel interrupted. "There, that's better. Tell me, do you consider me one of the young? I mean, as far as corruptin' morals is concerned? Don't answer that one, just keep it up—talkin' too."

I continued, "At present the puritanic faction of Circumlunans, composed somewhat more of those of Russian heritage than those of Americo-West European extraction, is in the ascendancy. With the lifting of the Interdict, they are demanding that not only we actors, but all Sackabonds not doing vital part-time technological work for Longhairs be deported to Earth. The great majority of Circumlunans don't want this at all—we're almost their sole source of fun and frenzy—but being respectable bourgeois technocrats to a man (and a woman) nearly, they daren't speak out against the highly vocal hyperpuritanic minority. The only solution for us, of course, is the age-honored one of buying off the Establishment with Circumlunan-acceptable cash—meaning funds available on Terra for buying Moon-short elements and materials the Circumlunans still find it difficult if not impossible to synthesize. It's to win that cash to defend from deportation all Sackabonds, but in particular the personnel and properties of the La Cruz Theater-in-the-Sphere, that I've come down to earth, Rachel Vachel."

I could feel her quiver with new excitement under my fingers. "You mean, you're goin' to put on *shows* down here to raise funds? No, don't stop what you're doin'—remember, you got your reputation for great sexual laxity to maintain and I got my daddy to spite. But in that case why not star with the Dallas Little Theater, with the title role in *Death Takes a Holiday* for a starter? I'm sure I could swing it and Daddy's got pots!"

"Alas, princess, the doctors assure me that even with constant exoskeletal support and large periods of rest, I dare not stay more than a week on Terra, or at a risky most, two, without suffering large permanent physiological damage. They expressly warned me against—"

I cut off that one quick, and the thought behind it too. Among the activities against which they had expressly warned me was the one in which I was now engaged, and I didn't want to start questioning my knowledge, superior to that of any doctor, of my own psychosomatic needs. Especially not now, when I was aboard the primeval rocket and the countdown started.

I contented myself with saying, "No, princess, I do not intend to put on any public performances down here."

She did not pursue her question, or appear to take note of my interrupted remark. With the gathering dusk and perhaps in some part because of my delicate manipulations, her eyes grew larger and more luminous. Her fingers slipping between my titanium shoulder girdle and head basket touched my cervical vertebrae. Her voice riding on indrawn and exhaled sighs, she said, "You know, Scully, I believe

I'm fallin' in love with you just a little bit—psychically, I mean, not only physiologically. Ever since I was a little girl I've had moods of despair where I wanted Death to come to me like a dark knight and carry me off—I wore out three tapes of Schubert's *Death and the Maiden*—and here you're doin' it. Why, you're just like Death in *The Seventh Seal*, leadin' me off in a dreamy dance—that is, if Max von Sydow had played the part 'stead of doin' the Knight. Say, Scully—no, keep it up—how are you ever gonna raise that cash down here you need to save your theater unless you put on shows? I'd give you some, except Daddy's a skinflint when it comes to pin money."

"I'll tell you a secret, Rachel Vachel," I said, my rumble somewhat thick, as she was shivering three fingers, thrust between my titanium exoribs, across my chest. What the devil, I'd already told her far more than I'd intended—I might as well, as Elmo would have put it, go it whole hog. "Before my grandfather lifted from Spanish Harlem, he had bought from a down-and-out Aleutian prospector a mining claim to an area near Yellowknife, Canada—I mean, Amarillo Cuchillo, North Texas. This claim was supposedly worthless, but the Aleutian, who had bought it from a Cree Indian, had investigated the area closely and discovered that within it lay the Lost Crazy-Russian Pitchblende Mine and he had drawn a map of the mine's exact location. My father treasured the claim and the map as an ace in the hole to revive the La Cruz fortunes in time of trouble. They were useless during the Interdict, but now that that's over and the time of trouble come for us and the entire Sack, my father has sent me down to sell the claim or seize the profits if someone else has meanwhile discovered it and been working it illegally."

"My, your pa must be quite a . . . a dreamer, Scully," Rachel Vachel murmured languidly. "That sounds to me just like the million and one Lost Dutchman Gold mines down in Mexico, Texas. Oh, but I'm dead sure it's going to

work out fine in your case," she hastened to add. Then, the
dark-wondering peaking in her eyes, "Kiss me, Scully."

Carefully tilting my head so neither my titanium jaw
shelf nor cheekplates would touch her, I planted my lips
on hers. Her hands moved on my back between titanium T-
spine and exorib lattice. We kissed for some time with
small moans. Then she broke away with a slightly bigger
one, in which I heard faintly the whispered words, "Come,
sweet death . . ." and her voice returned to medium brisk
as she asked, "You didn't leave the claim and map in your
luggage, I hope? Daddy's sure to have that snooped, 'scoped,
and espioned."

"But surely your father is too honorable and courtly and
genteel—"

"Oh, he's the genteelest jail warden in all Texas, Texas.
Why do you suppose I have secret compartments in my
lingerie drawers? If he could only see right now— You know,
Scully, we must be making a most exciting scene: a Greek
goddess bein' elegantly seduced by a romantical black-and-
silver skeleton, the matin' of the mantis with the june bug—
just the kind of scene Daddy'll never let us stage in our plays,
the courtly old Cromwell! Where have you got the claim
and the map, Scully? You didn't forget and leave them up
there in the sky, I hope?"

"I keep them on my person, princess."

"That's nice," she murmured, gently stroking same. "Say,
Scully, what's your impression of the Mexican situation
down here? I mean *seriously*—no, you keep it up too—and
truly. Answer honest, now."

"I hope this doesn't offend you, Rachel, but my answer
must be: deeply disturbing. The childish and superficially
humorous servitude of your Spanish Americans, I mean
Spanish Texans, I find disgusting. And those cybernetic
yokes—abominable!"

"That's interesting," she murmured. "Now what's your
attitude on revolution? No, keep it up."

I must admit that her rapid and startling questions were

putting me off stride a bit, like one-two punches, no matter
how well they conformed to my own philosophy of all curi-
osities satisfied simultaneously. But I gathered my forces
and carried on, on both levels.

"Revolution in Circumluna and the Sack? No. Except for
the Longhairs' puritanic blind spot, we are all too intelligent for it up there. Besides, we are too deeply interde-
pendent and the Longhairs hold all the cards. Down here?
I don't know. From what little I've seen of them, hoping for
a Mexican revolution would be like expecting a revolt of
the babies. *Emotionally* I sympathize greatly with revolution. I identify. Among my most favorite roles are Cassius,
Dr. Stockman in *An Enemy of the People*, Danton, Lord
Byron, Lenin, Sam Adams, Fidel Castro, John Brown, and
Ho Chi Minh."

"Oh I can just see you as Cassius. You got that 'lean and
hungry look' to perfection. You're goin' to devour little
Rachel, aren't you? Go Waltzing-Matilda with her? Promise? Or Ho too—you have the Dr. Fu Manchu touch: 'Be-
ware, America! You got your napalm and atomic bombs,
but I got my black scorpions, my giant centipedes, my spiders with diamond eyes that wait in the dark, then leap!'
Golly! Or maybe I could work up a drama around that
legendary greaser figure of El Esqueleto—you'd be *great* as
him. Say, there's an idea! But Daddy— Oh, forget it. Look
here, dear, I admit I'm getting a fetish thing about that
skeleton of yours, but couldn't you get out of it for just a
little while? Mayn't you be underestimating your unmech-
anized strength? Your hands feel so *strong* on my funny
bumps."

I was deeply moved at that, I must confess. For some
reason I could now see more plainly again my lovely eight-
foot-two pale goddess in her artistically disarranged robes.
A mysterious silver light bathed her and made me utterly
reckless.

"Look, darling," I whispered breathily and rapidly, "if
we're careful it's not necessary that I—"

I do not know what would have happened next, or rather I know exactly what would have happened next, and a disaster to have missed it, or more likely a disaster to have enjoyed it—anyhow, Rachel Vachel pushed me away with a sharply whispered, "They're coming back!" I heard the footsteps myself then, growing louder behind us, and I nervously smoothed my Sack suit and evened my breathing. The next moment, her drapery and platinum hair in order, she was handing me a glow-tipped reefer, and saying coolly, "Here you are, Señor La Cruz, a Chihuahua Pot-Perfecto. Daddy always says a man can't smoke on tobacco alone."

As I shakily inhaled the first piney puff, I looked straight out at the horizon again and saw that my "mysterious silver light" was merely that of the new-risen moon, silhouetting one of the big antimacassar lighthouses. I realized somewhat groggily but with a clutch of anxiety that I had not only missed my big moment with Rachel Vachel, but was already breaking my date with La Cucaracha.

The patio lights boomed on. I copied Rachel Vachel in leisurely standing up and casually turning around, though I spoiled the effect a bit by clanking my exoelbow against my pelvic girdle. Just come through the gringo door were Governor Lamar and his four fellow bigwigs, all looking a shade grim to me, and Elmo, who looked worried.

"Most sorry to interrupt your tête-à-tête," the Governor said smoothly. "I trust you weren't bored, Señor La Cruz, and that my daughter entertained you adequately."

I could manage no answer save a swallow, which bobbed my overly prominent Adam's apple, and a somewhat jerky nod.

"Now go to bed, sugar," he continued. "We have business to discuss with the señor."

"But Daddy—"

"Sugar!"

With a haughty shrug and thinning of lips, the Honorable Rachel Vachel turned to me and said formally, "Good night, Señor La Cruz. I trust we have the opportunity of continuing our most interesting conversation some other *day*." And she stuck out her hand, palm down.

I pressed and bowed over it. Though not risking a kiss this time, I did lightly scratch her palm with my forefinger.

Showing no reaction whatsoever, she turned away and walked through the gringo door without looking to left or right.

From the emphasis she had given her last word, I knew I could expect no opportunity of further converse with her this night and must pin on La Cucaracha any hopes I had of getting my jangled nerves soothed, especially my frustrated parasympathetic system.

But to tell the whole truth, I was far, far more—oh, so much!—concerned about the five unsmiling, craggy-visaged Texans I now faced, and it was chiefly my sympathetic nervous system, that old adrenal-squeezer, that was sending. Old tales of the vengeances done in patrist societies on daughter-seducers and sister-stealers and mere lovers-up marched like a series of funeral corteges through my mind. I thought of Abelard and Chance Wayne. Rachel Vachel had as much as told me her father was a constant spier on her activities. Would he have omitted those in the patio? Wouldn't he be sure to have had the couch bugged? And I had blurted out not only my grotesque passion, but also the secrets behind my trip to Terra. I cursed myself for an Eros-besotted fool.

It seemed to me most ominous that all five power men were now equipped with paired side arms belted over their beautifully tailored suits, that in addition, anachronistic rapiers hung from the hips of Sheriff Chase and Ranger Hunt, and that all five were once more making their nerve-twanging chink-chink, scratch-scratch, etc., tune.

It struck me as particularly sinister that the Governor was plucking invisible lint from his vest *without taking his eyes off me*.

Then as Rachel Vachel vanished and her rapid footsteps

died away and I expected the worst, everything suddenly changed for the best, like at the fairy-godmother moment in a children's tale. I could hardly have been more surprised if dancing elves had popped from under the flagstones.

The five power Texans relaxed and favored me with friendly smiles, while with the most winning of these the Governor himself advanced toward me, saying, "Señor La Cruz, most honored and patient of guests, it's my pleasure to inform you that all arrangements save one have been made for your passage by chartered private rocketship to Amarillo Cuchillo tomorrow morning." And he lightly took my limp hand and pumped it warmly though carefully. His breath was redolent of bourbon.

He went on casually, "The one omission is most trifling and really unnecessary to correct except for reasons of courtesy. It's that we visit tonight and get the counter-signature on your jet charter of President Longhorn Elijah Austin. The old gentleman would be hurt to have missed a visit with you, and—*sub rosa*, sir—we want to continue a little political fence-mending."

I hesitated. The Governor's expression seemed totally relaxed and friendly, as free from guile as Tom Mix's. I said, "But I thought—"

"Yes, sir, exactly, you *thought*—and no blame whatever attaches to you for that. But— Elmo!"

My old friend—I suddenly felt that way toward him—was twisting his huge hat into what looked like a model of a saddle-shaped universe, and he was working his lips and actually blushing. "Scully, I mean Señor La Cruz," he choked out, "I was reshading the facts a little. No, I was really lying to you quite a bit in our earlier conversations—chiefly by exaggerating my own importance and my inside knowledge of the current political situation. There was once indeed a little wounded feelings between President Austin and some of the other great statesmen of our land, but I blew them up out of all proportions; that arming his Mexican houseboys, for instance, what a whopper! And for a fact I simply didn't know—that's how small a bug I am in the human menagerie—that what wounds there were had been completely healed and only in need of the lightest postoperative care. Just a low-down Texas bigmouth, that's all I am, Scully, and I hope you forgive me."

"Of course, Elmo," I said quickly, embarrassed at his abject groveling, for that was what it had been, despite the humor with which he had pillowed it. I had grown to like Elmo, rather as one likes a clown. And to see a clown deflated, stripped, or dissected is always bad, or at least uncomfortable, theater.

I abruptly turned back to Lamar. "Is it necessary that my interview with President Austin take place tonight? I had rather——"

"I'm afraid it must, sir," he interrupted me. "A soiree rather than a matinee, as you gentlefolk of the stage put it. Your jet leaves early tomorrow and I have already, pardon me, taken the liberty of arranging your reception by our beloved prexy. I can understand your desire for, nay, your medical need of, rest, and I assure you the interview will be very brief and your transportation to and from it both rapid and unfatiguing."

"Quick and peaceful. Over in a wink," Sheriff Chase confirmed, snapping his fingers once.

As I hesitated again, I felt my reefer sting my fingers. Quickly shifting my grip back on the butt, I took a very long drag.

Perhaps it was the pot that gave me the inspiration and emboldened me to act on it.

"It wasn't rest I was concerned about," I said gaily. "Your hospitalities have quite refreshed me. It was that I had the whim to take all by myself tonight, by moonlight, a brief nocturnal jaunt through the quieter environs of your great city of freedom, employing for that purpose the cat wagon with which Mr. Earp so graciously provided me. Let me do this and I shall be only too happy to bandy amenities with your prexy."

Frowning slightly and even more slightly shaking his head, Lamar said slowly, "I'm afraid it's already been determined that you travel by official limousine. A cat wagon would hardly have the requisite dignity—"

"Tell you what, Cotton," Sheriff Chase broke in, "we can bring the wagon along on a flatbed racer. Then soon as his meeting with Austin's over, the señor can begin this little private wander on which he's set his heart."

"A happy inspiration!" Lamar said, his frown fading. "And now come, gentlemen, our time is growing short."

The loud chink of Burleson's coins was like a cymbal clash that begins a jolly march. Fanninowicz's facial tic was a "Forward!"

I took a last drag of my reefer, crushed it in the nearest tray, and stepped out with my illustrious entourage, the rhythmic clash of my titanium footplates dominating the thud of their leather boots. My cape was handed up toward me and I swirled it carelessly around my shoulder girdle without breaking stride.

It occurred to me how villainous I was to arouse myself with one woman and then plan to satisfy myself with another. But such is human flesh—at least that of an audacious Thin with a perfectly tuned exoskeleton setting out on a planetary spree.

5 / President's Manse

Had Society done its duty to itself, Ben Thompson
instead of dying the death of a desperado might have
become a useful citizen. [Ben Thompson was an
early Texas antihero and often acquitted multikiller
of the late 1800's, himself finally shot to death with
nine bullets in an Austin variety theater.] But will
the moral be read aright and turned to profit? It
certainly will not unless Texas society purges itself
of the complicity and indulgence which have so
largely nurtured and developed the desperadoism
in men. His is a slow growth and it is Texas society
which encourages that growth by holding out the
hope to him of achieving both fame and fortune in
a career of murderous violence and professional
terrorism.

—*Galveston News*

THE DOWNY, glimmer-windowed hurtling nest of darkness
that was the limousine silently braked to a stop with a suddenness that mashed my face against my cheekplates. With
tiny groans the straps around my titanium rib cage and
belly support tightened almost to breaking, then were
merely snug again. Beside me, Ranger Commander Hunt
cursed a simple, "Jack it!" as the exoelbow of my outflung
arm took him lightly across his handsome Roman nose.

From the other side Sheriff Chase fumbled at my riding
harness but I brushed his hands aside and deftly unsnapped
the two straps myself. I was beginning to resent being
treated as an invalid or baby. When they had got out, each
almost tripping over his ceremonial sword—for such they
had explained them to be—I followed Hunt as swiftly and
surely as a tall metal monkey and found myself standing
in the moonlight on a springy black driveway, the four

other limousines drawn up in line two before and two behind, and debouching their passengers, while to the extreme rear I thought I could make out the flatbed bearing my cat wagon.

The climbing moon silhouetted a spire and highlighted several others and also the three towers and slate roof of a vast building some two hundred meters ahead. It looked to my scenery-trained eyes like a Gothic manse of old, specifically one of those fanciful carpenter's-Gothic edifices of the late nineteenth century in America, abristle with balconies, columns, and fretwork of Moorish, baroque, and other manners too numerous to list.

Not a single window of the place showed light.

There were no lights between me and it, only a low, pale wall with an arch of triumph to admit the driveway.

The limousines had all doused their headlamps.

It struck me that the stage had been set, not for a president's reception but for a ghost story. . . .

All it would have taken was one lighted window and a terrified beautiful girl in the foreground to make it the greatest of camp art.

As if he had caught my first thought, I heard Elmo, as he came up behind me, boom out with a little of his earlier free-and-easy, "That old miser Longhorn Elijah! He'll whup half to death a maid who leaves on a twenty-five watter over an escalator or in a john the instant someone has wiped himself. But soon as we pass the arch, Scully, the whole shebang'll light up like a veritable fairyland, I can tell you that."

A discreet chuckle I recognized as Governor Lamar's came from the figure approaching beside Elmo. He said, "Elmo puts it crudely, but it is true that President Austin is a thrifty old soul who lives a life as simple as Timon of Athens', providing a crushing answer to those who accuse our officialdom of private prodigality. Well, sir, do you feel able to proceed afoot? I shouldn't like for the sake of your dignity to see you make a horizontal approach in a cat

wagon or stretcher, unless you feel it medically manda-
tory."

"We'd drive you straight to the door," Commander Hunt
assured me, "but immemorial custom dictates that the
prexy's mansion be approached afoot by all and sundry."

"Two of us'll walk close beside you and support you, of
course," Sheriff Chase added. "Elmo, you take his right
arm."

"Nonsense, gentlemen, I am quite able to navigate un-
grasped and erect on my trusty exolegs," I replied lightly,
keeping out of my voice the gust of indignation I felt at
this further evidence that they considered me a hospital
patient.

And with that I stepped out toward the dark mansion.

Elmo stayed beside me, but fortunately for his ribs, which
would have got a titanium dig, he did not attempt to
touch me.

Professor Fanninowicz came hurrying up on my other
side, fumbling with wires and chattering, "Sir, for the sake
of science, may I attach damp electrodes to your——"

"No!" I rapped out.

"But may I not at least accompany you and observe—"
"Yes, but hands off!"

The dark figures that had emerged from the leading
limousines parted for us. I noted that they wore dark uniforms that included knee boots and black slouch hats, and
that they were armed with heavy laser carbines. Ancient
shell rifles or even antique powder-and-ball muskets would
have seemed more appropriate ceremonial weapons to
match Hunt's and Chase's swords. But then I remembered
what Rachel had told me of her father's efforts to introduce an actual glacier into Wilder's Japanese-delicate *Skin
of Our Teeth*. Hunt's Rangers, I decided as we passed them,
were lucky they had not been made to tote ceremonial
atomic bombs.

Then Governor Lamar, stepping uncomfortably close behind me, almost on my heels, called out softly but carry-

ingly, "Everyone move very slowly now! We don't want to
hurry Señor La Cruz, or cause him to strain his satellite-
enfeebled heart."

That did it. As if hearts did not have to work well and
efficiently in free fall merely to supply tissues with oxygen
and other nutriment! Tissues such as the cerebrum, of
which I now bet we spacefolk had twice the volume of
these bumbling Texans! All butt and no brain, like dinosaurs!

I stepped out at my fastest, taking giant strides, my hood
and cloak flapping behind me. In almost no time Elmo and
Fanninowicz were panting. Such was my rage that I ignored my surroundings, not pausing to ponder the function
of the trenches we were now passing, or of the slitted walls
of thick metal on their mansion-side edges, or even of the
dim figures crouched behind those walls.

But I did catch the gasping Fanninowicz attaching an
electrode to my pelvic girdle. He already had one affixed to
my shoulder yoke. The fine insulated wires faintly rattled
against the drive behind us. Since he couldn't measure my
body electricity, he was evidently hoping to find some in
my exoskeleton. I jerked the attachments loose and struck
his hands away with a blow of my wristplate that got out of
him an, "*Aiii! Teufel! Gottverdammter Knochen-Mensch!*"

"For bleedin' Jesus' sake, take it easy, Scully," Elmo
pleaded between puffs. "We're gonna get there *soon
enough.* And you know, even He didn't exactly race up
Golgotha."

Deaf to the connotative and allusive significance in his
words, I was busy planning my entrance speech, which
began something like "I'm sorry to have outdistanced my
Texas escort, Your Sublime Excellency, but such was my
eagerness and such their excess of adipose tissue—well, one
must admit, Prexy, that some of them sweat a mite easy. I
submit in all humility that at least the Texas Rangers ought
to keep in a little better physical trim. Of course with someone as courtly and delicate as Governor Lamar . . ."

I was darkly pleased to note that there were no longer footsteps behind us, even distant ones. The three of us were entering the shadow of the manse now. And as we passed under the great archway, with its ghostly bas-reliefs of guns, snorting horses, dead Indians, and the like, even Fanninowicz began to fall back, was gone.

Elmo panted, "One thing I want to tell you, Scully, and I really mean it this time, you're a true Texan of the Raven-Alamo breed. I'm proud to have known you." He grasped my hand with such obvious spontaneity and sincerity that I had no impulse to strike it aside. Then he too was gone.

I took two furious strides more, then began to slow down halfway through the third. My brain was starting to work again, just a corner of it.

Two scarlet beams sprang from the dark grounds, zizzling past me to either side. I smelled the reek of ions. I heard spluttering, crackling splashes behind me.

Turning, I saw the two laser beams scattering gouts of white-hot molten stone from the bases of the triumphal arch. Dimly I saw Fanninowicz rolling away, wrapped by his wires, behind the shelter of the pale wall. At least he had temporarily escaped the laser's light stiletto. Of Elmo I saw no sign.

Then from corners of the manse and grounds a dozen lights blazed on me—white lights so bright and hot I thought for a moment I was being disintegrated. If I hadn't had practice from childhood in avoiding looking directly at spotlights I'd have been blinded.

The lights didn't reveal a fairyland, unless you count toy soldiers four and a half feet high as such.

The grounds were crowded with the shielded emplacements of laser and lightning guns and other heavy weaponry. They were manned by barefoot Mexicans wearing brass cuirasses and brass helmets with colorful horsehair plumes. And all the guns were pointed straight at me.

The natural thing, especially for me, would have been to run like hell. It was pure rage that held me titanium-rooted

—rage at Lamar and the rest for having maneuvered me into this sitting-duck position, for using me as some sort of stalking horse in their war against President Austin; rage at myself for having dismissed them as bumblers and letting them convince me so easily of the untruth of Elmo's earlier tales.

I'd be damned if I'd let those bulky bastards—by now all safely crouched in the outside trenches, *their* trenches— see me run.

And still I wasn't shot down, though both Elmo and Fanninowicz had been fired on. Like their guns, the Mexican soldiers were staring wide-eyed at me—my tall and thin black form, my doubtless dazzling exoskeleton.

It was then I got the glimmer of inspiration and acted on it instantly. Raising my arms wide and high, so that all of my cloak was thrown back and my exoskeleton completely in view, I thundered at my loudest, "I am Death! *Yo soy la muerte! Yo soy el esqueleto!* Vamoose!" Then I brought my arms together and waved them horizontally apart, as if brushing all the brass-armored bent-backs off the stage.

They wavered. One ran. A silver-helmeted officer drew a bead on him with a pistol and was himself zizzlingly transfixed on the red laser beam of one of his own soldiers.

Then they were all in flight and I was tramping straight forward again, straight up the stairs leading to the spacious porch and the manse's double doors. These slowly opened outward at my approach, revealing that they were backed by great thicknesses of steel.

I faced another curve of muzzles and of silver-armored, staring, back-bent soldiery. I scattered them as I had those outside, and I followed them, still at my remorseless steady stride. I was beginning thoroughly to enjoy my role of Death the Disperser of Armies. Then I realized I was doing exactly what Lamar and Company had wanted me to: win them a bloodless battle. Even that didn't at once destroy my delight.

Then I saw ahead of me a semicircle of glass cases ten feet high. There were at least twenty of them.

I halted. Striking with all his fabled cunning and genius for the unexpected, Death had after a fashion stopped *me*.

Each of the cases contained a life-size human figure in natural flesh tones and with Terran clothing that ranged in style over the last 150 years. The earliest or oldest were about six feet tall. Then as the eye ranged around the semicircle, they grew in height to eight feet and more.

I recognized the Americans Kennedy and Johnson from my history prints. I realized I was looking at the presidents of Texas.

They looked grimly back at me—some old, some middleaged, some almost young. There were handsome faces, harsh faces, faces jowled and tiny-eyed with dissipation and greed.

In the dimness they seemed alive. I felt sure the earliest were wax. I was not so sure about the later. I recalled how the early Russians had mummified the bodies, or at least stuffed the hides, of their early illustrious dead.

Then I heard a rasping voice and looked up.

Four or five stories above me was a magnificent, domed skylight of stained glass, made darkly colorful by the moonlight it transmitted. Curving down from beneath it in a wide and graceful spiral came a stairway railed with dark, delicate metal tracery. Here at least was a glimpse of fairyland.

And also an ogre from same. An ogre from whose quilted bathrobe a jowled and purplish face protruded, inset with pig eyes and topped by tousled white hair and wearing askew a golden wreath. He leaned over the stair railing about a floor and a half above me, cradling in one beblanketed arm an antique double-barreled shotgun.

"Whar are my Mexican houseboys?" he roared. "Whar are you, you little buggers? They's an attack. Shoot down every mother-screwing Ranger or other rebellious bein' sets foot inside mah walls! Get the man with the base bullhorn!

Whar's my praetorian guard? Sound the trumpet! Ah, thar's one of the assassins sent against me, skinny bastard in a black minji suit, but it don't hide him from mah all-seein' eyes!"

I lunged rapidly sideways under the stairs. The parqueted spot on which I'd been standing was blasted. Two ricochets stung my forehead and side while at least one more *plinked* off my exoskeleton. A glass case cracked.

I raced toward the back of the manse, taking the avenue of retreat the silver-cuirassed Mexicans had used. Soon I had plunged into a dark, rather narrow, blessedly protective corridor. Behind me, President Austin's voice ranted, "Dead as a doornail, dead! Come on, you traitors all, and taste the Old Man's wrath. Sound the alarum bell!"

Then a younger voice cut in. "There he is! But don't spoil his face! Burn him down! Get the other!"

There was another shotgun blast, a scream, then even my corridor was red as hell with leaked laser light—just in time to show me, before the collision did, that the corridor abruptly changed from a height of fourteen feet to four and a half. The head space carried a moral so simple and carved so large that I had read it before the red light faded:

> WATCH OUT, ANYONE WHO'S TALL!
> MEXES, AREN'T YOU GLAD YOU'RE SMALL?

I was on my hands and exoknees as fast as I could fall and scuttling forward. True, the "Get the other!" might not mean me, and even if it did, the "get" might not mean "burn down," but then again they might—and I had already in the past two minutes learned something of Texas political acumen.

I heard a dull crash behind. Austin's body falling? Don't ask useless questions. Crawl faster, you idiot Thin!

I do not know how long my quadruped scramble through darkness lasted, surely much less time than it seemed then. I do know that I made an even number of right-angle turns, and by exercising choice at forks managed to make as many left- as right-hand turns, ensuring that I was headed at the end in the same direction I had been at the beginning. Twice I half crawled, half tumbled down short stairs, and once climbed up. More than once I gave thanks to Diana that my hands were horny-palmed, that kneeplates covered my kneecaps, and that my motors kept purring happily. I thanked her too that I had practiced crawling as well as walking, up in the centrifuge. I also gained a certain respect for the maze-running abilities of the Mexicans who, surely often carrying trays of drinks, food, etc., had presumably regularly treaded these inky corridors in the manse of the light-penurious Austin. Or had they used flashlights? Somehow that seemed unlikely, but I wished I had one now.

From time to time an action-insulated corner of my mind thought thoughts: such as that the morale of the Rangers must be zero that they hadn't overwhelmed the manse by themselves, but waited for the accident of my aid. But maybe it had been essential to keep the political war secret and not destroy this Texas White House.

As I right-angled right after a particularly long stretch of Mexican corridor, I heard a thumping scuttling behind me. A thin blue beam narrowly missed my withdrawing foot and there was the faint smell of singed plastic where it struck the wall.

A voice rebuked, "Cut your power, you dumb-headed lightning plumber! Orders is to paralyze him, not fry him—'less we have to."

I was not greatly reassured.

Thereafter I kept hearing the sounds of my pursuit. It did not gain on me. I was grimly pleased that my motored titanium was performing as well as their flesh.

Suddenly the ceiling rose. I was in a large room dimly lit by moonlight coming through windows and open Texan and Mexican doors. Food smell and round, hanging shapes suggested a kitchen. I lifted to my feet, feeling a surge of dizziness and weakness, but I mastered them, tonguing down pills and water. I made for the Texan door in great strides, crashing down pots and cutlery. I heard angry calls from the crawl space behind, but I was out of line with it.

I stepped outside. I was on a narrow porch and at the head of a steep flight of stairs. I heard an equine snort and a low, chilling laugh—and I stopped.

A few yards beyond the foot of the stairs stood a huge white horse with black harness and silver-looking bit and harness rings. Astride it was a figure all in black, from under whose black slouch hat silvery hair cascaded.

Then Rachel Vachel's face lifted out of shadow and in a blue of movement her black-gauntleted hands drew lightning pistols from the black holsters at her side and directed them toward me.

I had never faced, it seemed to me, anything as icy as their needle muzzles and her gaze. Of course, I told myself bitterly, she had been in on my betrayal from the start, casually using her seemingly naïve wiles to brainwash me and soften me up for her father. I ought to have known you couldn't ever trust a society pinko. I tasted bitterness, and not only from an antigrav pill that had been slow in going down.

I heard rapid steps behind me—two sets of them—and cries of "There's the black bastard!" "We got him." "Don't move a muscle, Skinny." My arms were grasped from behind and a sharp muzzle pressed against my temple.

Then with only the faintest whisper of ionization and only its most ghostly acid perfume, two tenuous needle beams sprang from the tips of Rachel Vachel's pistols and bypassed my cheeks inches to either side.

The grip on my arms relaxed, the muzzle ceased to prick my temple, and there were soft yet ponderous thuds on the porch to either side of me.

"Greetings, Captain Skull," she called up to me. "Now hustle down fast and hop up behind me. Those two Rangers are out for a half-hour, but even with the morons opposing us, it's a sin to waste time."

Suppressing surprise, for a moment, and other emotions, I took the stairs two steps at a time, watching my feet narrowly, but calling back, "You mean we can escape? The Rangers haven't the manse encircled?"

"Hell, no. Like all Texas wars, this little scuffle's been all false front. Kick up your leg now and give a jump with the other. I'll yank your shoulder."

"But Rachel," I asked as I complied and found myself astride quivering horseflesh, and my exosternum pressed to girl, "how did you know you'd find me here? How did you guess your father would use me to—"

"Easy as guessin' a rat'll bite," she answered scornfully. "Now wrap your arms around me. All you got to do is figure out the sneakiest, safest course and you got Daddy's mind read to the base of his spinal cord. See, I even stole your luggage and got it at my saddlebow. How's that for service?"

She turned in her saddle. Her pale, thinly smiling face was close to mine. "Now confess, Scully," she said. "Aren't you just a mite surprised to discover that the silly little-theater gal (only she's a loose bitch too) and giggly Governor's daughter is in actuality Our Lady of Sudden Death, the Black Madonna of the Bent-Back Underground?"

"Well, yes," I said truthfully. "I mean, no—"

She gave another of her chilling laughs. "You menfolk—" she began. Then her eyes, scanning my forehead, showed sudden concern. "You're hurt, my lover."

Evidently the shotgun ricochet had drawn blood. "It's nothing," I told her.

"It had better not be," she told me seriously, "because you got a lot more to do tonight. Pull your cloak and hood around you, your bones gleam too bright. And hang on tight now," she added, turning front again and picking up the reins. "Oh, you can feel me up a bit if you get the chance —wow, your skeleton's still like ice. But hang on for your life, because it's a far greater cause than even my lover's precious existence that's now at stake!"

She touched with her heels the great white beast's flanks and we were soon going through tree shadows and silvery spaces at a ponderous gallop, which caused me to jounce considerably and not only to lock my arms hand to elbow around her waist, but also to steady my flapping legs by clenching them against the great heaving white barrel below me. In my brain there had gathered a certain bewilderment.

"Where are we going?" I asked.

She replied, "To the central point of tonight's riotous revolutionary assembly, which happens to be the bandstand corner of the Greasertown cemetery."

We galloped on through the moonlit night, my mind now truly a welter of confusion.

6 / In Church

La Muerte Alta, La Muerte Alta,
Alta como libertad,
Y viene, sí, viene
Aquí de la eternidad.

El Esqueleto, El Esqueleto
Quiere Texas caminar,
Porque él caza, porque encuentra
Muchos gringos que matar.

Y seguiremos, sí, seguiremos
Muerte donde él caza,
Y mataremos, sí, mataremos
Texans, hombre y dama.

—"Song of the Bent-Back Underground," sung to
the air of "La Cucaracha"

There follows a spirited free translation by
Rachel Vachel Lamar.

The tall grim reaper, the tall grim reaper,
Tall as all of liberty,
And he is coming, yes, he is coming
Here from far eternity.

Sir Skeletony, Sir Skeletony
Wants to travel Texas through,
Because he's hunting, because he's finding
Many gringos' bones to chew.

And we will follow, yes, we will follow
Death to where the oceans curl,
And we'll be killing, yes, we'll be slaying
Texans, every man and girl.

RACHEL DASHINGLY REINED in our mount and walked him
up the broad low steps before the church, whose pink and
pastel-blue walls were now only two shades of silver in the

moonlight. The night was eerily silent. I saw no signs of life in the cemetery—a good thing under these lonely circumstances, I suppose—or around the bandstand, or even in the church itself. It made me wonder at her talk of a "riotous, revolutionary assembly." I was, however, rather glad not to see La Cucaracha. After a half-hour of rocking embrace with Rachel, my titanium jaw shelf often resting on her shoulder, close to her neck, my desire was focused almost entirely on her, even though our closeness came chiefly from the necessity of my riding pillion. And the thought of my earlier infatuation with a—well—midget had come to seem almost grotesque. Moreover, I wasn't at all sure of how Rachel Vachel would have welcomed La Cucaracha. Or La Kootch Rachel, for that matter. And if "welcomed" is the word. Women are apt to develop toward each other strange animosities, in which the best interests of the man involved are totally ignored.

The tall doors of the church opened to a wide slit, spilling out dusky yellow light and three barefoot bent-backs in brown hoods and hitched-up brown robes. The first two carried a light stair of three steps and set it beside the horse so that one of my footplates brushed it. The third crossed his arms and looked up at Rachel, dignity and pride in his searching eyes, fanaticism in the clench of his swarthy jaws.

"How is the night?" he intoned.

"Dirty and dark," Rachel answered.

"What lines the way?"

"Danger and death." After a pause she continued, "I bring him whose coming has been foretold. You've been informed, Father Francisco?"

A nod of the brown hood. "Guchu and Rosa Morales brought word."

With a small snort of contempt that I did not understand, Rachel said, "Well, he's here now anyhow. Climb down, darling!"

"But—" I began, then realized I had too many questions to

choose between. I should not have let her con me into
spending our ride reciting "Lepanto" in her pale seashell
ear, with "The Congo" for encore. I ended by asking tamely,
"Aren't you staying?" as I steadied myself on the brick pavement by catching hold of the back of her saddle. Between
my ears I was still rocking from the gallop.

"No, sweetheart," she told me, leaning down, "I gotta
maintain my persona as the flibbertigibbet Honorable Miss
Lamar." She grasped my head by my ears, a not unpleasant
sensation if one goes along with it, and faced our faces at
each other, close. "Look, Scully, you just trust in me and do
as you're told, but don't take crap from anybody *and*"—she
shook my head, not entirely pleasant—"*Don't have anything to do, you hear me, with that man-eatin' Rosa Morales!*"

"But I don't even know a woman named—" I began. Suddenly her face tilted, her lips pressed mine at an angle of
ninety degrees, speech gave way to a subtler mode of communication, our arms went around each other. Time halted
in midtread. Then, as suddenly, Rachel Vachel pushed away
from me with a somewhat extravagant and alarming "Until
doom, My Captain!" and a more sensible *"Hasta mañana!"*
and, wheeling her horse, made off down the steps. A tail
of my cloak had caught in the harness and I was spun
around—157 pounds isn't much inertia—before it tore loose,
so that my *"Hasta luego!"* and wave of farewell were a
rather drunken-looking performance as My Lady of Sudden Death galloped off into the black and silvery night.

The experience left me somewhat dizzy, so that I was
grateful for the limited support of two of the little brown
friars as they walked on tiptoe and with arms upstretched
to touch my elbows and guide me through the slit between
the doors, which were closed at once behind us.

I stopped and leaned back against them, tonguing down
pills and drink. As my vision cleared, I studied the remarkable sight before me.

I was in a long room a few feet more than Texan tall.

Its violet, pink, and pale-blue walls and its darker-blue ceiling studded with a few silver-and-gold five-pointed stars were lit by flames, which are perhaps the strangest and most beautiful of gravity phenomena, though they can be reproduced in nullgrav in a carefully controlled wind tunnel. The flames rose from white cylinders and spread a spicy aroma as well as light.

The walls were lined with somewhat crudely carved and colored plastic, or perhaps even wooden figures, derived about equally from medieval European art and Mayan and Aztec forms.

Centered on the far wall was the Crucified Saviour, Mexican small, the short horizontal arms of the cross suggesting the cyborg's yoke, though in no obvious fashion.

To either side of the pitiful earth-brown figure were two figures as tall as the roof, indeed serving almost as caryatids to support the flat blue heaven. By the symbols carved in large on them—angel, winged lion, winged ox, and eagle—they were clearly the Four Evangelists. But, though barefoot and clad in simplest robes, they looked like Texans. Their serene and somber features had on second glance a subtly gloating or menacing cast, while their casually positioned hands had as if by accident the attitudes of those about to draw pistols or crack whips, though there were no weapons depicted.

The remaining figures along the side walls seemed more inspired by the great Amerind cultures and were chiefly crouching or bent. Human males, females, gods, demons, angels, devils, animals—I was frequently unable to tell which was intended. Their colors were predominantly dark with flashes of red, yellow, bright green, and gold, chiefly in the eyes and often fanged mouths.

Randomly grouped, a score of Mexes in shirts and short pants knelt toward me on the floor of pounded earth. Hams on heels, arms crossed on forward-bent torsos, heads acutely upturned to show eyes white-circled with dread, they more than any of the carven ones reminded me of those early Mexican forms in which a stocky human figure is compressed into a block.

Behind the altar, which either regularly stood or had been dragged out from the far wall, four persons sat widely spaced on the only chairs to be seen in the room.

The first was Father Francisco, who, having hurried back, now reoccupied his chair.

The second was a very burly young Mex, built as a bull though looking no taller than the four-and-a-half-foot Mex maximum. Even at the distance I noted the white flash of his teeth in his dark face as he gave me a confident, challenging smile.

The third was a wild-eyed scowling Negro in orange-and-yellow robes—yes, by Diana, he was the same babbling Zen Buddhist who had earlier drubbed my head basket.

The fourth was La Cucaracha. She had kept her rendezvous after all, though in a fashion quite unexpected. It burst on me that from her first seductive smile she had been planning to use me in this preposterous revolution. She was as bad as Elmo or Governor Lamar. But somehow in her I forgave it. Love has an infinitude of beginnings.

Father Francisco leaned toward and spoke briefly to the young man beside him, who raised toward me a fist on bent arm and called, "I am El Toro, comrade. Please to come forward."

I complied—though with a mental reservation on the "comrade" part—feeling theatrically at home in the place. My grotesque figure matched the carved ones, which lacked a good conventional representation of death.

The bent, kneeling ones hobbled out of my way on their knees, keeping faced toward me as I moved. Their dread seemed if anything to increase. It must be a very great power that kept them from staggering to their feet and hobbling off.

Standing very tall, I placed my hands on the altar table, leaning slightly against it, and looked the four back and forth with grim dignity.

But not for long. La Cucaracha sprang up onto the altar, threw her arms around my head, drew it down, and showered my face with kisses.

I should have been repelled, I suppose, especially after spending a very exciting, most romantic evening with a girl my own size. Why, I had even been thinking of La Cucaracha with contempt as a midget and my earlier infatuation with her an aftereffect of space-flight drugging. And I now knew she was also a political opportunist.

But, somehow, having her here in the flesh—and Rachel Vachel away until tomorrow—made all the difference. Once again I sensed her dancing aliveness, her wholly feminine muscularity. I even found myself comparing her swifter kisses with Rachel's, and they came off very well. As for size, that is a tricky business. Although almost as tall as myself, Rachel Vachel had a mass three times my own. While mine and La Cucaracha's masses were approximately equal.

I showered kisses back.

"My silver bones man! My most estimable and passionate!" she cried as we took breath. "Ah, *querido,* I knew you would choose to become a hero of the Revolution, the—how do you say?—supreme *figurehead* of the Bent-Back Underground!"

I had no intention whatever of becoming any such thing. I was still fully determined to fulfill my mission on Terra as quickly as possible and then get up out, no matter what amorous interludes might embellish the period. Of course by running away from the President's manse with two stunned Rangers behind me, I'd probably cooked my chances of that jet-special trip to Amarillo Cuchillo tomorrow, if there'd ever been any chances. No, of course there hadn't— that had just been part of the bait—I'd been thinking like a fool. Still, I'd find a way—

But by then we were kissing again.

"Cease this improper behavior at once!" a stern voice drove into our building rapture. It was that of Father Francisco. "A church is for worship only, or for the plotting of revolt blessed by God. It is not for the arousal and enactment of carnal desires, Rosa Morales!"

I felt a small surge of apprehension and even a speck of guilt at realizing that La Cucaracha was the "man-eater" against whom Rachel Vachel had warned me. The Governor's daughter would doubtless cut me forever, if she could see what I was doing, and maybe try to cut me apart. Still, she wasn't seeing, she'd be away until tomorrow—I wasn't even losing my chance at her by my present actions. Besides, her prohibition made La Cucaracha only more desirable, gave an added zest to my desires. What man doesn't love a man-eater?

"Pah!" Rosa informed the outraged religious, turning toward him, her fist on her hip, but her other arm still around my neck. "If the church is not for love, *padre*, what is it for? The bending of the knees to *you*? The frightened mumbling of un-understood prayers and petitions? The silly shy behavior of the white Texan Sunday school?"

While Rosa chattered on and Father Francisco fumed, El Toro was watching us with a white-flashing, amiable, but impatient grin, his fists on table edge with elbows up. He now said, laughingly yet sharply, "Rosa, I have warned you many times revolution and passion do not mix. Especially passion directed at one chosen to play the role of almost a god in our uprising."

"Oh, you hypocrite!" Rosa cried out at him. "Especially when your own continuing role in the revolution depends on a feature involving at least two peasant girls per night. Do not hark to him, *mi amigo*," she told me. "He merely hates me because I refuse to fall into his arms along with his trembling, shyly adoring, illiterate, fifteen-year-old stupids!" And she snapped finger and thumb contemptuously at the brawny young Mex.

However, it did seem to me that El Toro had made at least one valid point. I glanced to see how my "worshipers" in the body of the church were taking my display of all-too-human behavior. To my surprise, they were kneeling toward me as frightened-eyed as ever.

Rosa drew my face back toward hers with soft fingers on my cheek. "Do not believe the jealous and censorious ones, *amadísimo* Señor Christopher La Cruz. Revolution and the making of love go together like rice and beans, like meat and chili sauce. It is only the joys of amorousness that make endurable the exhausting meetings, the interminable plottings-around-tables, the unceasing danger of discovery. *Ai mi*, that is of the truest, Cristobal *queridísimo*."

And she brazenly resumed her kissings and embracings, and I went on brazenly enjoying them. We hardly heard the *padre*'s doleful, "Oh, my daughter, my poor daughter dancing with her high-heeled shoes and painted lips toward hell," or El Toro's controlledly bland, "What I do not understand, in truth, is what of erotic interest you discover in a living skeleton, Rosa. Now a man of flesh and muscle, a strong man, a man *muy hombre*. . . ."

But we were shocked apart by a roar-screeched, "Stoppit! You're driving me out of my skull! For freedom's sake, I can consider collaborating with a metal construct from which dangles the simulacrum of humanity like a hanging jumbee, but to be forced to watch firm flesh embrace such ofay offal dropped from the sky—"

It was, of course, the Buddhist, his arms waving, his contorted mouth a-hang with loops of spittle.

"Shut up, Guchu, you foreignor with toppled mind, you black bees bonnet!" Rosa snapped at him.

"I'll set myself afire, I'm warning you," he threatened back.

"Gentlemen! Gentlemen!" I thundered my deepest, jarring the altar table with decisive planting of my spread-fingered hand. "And my most darling Rosa," I added softlier. "Most potent, grave, and reverend signiors"—why, it fit them better than it had the Texans!—"my very noble and approved good masters, I am the unhappy subject of these quarrels. Yet I have not been permitted, or perhaps I should

say, given full opportunity, to express my own outlook on
the matter. I am moved by the plight of the underprivileged
in Texas, I sympathize with the aims of the Bent-Back Underground. But I am in fact and figure an extraterrestrial,
and one who has not spent twelve hours on your planet. As
a Circumlunan of the Sack, I am bound to uphold the
truce on which the lifting of the Interdict is based. I am
pledged to my own home-world not to take sides in any of
your quarrels and to maintain a complete neutrality in all
matters." At this moment, however, I unobtrusively slid my
hand to Rosa's slipper and covered it gently, to assure her
that my "complete neutrality" in no way applied to our
budding and now hothouse forced relationship.

"Moreover," I continued. "I am here in Dallas, Texas,
Texas, purely by accident. My spaceship was supposed to
land me in Amarillo Cuchillo, where I must conduct pressing business on which rests the continuing safety, nay, the
life of a large section of the inhabitants of my world. They
must be my first concern. So, much as I sympathize with
your revolution, much as I am honored by your invitation
to participate, I must with great regrets decline."

"But, *amiguísimo*," Rosa protested with a childlike wonder and injured innocence masking utter dishonesty, in a
fashion characteristic of all women, "in agreeing to this
rendezvous with me, which I have faithfully kept, you
agreed to all else surely. I trusted you—"

"Claims to be a man, but does not act like one," El Toro
put in scornfully and I think more for Rosa's benefit than
mine. "It becomes clear that with utter lack of muscle—
aye, and of *cojones*—goes complete absence of courageous
heart."

"False heart as well as false flesh. No more dickering with
this death dingus, I say," the Buddhist Guchu half chanted,
half raved, while Father Francisco put in reprovingly,
"Though tolerating them for revolt's sake, I have always
warned you against foreignors, children. And now you see

in this creature from Limbo, this dubious being from the lower stars—"

Though angry with their imputations of weakness to me, especially in the genital department, I controlled that emotion and once again thunder-rumbled, "Gentlemen! Gentlemen!" It is remarkable how a voice like an approaching storm catches the attention of others and silences their disputes. Filing away this valuable theater datum, I continued, "Moreover, your plan to use me as a figurehead for your revolution, though most picturesque—and flattering to me—is unfortunately quite impractical." And I gave them a very brief account of how I had scattered the battalion of houseboys at Austin's manse, ending with "And so you see, gentlemen—and dear Rosa—that instead of flocking to me, your peasants and cyborged proletarians would fly from me in terror."

El Toro, who had listened with searching interest to my account, now said, "Ah-ha, comrade, I see that you are perhaps not a coward, only deplorably ignorant of mass psychology. Any leader, in particular one of supernatural character, *must* be dreaded as well as loved. Fear and followership are but two sides of one coin. You may trust us to present you in such a way that the repulsion you generate in others is always outweighed a little by the attraction."

"You speak truly, my son," Father Francisco nodded. "Even God the Father rules firstly by the wholesome fear he strikes into his creatures."

Guchu did not comment, at least in intelligible words. He had sunk to a staring-eyed growling and muttering, rocking all the while rhythmically in his chair.

Rosa said eagerly, "Also, *amado,* there is your desire to reach Amarillo Cuchillo. We will take you there, as last stop in a series of northward-trending revolutionary rallies long planned. Can you not serve the Revolution for a month?"

That last bait did attract me for a moment, even though a month was twice the maximum terra-time the doctors had given me (doctors always leave margins of safety), until

I realized that Rosa's month most surely meant two or four, if it was not bait purely.

I said, "Gentlemen—and dearest, most solicitous Rosa—I must still decline for several unimpeachable reasons, of which the first——"

"Bah!" El Toro interrupted. "A weakling to the core, as I first surmised. No muscles. No *cojones.*"

Father Francisco stared through me, shaking his head contemptuously.

Rosa jerked her foot from under my hand and stamped with her heel, not quite on my fingers but very close, and spat at me, "*Cobarde!* Coward! Oh, most trusted and now most unmanly one! *Aii, aii,* how this poor girl, thees *muchacha muy miserable*, has been deceived!"

I really got angry then. I made no effort to finish my rejoinder, in which I had intended to offer to appear in one or two revolutionary benefit performances, one might call them, in exchange for transportation north. Instead—

"*Stoppit!*" With a blood-curdling screech, Guchu sprang up from his chair, then, dipping low, snatched up a red container and began to gush its highly aromatic contents on his frizzy head, the while he pranced about, yelling, "I can't *stand* it anymore! I'm going to set myself afire! You all groveling to that feckless, fistless, filthy, frightened jumbee with no sinews, no guts. Gonna set myself afire for *sure!*" And he snatched out of his robe what appeared to me to be a small device for making a spark or flame jet.

"Comrade, control your Oriental eccentricities," El Toro roared at him.

"Heathen!" Father Francisco cried out. "You shall not set yourself afire in my church!"

"*All* bees bonnets!" Rosa commented to the blue ceiling with an indignant rat-a-tat-tat of her heels.

"Stoppit, you dumb niggar! STOPPIT!" I thundered, pulling out all the stops.

He stopped. Truly, a trained actor has inordinate—in

fact, most unfair—advantages over groundlings, even politicos.

I deliberately leaned forward, setting my jawplate on my doubled-up right hand, gave them all a medium-fast scan, my expression at its skullfulest, and said, "You low bandits. I am deeply offended by the aspersions you have cast upon my musculature and my manhood. I pass over the point that none of you has had the wit to realize what a powerful diaphragm I must have to support my magnificent voice. I suggest——"

"I know of no way to duel with the diaphragm muscles," El Toro interrupted somewhat contemptuously, yet studying me thoughtfully too.

"Except in a shouting contest," Guchu put in, suddenly more intelligible and, strangely, quite cheerful. The red container and firing device had vanished, though he still dripped odorously. "And that's all we've been having from him—words, words, words!" His voice chuckled off. He twice inhaled deeply and his grin became ecstatic. "Hey, that's not bad, man."

"Oh, you tricksy villain!" Rosa put in, shaking a finger at the Black Buddhist. "You pretend these self-blazes only to take gasoline trips."

"I did *not* intend a shouting contest," I said quietly, "although a duel with diaphragms is by no means impossible. Suppose we should hold our noses tight, take deep breaths, then press open mouth to mouth tightly, to determine who can break the other's eardrums? But I do not suggest such a contest either. I propose one with the outer skeletal musculature."

"But that way you'd have the advantage of your metal and motors," El Toro objected. "Not that I don't think I couldn't bend double any of those pipestem rods," he added, scrutinizing them.

"I was intending wholly to forgo that advantage," I replied. I did *not* tell him one reason for this decision of mine: that I had suddenly become aware that I had let my batteries run low. While tonguing pills, etc., into my Inner Man, I had neglected my titanium Outer One. Even in a powered fight I would do badly. And now I recalled that Rachel Vachel had absentmindedly galloped off with my luggage with its precious battery freight still at her saddle-bow. Drat the huge, gangling girl!

Without otherwise changing position, I removed my right hand from under my jaw, undoubled it, and moved it slowly from side to side, writhing its fingers and turning it, now palm to the Revolutionary Committee, now knuckles.

"You will observe," I said casually, "that forward from my wristplate, my fingers, thumb, entire hand, are completely naked and have no mechanical backing whatsoever. I propose simply a contest with the strongest of you at gripping—wrists not to move, forearms flat on table. Positioned so, we clasp hands and squeeze until one gives up, either by crying quits or by straightening fingers and thumb." And with a soft clank of my exo-radius-ulna, I laid my forearm across the altar in El Toro's direction.

"Lemme at him!" Guchu cried happily, waving in circles a bent arm with fingers clawed. "I'll mash his pinkies to mush. Yoo-hoo, sky-birthed! Prepare to have your hand crushed."

"He is mine," El Toro asserted, thrusting the Buddhist back with a sidewise brush of his brawny arm. He took out a cigar, lit it, and clamped it between his strong white teeth. For once on Terra I was smelling true tobacco smoke, not weed fumes. The Mex sat down across from me, rolled the sleeve on his right arm back to his big biceps, but did not yet lay down his forearm.

"I still have doubts, señor," he said, "that your hand is not somehow reinforced with metal, either invisible or surgically implanted."

"I will check that," La Cucaracha told him and, kneeling on the altar, took up my hand after glancing to me for permission. She fingered it most thoroughly, here and there digging in her nails. "I find it bones and flesh only, tough-

skinned, the hand of a worker," she told El Toro. Kissing
two fingers of her own hand, she laid them for a moment in
my palm, and then, with a grin toward me, laid down my
hand again and, still kneeling on the altar, commanded,
"Begin!"

Leaning in from the other side, Guchu began snapping
his spatulate fingers. "Come on, Bull Boy," he cheered.
"Pulp him!"

Father Francisco, obviously gripped by mixed emotions,
said sternly, "It is not lawful to have sporting contests of
any sort in church and especially on the high altar of God.
Except to decide questions of revolutionary policy," he
ended weakly, his eyes now eagerly watching the table between me and the Mex.

El Toro slowly let down his bulging forearm and carefully positioned it. We clasped hands lightly, getting a comfortable position. My hand, though somewhat bonier, was
bigger than his, which felt to me both soft and wet.

Without warning he gripped most powerfully, breath hissing out around his teeth-clenched cigar with an almost
"Hah!"

I merely matched his grip, staring serenely into his brown
eyes which showed amazement. Then I squeezed a little.
He squeezed back, puffing his cigar furiously. I squeezed
harder, the muscles below my elbow beginning to bulge my
Sack-suit sleeve like hard salami sausages, Flexors digitorum profundus, digitorum sublimus, pollicis longus woke
and got to work, also the nineteen small muscles in my
hand, mostly under tough palmar aponeurosis. He squeezed
back desperately. The forward section of his cigar, bitten
through, dropped to the table and smoldered there. I increased the pressure. Spitting out his cigar butt with a sudden soft but anguished "Aiii," he let his fingers go limp and
they straightened. I instantly spread my own, continuing to
gaze poker-faced at El Toro, who began gingerly to massage
his punished hand.

"Un milagro," Father Francisco breathed, crossing himself.

"I'll be a ring-tailed ofay," Guchu exclaimed.

"*Amado muy bravo!*" Rosa cried. "*Olé!*"

El Toro started to reach his left hand toward me, then shrugged and made it the right. "*Camarada*," he said solemnly. We shook hands carefully, yet quite firmly, he wincing but keeping up a grin. "You are a most surprising *hombre*," he said. "But *hombre, muy hombre.* Guchu, this man has muscle, make no mistake."

Really he could have figured it out before getting hurt. And despite the *padre*'s comment, there had been no miracle whatever in my performance. Finger-gripping is simply one activity a human does as often and with as much strength in free fall as in a gravity field. Maybe more. You need only featherweight muscles for most work and maneuvering in nullgrav—muscles having perhaps one twentieth the strength of those in a being forever battling terragrav—*except* for your hands (and toes, if you're resourceful). At least, so it had been with me, working from earliest youth on costumes, props, scenery, and so on for my father's shows. Also I had done many small sculptures of most recalcitrant clay, some with one hand. (Father would tie the other behind my back.) Another point: even on Terra fingers are light as mice, so finger manipulation is an activity on which gravs have plus-little effect.

"*Olé!*" La Cucaracha cried again and began to dance up and down the altar with much rat-a-tat-tatting of the heels and many a swing of her delightful posterior. At the same time she began singing in time with her dance a catchy song beginning, "El Esqueleto, El Esqueleto!"—this with a grin toward me.

In hardly any more time, El Toro and Guchu took up the song too, Guchu clapping hands in time and El Toro banging his good one on the altar. Only the *padre* remained aloof, now scandalized, now smiling in spite of himself.

I found myself clapping too. Listening carefully, I made out that the song was a revolutionary one about the coming of the Tall Death, El Esqueleto, and I began to feel strongly

the pull of this part. To play Death himself before audiences
who both feared and adored—what a challenge! Or rather
what a cinch part, a sure hit!

Rosa ended her dance in an electric storm of stampings.

I rumbled impulsively, *"Señores y señorita sublima!* If
you'll guarantee to get me to Yellowknife within three
weeks, I'll guarantee to make at least a trial appearance
as El Esqueleto."

"My hero!" Rosa cried, running to me along the altar-
top. *"Mi heroe de la revolución!"* We embraced most
warmly and the kissing shower began again.

Nor did we interrupt it when we heard the great doors
open behind us and bare feet come running across the dirt.
Or even when there was the measured thud of the hooves
of a horse walking. In fact, the only thing that made us pull
apart was Rachel Vachel calling out, "Lover, I forgot your
luggage, so— *What are you doing huggin' and lovin' up
that prancing, squashed-down, she-greaser hot-pants, Rosa
Morales?"*

She had ridden her white horse into the church. The
kneeling ones had at last sprung up and scattered to the
side walls. The two Mexes who had run in ahead of her had
darted behind the altar and were excitedly conferring with
El Toro, but I had no attention to spare for anyone but
Rachel Vachel. The Black Madonna's pale face and deadly
eyes were paler and deadlier yet with fury.

"I am merely joining your revolution, dear," I called to
her with consummate adroitness.

Never has a clever remark of mine been more completely
ignored. Clearly the two women now had ears and eyes
only for each other.

Quite unintimidated by Rachel Vachel's size and anger,
Rosa snatched off her high-heeled shoes and, grasping them
as weapons, jeered, "Hot pants you denominate me—when
it is well known you patronize our revolution only to obtain
the embraces of some of the cruder and badder-tasted members of our following!"

"I don't give a hoot what you say about me, you Juárez whore," Rachel retorted, "just so long as you keep your cotton-pickin' hands off Captain Skull. He's my property."

"Your property! Did you not now but witness how fiercely he fondled me? And he has most recently, let me inform you, fought a duel with El Toro, with myself as the prize, and won! He is mine, I tell you—mine, mine, mine!"

I made a last and most risky effort, though I stated only purest truth. "Lovely ladies," I rumbled, "cease this disastrous quarrel. I love you both *equally*."

"He is bees bonnet, but mine, affianced in Holy Church —you Texan man-stealer!" was La Cucaracha's answer.

"He's ravin'. While single-handed routin' two hundred soldiers, he got a head wound, which is somethin' you'd never notice or comfort him for, you midget bitch, you Chihuahua in rut!" was Rachel's interpretation.

A hand grasped my shoulder from behind. It was El Toro's, who said to me rapidly, "Make no interference, *camarada*. They must fight it out themselves for—*ay, Dios!* —is it the twentieth time? Each thinks herself the heroine solo of the Revolution. Meanwhile I am told that the crowd has gathered. You must instantly prepare your speech to them, *camarada*. I will introduce you briefly. You'll enter beside Camarada Lamar for maximum effect—your costumes match—if she's still in shape to walk."

"*Elefante! No, jirafa!*" Rosa was meanwhile shrieking at Comrade Lamar. "And no good in bed either, as all males testify."

Rachel's hands dropped to her lightning pistols.

"That's right, shoot me! Kill me in Holy Church," Rosa responded triumphantly. "Prove you are no true daughter of the Revolution, but only arrogant Texan."

Rachel's hands came together and unbuckled her gun belt, let it drop on her mount's croup. Then she vaulted down nimbly and, touching her horse, pointed to a side wall and ordered, "*There*, Silver!" The beast obeyed docilely, joining the white-eyed Mexes crouching among the demon-eyed carvings.

Rachel Vachel walked steadily toward the altar, swinging her black crop. "I'm merely going to turn you over my knee," she announced casually, "and lambast the skin off that over-active and overambitious ass of yours."

"And I—oh, I shall rip your most unattractive flesh to even less attractive tatters!" Rosa replied, raising her spike-heeled slippers.

I watched with a deep concern and horrid fascination, but somewhat abstractedly. I was very busy reviewing my Spanish and putting together the first half-dozen sentences of a revolutionary oration by Death the Liberator—I knew if I got them exactly right, the rest would be a breeze.

Suddenly, sacrificing what help-in-altitude the altar gave her, Rosa leaped down, sprinted at Rachel, and at the last instant threw up her bare feet, so that she sailed through the air, a straight-legged projectile with heels aimed at her opponent's midriff.

Rachel slipped aside with startling litheness, caught loose hold of Rosa's waistband, and gave a tug that accel-erated her progress through the air; Rachel also got in a slash with her crop.

But Rosa, reaching sidewise with one of her slippers, had ripped Rachel's shirt across at the waist and scored the flesh beneath. Now she landed on the hard earthen floor in a painful skid, which she quickly turned into a roll and was on her feet again, instantly springing back toward her more than twice as tall adversary, who stood crouched and ready.

Again at the last instant Rosa launched herself through the air, this time headfirst. Again Rachel slipped to one side.

But Rosa had launched herself not straight at her oppo-nent, but toward one side—and she had picked the right one. At the instant her head thudded into Rachel's belly, the Texan girl brought her hand down on Rosa's neck in a vicious chop.

Rachel sat down heavily and turned a pale shade of green.

Rosa, rolling away, writhed on the dirt, clasping her neck and crying feebly, "*Aii, aii, mi cabeza!* Oh, my poor head!"

El Toro, running forward, called authoritatively, "All right, all right, fight's over. Declared a draw! Now we get out there before the crowd riots."

I told him about my weak batteries. He helped me over to Silver, from whose saddle my three bags still hung, and we effected rapid replacements. I felt surging with mechanical power once more.

Meanwhile the girls were staggering painfully to their feet, both bent over.

"Come on, come on!" El Toro ordered. "I go first with Father Francisco. Rosa, you follow with Guchu. Lamar, you're beside El Esqueleto—and get that cloak around you tight, *camarada,* and throw forward your hood—we don't want to flash that skeleton until you start to speak."

Rosa, still reeling a little and moaning and holding her head, took Guchu's hand and inquired, "Does the back of my skirt still exist?"

"Sure does," the Buddhist told her, "though I can't vouch the same for your underpants. But don't worry, you look fine. Just spit on your hand and wipe the dirt off your face."

Rachel, composing her features and holding herself erect with difficulty and I was sure some pain, took light hold of my hand, holding it shoulder high, as if we were about to dance a minuet. She said to me out of the corner of her mouth, "You loose-livin', false-hearted dastard, you. I still think I'm going to up-chuck."

"If you do, play it straight," I told her in the same fashion. "It will vastly impress the audience to learn that you are here despite serious illness. Come on now, let's make a good entrance. Tum-te-*tum.*"

"That's right, the play's the thing," she replied somewhat unenthusiastically.

Father Francisco, passing Rosa with his robes a-flap, said, "Fifty Hail Mary's, my daughter, and fifty Our Father's. Señorita Lamar," he called, "examine your Protestant conscience and *please*, not again to ride the horse into my church."

The doors before us swung open, four bent-backs pushing each, and we walked down into a shallow sea of torchlight, swarthy faces, and noise.

7 / In the Cemetery

I met Murder by the way—
He had a mask like Castlereagh—
Very smooth he looked, yet grim;
Seven blood-hounds followed him:
All were fat; and well they might
Be in admirable plight,
For one by one, and two by two,
He tossed them human hearts to chew
Which from his wide cloak he drew.

—"The Mask of Anarchy," by Percy Bysshe Shelley

SNUGLY WRAPPED IN my black cloak and hood, I sat toward the back of the bandstand in the endmost of a row of chairs occupied by my new comrades from the church.

Outwardly I was serene. Inwardly I was critically furious at the performance being put on by the Revolutionary Committee.

It had no oomph. It lacked pazazz. In short, it was lousy theater.

And as for rabble-rousing fieriness, well, it wouldn't have ignited phosphorus.

It wasn't that they didn't have a big and potentially responsive audience. From the bandstand to the flower-embowered moonlit little houses, and spreading into the street on one side and the cemetery on the other, was a dense expanse of intent little faces, with here and there a torch streaming in the gusts of wind as fascinatingly as the candles had burned upward. And the crowd *did* respond at times, but only with scattered listless applause and weary cheers that I could tell were directed by a few dispersed claque leaders. All the while, like a burning evergreen forest, there wafted from them to us the piny odor of pot.

The crowd was so huge and the whole meeting so open that I asked Rachel out of the corner of my mouth, "Darling heart, how in Terra are you allowed to get away with gatherings like this? A deaf, blind man could smell it five kilometers off. Your pa and the Rangers may be a little slow on the uptake, but—"

"You faithless cad, how dare you speak to me?" she replied, likewise *sotto voce*. "Yeah, those greasers stink, all right. Come the Revolution, they'll scrub and take showers and like it! The fact is that Daddy and the others are convinced these meetings are just a harmless catharsis for Mexes, the emotional equivalent of Coca-Cola, but—"

"And how right they are, sweetheart," I thought but did not say.

"—but tonight we'll show them different, won't we, you blackguard?" she finished, squeezing my hand. The deeds and words of women engaged in the love game rarely match.

"Beloved, you haven't the faintest dream of how different," I again thought without words, contenting myself with returning her squeeze. She permitted this for a long moment, then angrily jerked her hand away.

I blinked at a brightly haloed, rather long flash of white light beyond some low hills beyond Greasertown. It was as if a brighter moon had started to rise there, then decided not to. I glanced around uneasily, using eyes only, but no one else seemed to be concerned about the phenomenon.

A half-minute or so later, there came a shattering *boom* and a great gust of wind out of Greasertown. I am stage-trained to show no reaction to loud sounds unconnected with the play, to scuffles in the audience, or even the smell of smoke; but this time it was hard for me to hold still and I marveled that beyond a few jerks of startlement around me and brief over-shoulder looks by members of the audience, a few rising to stare, there were no reactions from actors or observers. I touched Rachel Vachel's hand and looked a baffled question.

"Blastin' operations, I presume," she whispered with a slight shrug. "You've got to expect those all the time in Texas, Scully. Most likely from one of those new outsize oil wells. They've been working on those twenty-four hours a day."

And now my attention was riveted by a dark cloud, ghostly gray in the moonlight and shaped like a slender toadstool, risen from the point on the horizon where I had seen the flash. Even as I watched, it grew taller. A most menacing specter. It made me shiver. Yet no one around me seemed to take note.

I decided that Texans, and perhaps especially Mexican Texans, were stolid creatures indeed, and in addition permanently doped with weed—which perhaps accounted, it occurred to me, for our revolutionary performance beginning and continuing as such a gutless turkey. First, Father Francisco had opened the meeting with a long, inaudible prayer, then delivered himself of some homilies conveying that the practice of revolution was something like going to church, a duty-enforced activity such as prayer, confession, and masses for the dead.

Next Guchu had done his act, sprightlier at least. He kept waving his staff and bounding out of and, purely by accident I believe, back into the two spotlights the bandstand boasted, so that for the audience he was continuously appearing and disappearing, his orange-and-yellow robes flapping from being into nonbeing. Likewise, he was using the mike half the time and not using it the other half, so that, especially for those farther back than the tenth row, his voice was alternately a raucous roar and a faint screech. As for what he actually said, well . . . "Kill the ofay in crib and catafalque! Kill the ofay in yourselves. Red heavens and green hells and God a gray fume binding them" might, like his whole act, have been barely acceptable in black comedy, but hardly here.

Even the female and child—and so, presumably uncyborged—Mexes seemed more puzzled than amused by his antics.

Now El Toro was orating, and a little more to the point, too—that is, if what I took for a series of punchy but unrelated sentences cribbed from the writings of Marx and Lenin, rather poorly translated into Spanish, might be considered an oration. But he worked too close to the mike, so that his every fourth word blared out of recognition. None of the speakers, for that matter, had the faintest idea of how to use a mike.

Besides, El Toro spent too much time flexing his biceps, sometimes one—simultaneously showing off his unimpressive profile—sometimes both together, accompanied by a white-toothed glare. He may have thought he was symbolizing the strength of the working, or rather, cyborged, class. To the audience, I think, it gave the impression that he intended to conduct the entire revolution without assistance, in the fashion of the primitive cartoon character Mighty Mouse, or else that he was advertising a course in body-building. It made *me* think of some of our worst athletic types in Circumluna, forever showing off their bulk of unneeded, unaesthetic, striated muscle.

Neither of the women had spoken, I suppose in accordance with the ancient habit of latin males of hogging all the available lamplight. I was sure La Cucaracha could have done a snappier job than any of them, while even one of Rachel Vachel's recitations of one of her revolutionary poems would have been preferable. I was sure she must, in her spare moments, have dashed off a whole lingerie drawer full of them, beginning with lines like "Shuck off, ye Mexes all, your servile yokes," and rhyming that with such gems as "And take at tyrant Texans healthy pokes."

Just then I heard El Toro saying, "And now, comrades, it is my great privilege and colossal pleasure to introduce one who, though from another sphere—"

He was introducing *me*. And he was going to take a half-hour to do it, as is the custom with all masters of ceremony, whether ragged revolutionaries or reactionaries clad in as somber stylishness as banks. During that thirty minutes he would say badly everything I intended to say, putting the audience totally to sleep and leaving me nothing to do but take one bow, or conceivably two.

Filling my chest, I stood up and let off with a growl intended to shiver and split the tombstones in the cemetery. Then I walked forward, deliberately stamping my titanium footplates on the bandstand's aluminum floor, so that it rang out like a cacophonous gong and was very likely dented.

I kicked over the mike, placed myself precisely at the convergence of the spotlights, threw back my hood and cloak, and said in my saturate-the-Sack voice, spacing the words rather widely and the sentences even more so, "*Yo soy la muerte. Pero la vida también. Qué vida!*"

My audience, who looked like a beach of dark pebbles each topped with darker sea moss, shrank in terror, gasped in awe, and burst into laughter.

I offer no explanation as to how I could achieve this merely by saying, "I am the Death. But also the Life. What a Life!" accompanying the last with a shrugging of the shoulders, a spreading of the upturned hands, and a certain cocking of the head that gave the impression I had winked, though actually I had not.

The actor's high art is a mystery.

Naturally El Toro, misjudging everything, thought the laughter showed I'd wrecked the scene, and naturally he tried to circle in front of me to save it, though in that stage position he would have been well underneath the beams of both spots.

I rammed him into his chair, not with a contact shove— which if successful merely moves the body and often has unforeseen comic consequences, such as an overturned chair plus pratfall—but with a faked, or theatrical, shove, which never touches the body but stuns the mind and is foolproof.

Grinning widely at my audience, I confided to them in a

voice that carried to the back row as clearly as did my gleaming teeth, "Comrades of the Revolution! As you well know, I come from a *very* far country and over an electrified fence which only *I* can cross, a fence high as the sky and dark as all mystery. It was a long and hungry journey. The pickings were slim, as you can see for yourselves." I somewhat elaborately indicated my gleaming skeleton and the hardly less slender, black rest of me. "But now, comrades," I continued, ogreishly leaning forward, "now that I am in *Texas*, I intend to feed well." And I gave them another long flash of my teeth, somewhat hastily adding, for several of my audience appeared about to run, "*All* of us shall feed well, comrades."

I faked tossing something into the air. I thought of it as a small human head, so presumably my audience did too. I narrowly watched its ascent and fall, and at the last moment ducked my skull sideways and snapped my jaw on it, with a canine growl that I made suggest also a crunch.

I chewed with relish, then swallowed with a head-rocking bob of Adam's apple. "That was Chaparral Houston Hunt, Vice-Commander-in-Chief of the Texas Rangers," I explained. "Tough, but juicy."

My audience also ate it up—my acting. I mean—ate it up so much that I repeated that bit with the fancied heads of Sheriff Chase and Mayor Burleson. Then I decided it was time I state my simple revolutionary platform.

"Yes, comrades, you and I shall feed very well, once the Revolution is won. Free banquets for all! No more work! Free clothing—wardrobes of the most beautiful! Travel everywhere! Homes too luxurious for anyone to wish ever to leave! Two women for every man! And," I added, since I could see dark feminine frowns in the first rows, "a wholly faithful and ever attentive husband, gallant as a grandee, for every woman!"

A diversion was needed before they puzzled too long over that amazing paradox. Accordingly, a dog yelped, as though demanding food, or more food. I looked about to see where the hungry animal was. My audience began to do so too. I glanced under the chairs of my comrades on the bandstand. I even knelt and looked under the bandstand itself, my lips open all the while, as if in wonder, but unmoving. I shaded my eyes, gazing into the distance. The yelps continued. My audience was consumed with curiosity.

Then I faced front and smiled, raising my eyebrows and one finger in the fashion of one who has suddenly discovered the solution to a problem. I tossed up another imaginary head. The yelping became wildly eager. I caught the head with a crunch of my side teeth and the yelps changed to snarly, greedy mouthings.

I am by no means the Luna-Terra pair's greatest ventriloquist, but I have as much command of that limited art as is proper for its greatest actor. I also sing and dance and do the free-fall equivalent of juggling, which involves bouncing resilient objects off a surface.

At any rate I pleased my simple audience, who were altogether charmed to discover that the yelping dog had deceived me by hiding inside me. When their laughter and applause began to fade, I explained, "That was Governor Lamar," and I tossed up another head and captured it with my mouth, this time omitting the crunch. I grinningly rolled it about inside my cheeks and finally swallowed it without chewing.

"And that was his beautiful daughter, who spends your rightful wealth in tinseled theatrical displays," I announced, licking my lips. "Very tasty."

Through the renewed laughter, chiefly male, I spotted Rachel Vachel's gasp and stifled giggles behind me. If they had been any louder, I'd have thrown something at her, probably the mike at my feet. An actress who breaks up because of private onstage jokes doesn't deserve the name. Of course I probably shouldn't have started making gags like that so soon, but at times one must instantly follow all inspirations of the muse.

I decided I could now risk feeding my audience a little

more brain food. *"Silencio!"* I decreed, and when they had quieted, I said, "Comrades, you are genial and generous. Far *too* generous. It concerns you that one mangy dog go hungry, and delights you that he be fed. Think equally of yourselves, I command. Think of your own empty bellies, I say." (Since it was well past suppertime, I knew most of them would be feeling a bit hungry.) "For 250 years you have been starved, enslaved, and exploited by the white Texans. That is something not to be endured—not by you and certainly not by *me*. It is to demand, in your name and with your help, payment in full—aye, and time and a half for overtime and double time on Sundays and holidays —for that quarter millennium of distasteful servitude, it is to achieve those things, I say, that I have come striding from my far country!"

And purely for the sake of variety, I drew myself up tall as I said that and drew close around me my cloak, reversed to show only its scarlet lining.

Instead of being soberly impressed, or rather in addition to being impressed, my audience all laughed hugely.

Leaning toward La Cucaracha, who sat at the opposite end of the chair row from Rachel Vachel, I asked under cover of the joyful noise, "Why am I getting a laugh on the red cloak?"

"Because our bill collectors traditionally wear a red suit," she replied with commendable brevity, beaming at me.

"Go, man, go!" Guchu cried encouragingly.

"I think he goes too far," Father Francisco also took advantage of the opportunity to put in, mutteringly. "I think he is of the devil."

"Contrary to my first expectations, you're doing excellently," El Toro assured me. "Only harken to the wise father. Don't go too far."

"What sort of revolutionaries are you?" I demanded of them in a contemptuous hissing whisper. "Too far? You haven't seen anything yet. And you, *padre*, just watch my devil's smoke!"

And in a swirl of red cloak I turned my back on them before any could reply.

Taking advantage of the dope I'd got from Kookie, I pantomimed a bill collector walking up to the tall door of White Texas, rapping on it authoritatively (footplate stamps, hidden by my cloak, providing the noise), pounding on it when that got no answer, and finally telling the one who opened it, "Señor Gringo, I intend to stand here, to your great shame, until you have made payment in full —aye, and in double measure, running over—to each and every noble Mexican, noble Indian, and noble Negro, alive or dead!"

As the applause for that act faded, I turned slowly on my audience with a great pointing finger that took them all in. The red of my cloak had entirely vanished; I was all black and silver again. Leaning toward them confidentially, with the effect of elbow on knee and chin in palm, and driving home my points with slow forefinger shakes of my other hand, I said in my deepest voice, "You laugh. You enjoy yourselves. That is well—now. But you and I, comrades, know we will never get anywhere at all by standing at the door and asking, or even demanding. Never did even a husband get his wife by such behavior. You and I know we must burst down that door and seize what is ours by right. You and I, old comrades of the Revolution, know we must *fight*, that we must risk death, and if necessary deal death, to achieve our aims."

Suddenly I was no longer Christopher Crockett La Cruz, juvenile leading man of the Theater-in-the-Sphere. I was no longer a gangling and sex-struck spaceling caught up in a perilous but ridiculous Terran brouhaha. No, I was Cassius working on the noble Brutus. I was Sam Adams inciting puritanic rowdies called Sons of Liberty to perpetrate the famous floating tea party. I was Camille Desmoulins demanding the storming of the Bastille. I was Danton roaring for the head of Louis XVI. I was John Brown forging the sword of Abolition. I was Lenin telling the wavering Congress of Soviets, "We shall now proceed to construct the Socialist order!" I was Comrade Mao beginning the Long March. I was Malcolm X founding Black Nationalism. I was Senator Whatshisname rising to demand a vote of censure against that administration's war policy in Vietnam.

What I said was, "Comrades, you outnumber your oppressors ten to one, and now you have my help from beyond the grave. True, your oppressors are bigger than you, taller than you, and they possess engines of infinite power. But they are big with the soft bigness of men whose bodies have outgrown their untried, unforged courage and conscience. Outside they are tall, but within they are pygmies, moved only by vanity and greed, knowing nothing of true want, which is the mother of all true feeling. While no engine is as powerful as the man who seizes and controls it.

"Have you never seen a man sweating and writhing, struck down by bite of scorpion or spider smaller far than he? Mighty armies have been conquered by invisible bacteria. Comrades, your foes are few, and they have been weakened by sloth, greed, and corruption. Be you as scorpions and spiders! Now is the time to strike!"

There was a hiss of surprise behind me. So I was startling my colleagues too? So much the better!

I stood tall again, eerie and distant, yet my comrades' friend. Now I was Frankenstein's monster, I was Danton on trial, I was Lazarus returned, I was Lon Chaney in *The Phantom of the Opera,* I was the fourth horseman of the Apocalypse, dismounted.

"Comrades," I pronounced, "only you and I know the great gap between talking and action, between words and deeds. Only minutes ago, I amused you by pretending to eat the heads of some of the puny great ones of Texas. That was funny, I trust—good theater, as we say—and also, I hope, a prophecy now for something that is not theater.

"But only short hours ago I laid my hand on the shoulder of President Austin of Texas and he died. The Longhorn dictator is dead! *I ate him.* That is fact—fact like the death of a child or of a cockroach crushed underfoot."

Now I heard footsteps behind me, but I ignored them, determined to finish my serious pitch, driving it home as forcefully as I had my comedy.

"Comrades, it is one of my qualities that I can eat—and eat and eat—without ever becoming less hungry or growing a grain fatter. Death is never sated. Be you like me! Arise, destroy, feast! If in doing this you die yourselves, you only cross to my side of the fence and from there continue the battle. So you are invulnerable. My hand is forever over you—in comradeship and love. Let our watchword be Vengeance and Death!"

I liked that so much I repeated it, this time with a falling, rumbling inflection like lights being turned off. *"Venganza y muerte!"*

I calculated there would be five seconds of stunned silence, then ragged cheers growing to a roar.

I got exactly three of those first seconds—genuine stunned silence, all right.

Then great searchlights trumpeted on from all around, blasting us with high-pitched violet-white light.

Bullhorns and sirens glared on blindingly, shaking us with dazzlingly white noise.

Their pandemonium hid for moments the ponderous slow tread of huge horses closing in on my audience saddle to saddle on three sides, leaving open only the way back to Greasertown.

Then the darkly hooded Texans riding those horses cracked out simultaneously their long electric whips. There were blue sparks in a great semicircle. The fringes of my audience shrieked and writhed.

I turned around. Except for one figure besides myself, the bandstand was empty. The footsteps I had earlier heard had been my comrades of the Revolution taking a powder: El Toro; Father Francisco; Guchu, who had cried me on; La Cucaracha, who had proclaimed herself my eternal beloved;

and all the other loyal ones whose names I hadn't had time to learn.

The one exception was Rachel Vachel. She was sitting in her chair, arms folded across her chest, gazing at me a cold question that I could not decipher.

I was glad that at least one had not fled. But why, I had to ask myself, wasn't she using her lightning pistols, or at least standing at my side?

Beyond her, more horsemen and at least one large vehicle were closing in on the bandstand.

Shouts and screams behind me made me turn again. What I saw paralyzed most of me, so I could only stand there, moving eyes and head.

They say actors are always playing parts, even in private life, that they can never truly feel. This one can. Now, expressing it in no fashion at all and so for no one's benefit but my own, I was simultaneously racked by exultation, horror, and shame.

My audience was attacking the Texans. They were scrabbling about for rocks—fragments of age-cracked tombstones, I suppose—and occasionally finding and hurling one. A few had managed to get past the whips and were clubbing at horses' legs and snatching at stirruped ankles. I watched while two of them were cut sizzlingly in half by the red beams of laser pistols. Three of them got hold of a whip by its insulated section and yanked on it while another Mex pushed upward the booted foot of the rider, toppling him from his saddle. They raced screeching to stomp him.

Yes, my audience was mounting an attack. And it was clear from my first glimpse of it that it had no chance whatever of success.

And all this while members and groups of my audience —no, of this mad revolutionary mob—were shouting, sometimes with hand outstretched toward me, my dreadful, melodramatic watchword. *"Venganza y muerte!"*

Believe me, each utterance of that idiot phrase struck me like a lash. I, and I alone, had caused these dark-faced, dwarfish fools to fight, to suffer real wounds, even to die, instead of running off safe, for it had been shown that the Texans' whips, at first at least, had been set only to shock and pain, not to kill or even stun.

I could no more have cried them on now than I could kill my father. Yet my mere motionless presence was causing them to keep up the hopeless battle, was sending more of them to their deaths. And my presence was in no way due to courage, but only shock and sheer stupidity. Yet so long as I stood there, I was their black flag, driving them on, forbidding retreat. Why, I had even promised the poor fools deathlessness, as the Old Man of the Mountains had the Hashishin. Oh, why hadn't my comrades told me that the play was over and I must run with them? Why had they left the ignorant actor to suffer or at least view the consequences of his vaunting performance? Perhaps even now I should try to call off the little morons dying and suffering agonies around me.

I might have tried it, but at that moment several actual lashes struck me, and I was enveloped in a cloud of blue sparks and ozone.

But I was not either killed, paralyzed, pained, or set awrithing. I felt only a slight tingling.

I realized why. Since my skeleton was exo, the chances were at least four in five that a lash would land first on it, grounding out neatly through my titanium footplates and the aluminum bandstand, rather than shock my flesh.

With this and the further realization that my seeming immunity to the whips would increase my imbecile followers' trust in me, I laughed wildly.

The bandstand was bumped and it rocked. I heard a familiar voice growl louder, "Cut those whips!"

I turned once more and saw mashed up against the bandstand, almost like an extension of it, the aluminum flatbed of a big truck. From it strode Sheriff Chase and Ranger Hunt, drawing their ceremonial swords. Possibly they had figured out that my power was of a mythic or legendary sort, lying in my impersonation of El Esqueleto or the Tall Death, and that therefore it would be highly appropriate and also impressive to the Mexicans if they cowed me or cut me down with anachronistic weapons.

Possibly. Yet by this perhaps shrewd action of theirs, they changed the whole situation for me and created for themselves a danger they could hardly have foreseen. Suddenly, for me, everything was theater again—theater in deadly earnest, perhaps, but still theater.

As those two big, gleaming, exceedingly sharp-looking rapiers came toward me, I crossed hands to touch three buttons on my wristplates.

One of them simply doubled the speed and strength of my exoskeletal movements. I put my exomotors in high. This was dangerous to me: a motor, meeting sudden resistance, might burn out; I might smash myself in a powered fall or collision. But it was also necessary, especially if Chase or Hunt were even moderately skilled swordsmen. The other two buttons untelescoped my slim canes, and this time I continued button-pressure until the final needle-tipped sections were extruded. I tossed off my cloak.

Then with a stamp that bounced me a foot in the air and with an uncalled-for but most enheartening "On guard!" I was upon them.

There are two basic ways in which two swordsmen can engage a single opponent armed with two swords. They can try to take him from opposite sides, forcing him to keep turning his head 180 degrees, cutting off his fastest lines of retreat, and aiming to pin him between them.

Or they can attack him side by side. To engage both their swords, he must face them chest on, presenting them with a wider and closer target than either of them presents to him.

In both cases, the doubly armed lone swordsman has available to him tactics that partially compensate him for his basic disadvantage. To begin with, he always has the advantage of a single command opposing a shared command: Hannibal versus Paulus and Varro at Cannae, etc.

Attacked on opposite sides, he can seek to overwhelm and kill one of his opponents with a very fast attack before the other can get at him, then turn and take care of that other.

Facing opponents who attack him side by side, he can concentrate more fully his attention and tactics, particularly if he has good and well-trained periferal vision and is ambidextrous, in both which abilities I rank high. By swift enough circling he can put one of his adversaries temporarily out of the fight.

In short, according to the tactics his opponents adopt, he has two basic tactics: the fast attack and swift circling.

In my first engagement with Hunt and Chase, I chose a third tactic. In fact, I invented it on this occasion. It has nothing whatever to recommend it, except that it will startle the enemy, though without harming them.

After a slow, one-two advance, I launched myself in a great and very rapid lunge at Chase, my right-hand adversary, seeking to catch his blade in a bind in high seconde and skewer him, meanwhile fending off Hunt's sword with the hanging guard. It was a great mistake.

One: I had not allowed for the actor's ingrained habit of always missing his opponent rather than hitting him. Two: I had not really allowed for the speedup in my motors, with no corresponding speedup in my nervous system. I took off so fast on my left foot that I couldn't get my right foot ahead to catch my weight.

There seemed only one thing to do. Parrying both their swords in seconde—simply shoving them aside the easiest way, that is—I doubled sharply at waist and shoulders, turning my lunge into a forward somersault straight between my adversaries. For a Thin, I am an excellent free-fall acrobat. The feat I intended was exactly like a forward somersault in free fall, but with one slight difference: midway I would have to take a tremendous bump on the head; I could only try to get spun far enough around so that it would be a crash of head basket rather than a crunch of frontal bone; I could also pray that the Longhairs had forged my exospine exceeding strong.

Perhaps Diana, almost overhead and smiling through clear sky, decided to be kind and worked a miracle. At any rate, there were simultaneous great bongs, bass and treble, of titanium and aluminum. My sworded arms thrown backward gave my upper body forward impetus. The weight of my footplates drew me down to a landing on them. There was bandstand left to land on. Though reverberating and groggy from head to foot, I managed to keep my balance and turn around and get both swords up and engage Hunt and Chase as they came at me side by side.

At that point I resolutely turned my brain off, especially its schemy sector, and let reflex and training take over. I defended only. I fought no habit of mine, including the actor's habit of never laying sword point or edge on his adversary. In fact, now—for me, at least—the duel had become rather like that fabled one in the American Civil War, where an actor on the Union side meets in battle an old fellow actor on the Confederate side and yells, "Primes, cully, primes," whereupon they most spiritedly fight the duel from *Macbeth* to the great edification of their fellow soldiers on both sides.

As my body and nerves recovered, I automatically went on the attack, cautiously this time. Hunt and Chase proved to be mediocre duelists. I drove them back across the bandstand. Yet I scrupulously avoided pricking or scratching them with my point—actor's habit completely in the ascendancy, or perhaps by now I was beginning to realize that my only chance of surviving this first and thoroughly lost battle of the Bent-Back Revolution lay in my not killing or hurting anyone.

Nevertheless I cried, "Fight, cowards, fight! There'd never have been an Alamo if the place had had a back door!"

Hunt and Chase obliged by fencing more furiously and worse.

With a sudden bind in tierce followed by a heavy beat in seconde, I sent Hunt's sword flying out of his hand. Then, having both cane swords to use on Chase, I disarmed him too. I stood menacing both men, whom I had almost driven off the front edge of the bandstand.

Between them, I saw the last of my audience-army running madly toward Greasertown, away from the pursuing whips. My little assassins, drugged like the old man with hemp, had at last admitted defeat. Here and there lay a few unmoving bent-back bodies. At that moment, the last half-dozen Mexes in flight—my pitiable rear guard—paused to raise clenched fists and shout toward me, *Olé*, El Esqueleto! *Venganza y muerte!*" Then they were running again and the pursuing Texan cavalry cut them off from my view.

Perhaps it was that little cheer, perhaps it was hearing Governor Lamar's voice from the flatbed that roused my idiot optimism again. Suddenly my brain was back with me, full of melodramatic plans. I would seize Lamar and, menacing him with a sword, demand my release. I would—

As I turned, full of wild speculations, Rachel Vachel, risen at last and come forward, was facing me.

"My hero!" she cried as she lifted her arms toward me. "Oh, Captain Skull, that was most brilliantly dueled! I doubt another man in the universe could have—"

Her face was radiant. I lowered my cane swords to either side. What I did not notice until too late was that in one of her hands she held her black crop. With it she touched me neatly on my naked neck, like a fairy godmother enacting an enchantment.

Pain shot through me, followed by paralysis of all parts below my head. I heard myself sit down with a clank on the aluminum. My upper body would have sprawled forward, doubled over, except that my useless outflung arms kept me propped up, while my eyes first stared hurt, then glared hatred at my betrayer.

There were loud sighs of satisfaction from Chase and Hunt behind me.

Meanwhile Lamar came hurrying from the flatbed, followed by Mayor Burleson and Professor Fanninowicz.

The Governor's courtly features were red with rage. He grabbed his daughter by her upper arms and shook her.

"Sugar, I'm intensely angry with you," he said in tones that were both well and yet barely controlled. "I'm going to lock you in your bedroom for twenty years."

"But, Daddy, I saved your life," she protested in a voice that went up an octave and back at least a decade into her past.

"That's not the point. Sugar, I'm *ashamed* of you. It's a scandal. Dressing like a man. Wearing pants, when there hasn't a lady of the Lamars rode anything but sidesaddle for two centuries. Ten years' bedroom confinement for you anyhow."

"Daddy, you're in a temper. What's soured you? Didn't you get President Austin?"

Here I began to have difficulty following their dialogue. It wasn't that my consciousness was wavering—no, above my neck I remained fully alive, though paralyzed below, so far as sensation and voluntary muscles were concerned. It was that Fanninowicz now knelt beside me, his whole face gleaming like his monocle, and began to finger my exoskeleton with little gasps of pleasure as he traced the courses of its cables and the myoelectric leads to my skin. He even began to palpate and pinch my numb flesh, softly chortling with wonder at how little there was of it over my big bones. It was vile, but I endured it (what else?) and concentrated on what Lamar and Rachel Vachel were saying.

He answered her question pettishly.

"Oh, we got Austin all right. But then his Mex houseboys, who'd run away, laid an ambush for us. Beamed three Texas Rangers *dead*. Missed *me* by just *that!*" He spread forefinger and thumb. "And by the time we'd dropped a mini-atomic bomb on them, they'd scattered so I don't think we got more than fifty percent."

"Aw, cheer up, Daddy, you probably got more'n you think. And you know yourself how your nerves get whangled when you're wearied and stayed up too late and not had your proper liquor and weed, and been threatened with death, like when you catch cold."

"Don't you try to soften me up, sugar. I'm making it five years and not a day less. And what I say goes."

"That's right, Daddy, it sure does," the incredible female agreed contritely. "Gee whillikers!" she added with a grin. "And now it goes double. I forgot— You're president of Texas!"

"Even *that's* in doubt," he said, his voice almost cracking. "The Establishment Council's been talking of Burleson and Hunt too, and even Ma Hogg. Not that I hold it personally against you boys," he added quickly.

"Course not, Governor. Course not," the soothing deep-throated replies sounded around me.

"And that's not the point either, sugar," Lamar continued, grabbing his daughter again. "It's you. It's you I'm ashamed of. Wearing those pants that show off your legs as if you were bare-naked. Consorting with filthy, stinking, low revolutionaries—"

"But, Daddy, I *had* to dress like this so as to be able to consort with them so as to be able to learn their revolutionary secrets. It's a mighty big thing I've done for Texas. I admit they smell bad, but I bore it so as to——"

"Secrets!" he interrupted scornfully. "Sugar, there aren't any revolutionary secrets. Again and again I've told you to keep out of politics your cute little nose, that reminds me so of your sainted, admirably docile mother's. We've known all about this revolution for years. It never gets anywhere. It's just a safety valve for the greasers. I admit that President Austin's arming his houseboys has tickled it up a bit, but that doesn't really mean anything. No, sugar, you've been wicked and disobedient, and it's five months locked in the bedroom for you."

Here Fanninowicz tried to examine the containers in my

cheekplates and I snapped at his hand, almost getting a finger. He appeared to bear me no more resentment than if I'd been a surly chimpanzee under restraint. He merely turned his attention to my wristplates, his fingers hovering over the buttons in a spasm of fascination and hesitation.

"You cain't mean it, Daddykins!" Rachel Vachel wailed. "What's more, it's just not true what you say about knowing everything about the Revolution. It's been changing, Daddy. There's niggers in it now, niggers from the Pacific Black Republic. And there's Injuns too."

"Sugar, you can't sweeten me, no matter what you—Niggers from the Black Republic, did you say? And Indians? Not *Comanches*, I hope." His voice went high.

"Yes, Comanches, Daddy, and Apaches. And there's spacefolk! The La Cruz person admitted to me that——"

"That's another thing I'm holding against you!" he interrupted her. "Early this evening you were snuggling concupiscently with that low Sackabond actor, who on his own admission is no more than a dirty-minded court jester to the mad Longhairs of Circumluna. I *saw* you. I always knew acting and actors would be your ruin, sugar. My sentence remains the same: five months in a locked bedroom, on pinto beans, corn pone, and Coca-Cola."

"But, Daddy, that was my greatest hour. I was bein' a better li'l ole *agent provocateur* than the best pros turned out by Hunt Espionostics. You think I enjoyed it? It was like snuggling up to a giant spider. But I called on my deepest wells o' courage and—"

I would have said something ferocious then, except Fanninowicz chose that moment to press experimentally one of the buttons on my right wristplate. My right cane sword retracted, scraping aluminum, while the German beat his knuckles together and softly tittered in ecstasy. I sagged toward that side.

"And that's not all, Daddy," Rachel was saying. "There's something else I got to tell you, but it's a private sort of thing and I'm a little embarrassed about it. Would you other menfolk mind stepping out of hearing for a minute? Just to humor poor little me?"

With murmurings of "Sure thing, Miss Lamar" and "Anything to please the Honorable," Burleson, Hunt, and Chase went to the other end of the bandstand, the last dragging the reluctant Fanninowicz.

Rachel took hold of her father's lapel and drew his face close to her own, meanwhile bending down, so they were both very near me.

He rasped in an angry whisper, "What's all this, sugar? You're not going to tell me you've been *intimate* with this sky-born abortion?"

"Shut up, Daddy," she whispered with something of a return to her old authority. "Remember how Icky Elmo said La Cruz had large mining interests in North Texas and he denied it? Well, he has 'em, Daddy, as he admitted to me while reelin' from my charms. And I didn't do a thing more than Ma would have done when so much was at stake. What's more, his mining interests consist of the original map and claim to the *Lost Crazy-Russian Pitchblende Mine!*"

"How can you be sure of that?" Lamar demanded sharply, though keeping his voice down. "I even had the linings of his luggage unstitched and all areas chemicaled for invisible inks, and there wasn't a document of any sort discovered."

"He carries them *on his person,* Daddy. He told me so. So all you have to do is search that creepy-crawly black suit of his at some moment when those vultures over there aren't around, and you'll be the sole owner of the valuablest property in all North Texas and maybe the world!"

Tears came into Lamar's eyes. In a tremulous whisper he said, "Sugar, I've misjudged you unforgivably. You're a true Lamar of the finer sex, perhaps the truest and finest ever drew breath. Of course I'll still have to give you one day's room arrest, so the others don't smell a rat. But after that— Why, if you like, I'll put a million on the line to hire Nembo-Nembo out of Florida Democracy to paint your 3-D portrait —they say he's the world's greatest. I'll underwrite a production of *Texiana* with a solid-gold surrey and diamond-encrusted hoopskirts on all the chorus girls and——"

"Señor Lamar!" I interrupted, unable to bear her perfidy and his stupidity a moment longer. "There are a few other secrets your dear daughterkins hasn't told you. Such as what she really thinks about your lousy taste in theater, your anti-macassar lighthouses, and your provincial, yokelish notions concerning the intercourse of the sexes. Do you know what she calls you? 'The genteelest jail warden in all Texas!' 'The courtly old Cromwell!' While hidden in her lingerie drawers, she has—"

Again the fairy-godmother wand reached out, this time touching the center of my forehead and bestowing on me the benison of oblivion.

8 / *The Invisible Prison*

I never saw a man who looked
With such a wistful eye
Upon that little tent of blue
Which prisoners call the sky.

—"The Ballad of Reading Gaol," by Oscar Wilde

As CONSCIOUSNESS WORKED its way back into me, starting deep inside and moving blindly toward my eyes, the first thing I became aware of was pain.

The pain was everywhere and came mostly from being tightly tied with a thousand ropes or a hundred thousand hairs to a flat, hard surface with wide cracks in it. But I was thirsty too. There was only enough moisture in my mouth to glue my tongue to its roof. And I had the kind of weakness that told me I needed food, though the thought of food nauseated me. I also needed some sort of pills. On top of that my feet were burning up.

My head was tied, left ear down against my left shoulder, numbing the latter and mashing it into the flat, cracked surface. The down ear, mashed too, heard only my thudding heartbeat.

The sound frightened me. It was very labored. My arms were strapped down to either side, so that I lay on my back in a cruciform position that was symmetrical except for my head turned to the left. The contact between my dorsal flesh and the flat, hard surface was intimate. I realized I was naked.

I tried to think where in the Sack or Circumluna was a surface like that. The only one I could recall was a big abstraction made of thin slabs of rare moon-marble. So Murray the mosaic-worker had decided to incorporate me into his greatest work of art! Visualizing carefully from onlooker viewpoint, I decided the effect would be striking, moving, even beautiful.

But did they untie me at intervals so that I could rest, drink, and eat, or was I a permanent part of the mosaic? There seemed something wrong about using a highly talented actor for such a purpose, no matter how tremendous the effect. But then artists and photographers are single-minded clots. Some of them won't even read a book or go to the theater.

Photography reminded me that I must explain to Murray that a good life-size solidograph of me portraying naked agony would do just as well, or even better, for his mosaic and free me to go back to the La Cruz Theater-in-the-Sphere, where I was needed and could express my own varied inward visions, not just one of his.

By now the burning sensation had traveled up into my calves.

Into my darkened mind there floated a dim picture of Rachel Vachel and Fanninowicz gloating over me, the latter saying, "Clearly he will require no other restraint," the girl agreeing, "That's for sure, Fanny. He looks as if he'd been glued down yesterday with a quart of sticktite. Or like a mashed giant spider."

So Terra's most hysterical personality-changer had also been a sadist. I hoped I had paid back my tall inamorata well in the only coin women understand, before returning to the Sack. Why in Pluto's name had Murray tied me down so cruelly? I wished there weren't so many gaps in my memory of the last half of my trip to Terra. Evidently when gravitation sickness had struck, it had struck hard.

The picture was replaced by a motion one of Fanninowicz battling wildly with Chase and Hunt. The professor's mouth was open and working, as if he were shouting at them, although I now heard nothing. From time to time he pointed behind me. He was the more active fighter, but the two bigger men were drunkenly getting the better of him.

A bottle crashed and splashed soundlessly. For some reason Fanninowicz was on my side and I desperately wanted him to win. It didn't make sense.

Then the vampire-smiling Rachel Vachel floated back again, but this time with her father. Suddenly I could remember sounds again, for Lamar was saying, "Don't you fret, sugar, we'll get those papers out of him if we have to skin him alive!"

For some unknown reason, this grisly sentiment made me laugh uproariously. The laughter came out as a strangling and highly painful series of dry croaks, but it helped wake me up. I dragged my eyes open.

My surmise had been correct. I was glued to Murray's masterpiece.

But something must be very wrong with my memory, because I didn't recall his Sack-famed mosaic being anything this huge or violently colored. He must have extended it and touched it up with seventeen different hues of paint —and Murray was an artist who favored sallow tones, such as me and my skin. And wouldn't even a clot of an artist have too much taste, or mere brute instinct, than to paint over the ghostly shades of moon-marble?

And why, besides myself, had Murray also glued to his revised mosaic many jagged fragments of brown, green, and clear glass, several smashed chairs and tables (how had he ever wangled those out of the Museum of Terran Domestic Artifacts and got permission to destroy them?), numerous pillows, a lightning pistol, an intact monocle, and—flat on his back—*Mayor Atomic Bill Burleson of Dallas, Texas, Texas*?

That last brought me back to reality with a bang. I simply couldn't see Burleson sacrificing himself for a work of art, especially another man's, something I myself might do in certain moods.

No, I clearly was back in Governor Lamar's patio and there had been a sizable brawl last night. Burleson, I now noted, had his head on a pillow and was snoring in the shade like a drunkard still well soused, while the burning sensation in my lower extremities, which had now reached my knees, was the morning sunlight creeping across the patio.

I *must* do something before it crawled high as my belly and chest, I told myself for a long frantic moment that ended as soon as I faced up to my helplessness.

My exoskeleton and Sack suit were gone. The million invisible hairs pinning me down were simply the force of Terran gravity. I could wriggle my fingers and toes. I could open and shut my lower jaw. Otherwise I could not bend a joint. The way my head was placed, I could not even look down at my body. I only got a foreshortened view of my left arm coming out from under my cheek.

I let my gaze wander out. The landscape, which last night had been romantic, now looked dismal and sunblasted, almost like Luna's. The few trees drooped. The truncated cones, small and large, shimmered in the heat waves like chesspieces designed by a computer. Else there was nothing but a plain of pale-brown dust.

Except for the big swimming pool, everything looked as dry as the inside of my mouth felt. Even the faintly blue sky appeared dehydrated, while I was robbed of billions of molecules of my slender supply of moisture by each breath I drew of the desiccated air.

Now through the last there came flapping across the pool two tiny swatches—yes, Rachel's description had been precise—of black-and-orange batik. With a longing that was almost worship, my eyes followed the delightfully erratic movements of the flutterby. For that must be the true derivation, mangled by comedians. How can butter fly? Every atom of me yearned toward and revered the delicate whimsical creature. She had conquered gravity, while *Homo christophorus sculliansis* definitely had not. She fluttered out of sight.

My longing altered without changing direction. Now I passionately wanted my exoskeleton, as if it were my metal Siamese-twin brother or a new-wed robot wife.

It must have been removed from me last night while I was still unconscious from the touch of Rachel's black wand or from further shocking or drugging, perhaps on the pretext of rendering me helpless or tormenting me, but ultimately so that Rachel Vachel and her father could remove my Sack suit and hunt through it for the claim to and the map of the Lost Crazy-Russian Pitchblende Mine. That made me chuckle again, despite torment to my uvula.

I scanned all the patio I could. Trusty Old Titanium was nowhere in sight, though he (she?) might lie hidden behind one of the couches.

Perhaps I was foolish to believe my exoskeleton would have been left in the patio, but I thought not. True, Fanninowicz would have taken it away with him if at all possible, but my last recollection of the professor was his enthusiastic manhandling by Chase and Hunt. Most likely he had departed under restraint or on a stretcher.

Someone else with a rudimentary sense of caution or tidiness would have taken it away. Why, they hadn't even bothered to take away Burleson, who lay snoring as sincerely as ever. Most of the others would have been close to dead drunk too. Might Rachel have taken it away? To fondle it in bed? Ridiculous! She hated me.

I recalled Fanninowicz pointing over me during the fight. At what? My stripped-off exoskeleton, I suddenly felt sure. Why would I have felt involved in the fight, unless it had been about my exoskeleton? I yearned for the impossible: that I could turn over and peer behind me. Though what use just looking at it would do me, I did not know, except to make me more miserable, if that were possible.

Then another reason occurred to me why my exo might have been carelessly left behind. All the Texans would have assumed that I would be utterly unable to stir without it. They would have forgotten, *as I myself had up to this moment,* the preternatural power in my fingers, toes, and jaw. And come to think of it, not even Rachel had seen my handshake fight with El Toro.

With a shudder of hope that made my hair rise (small but auspicious victory over gravity), I walked my left hand to my thigh, dragging my flaccid arm behind it. It was easy. My fingers found purchase in the cracks between the tessellations and hardly felt the weight they dragged behind them.

Now the task was more difficult: to walk my hand across my body, lifting the dead weight of my arm during the first half of the trip. But I am moderately hirsute around my crotch. By pinching hold of tufts of hair with outstretched fingers and then crooking them sharply, and by digging my rather thick, long fingernails into my flesh, careless of pain, I swiftly accomplished the job. Indeed, my hand proved to be a most able little five-limbed mountain climber.

During the trip my fingers felt the heat of direct sunlight, reminding me I had no time to lose.

The descent had been a breeze despite the friction between my dragged left arm and body. Now my left fingers blindly found cracks again and began to walk both away from my body and up toward the line of my shoulders.

Meanwhile I walked my right hand up toward my right armpit, to provide a cushion for my head, when and if it turned over, and also to be a brace and obstacle, so that my left hand would have its chance to turn my body over, not slide it across the pavement.

At the same time, by moving my jaw first right then left, I started to walk my head off my left shoulder, which had begun to lift, and across my chest. The stubble on my chin —I had not shaved since departure from Circumluna— helped, though in this area I made little progress.

My left fingers were really working hard now. Thumb and middle finger would crook in a crack, while my forefinger and ring finger groped forward seeking another crack, in which they could seat their tips and take up the crooking or pulling job. Little finger helped which pair needed her most.

A quarter of my back was lifted off the pavement now. There was a sharp pain in my left shoulder. I feared it would dislocate—ghost muscles are little use in holding together joints subjected to strain. My eyes, slit-lidded, were looking almost straight up into the bright pale sky.

There was a moment when I feared I'd never make it. But then my fingers found a providentially wide and suitably curving crack in which they could all pull together. My head rolled over so that it lay with temple on right shoulder, chin on right fist. My hips turned then, so that left was directly above right. For the present I let them remain that way, my body lying on my right side. Most of the front of my body was in shade at last, though other areas of it were newly exposed to the bright sunlight, which had now moved as high as my hips and was stinging me hard.

Suddenly feeling very apprehensive, I blinked my eyes twice, then forced them to look dispassionately toward the house end of the patio.

Facing me and grotesquely seated in a chair not four meters away was my exoskeleton with my Sack suit tossed across it.

But both my titanium humeri and femurs had been bent almost double, so that their cables curled and dangled. The delicate lattice of my ribs had been crushed in almost out of recognition. My head basket had numerous dents. One cheekplate had been bent out. While my Sack suit had been slashed to black ribbons.

Really, it had considerable power as a semiaccidental work of art. In fact, it brought tears to my eyes—tears that I hated because I now loathed any power of Texans to make me emote, but more because tears robbed me of moisture I could ill afford to lose.

For now my most urgent need was water, along with some sort of relief from the unending strain of gravity and the burning, dehydrating heat of the sun.

I would not ask Texans for help, even if anyone would come in answer to my croaking calls. I resolutely repressed from my mind the vision of Chase and Hunt demonstrating their drunken strength last night by bending my exo-humeri and -femurs, and tromping my rib cage. It had been to prevent that, of course, that Fanninowicz had fought them: he loved my exo even if he didn't love me.

There was no use whatever in regretting the past, or in gloating with a masochistic self-pity over the indignities done me and my dear exo.

My body must have known my intentions before I did, or else, already in the fringes of dehydration delirium, I was beginning to act by instinct rather than reason, for while I had been thinking those thoughts, my left hand had toppled my body over onto my chest. Now, aided by my fresh right fingers crooking and crawling under my chin, it was walking in a direction that would hopefully drag my whole body around and head me for the swimming pool.

My toppling over had left me with my right leg twisted under my left. But now my well-muscled toes got to work, first untwisting my legs, then finding cracks and aiding me to claw my way toward my new goal.

At last I was turned enough so that I could see it. Because it was almost brimful, my eyes could even glimpse from their slight altitude the great sheet of lovely glimmering silver. It made me think of how comfortable and snug I'd felt sandwiched between my water mattresses aboard the *Tsiolkovsky*, totally embraced by sheeted liquid except for a hole over my face.

My fingers and toes redoubled their efforts. I told myself that once I was floating on my back in that delectable H_2O, its cool erasing the sun's sting, my whole body exquisitely hydrating again—that then I could ponder my next move and easily conceive some brilliant plan to thwart my captors. But for the present I must concentrate on finger-, toe-, and maybe even chin-crawling, lugging my inert body to the reviving fluid.

The whole course ahead of me was liberally scattered with broken glass. I chose a curving and recurving route that would take me close to Burleson's feet, but miss the worst of the glass. Most of it would be through direct sunlight, but that did not worry me as much, now that my belly and chest were in shade.

I soon discovered that I could keep my head upright on my chin without the aid of my right hand, which was more efficiently employed like my left—stretched far ahead and finding cracks by which to pull myself forward, a job that my toes had to do blindly. Quick work with my chin would keep my head from toppling to either side or from falling forward, robbing me of my vision.

Of course my chin was getting well-scraped in the process, as was all of my ventral region, but this was inevitable.

At first I would walk a hand to and with a finger flick out of my path any but the tiniest fragments of glass.

But then my whistling breath, an increasing ache in my throat, dizzy spells, and a sense of being engulfed in almost unendurable heat made me realize I had only a very limited time left in which to reach the water, which would save my life.

Now I flicked out of the way only the largest and most wicked-looking fragments. My chin avoided most of the others, which accumulated under the top of my chest, where they scratched and stabbed.

As I approached Burleson in my giant-inchworm fashion, I saw his eyes open and stare at me, at first incuriously, then with a certain groggy but not overgreat horror, as if I were only one more grotesque denizen of the world of hangover. He lifted to his lips an open green bottle that his right hand had been snugged around, glug-glugged awhile, and relapsed once more into his shut-eyed sprawl.

It tells much about my desperation and depletion of resources at that time, that I did not then see anything the least funny about his actions. I was merely glad to get past the big slob's huge shoes, one more landmark in my advance.

I didn't bother anymore about the glass, though I was aware of certain new sharp pains in my chest and belly, and also of a warm slime that made travel easier. Actually I no longer saw even the glass, I saw only my watery goal. My fingers, toes, and chin were moving on their own initiative. I had turned into a team of two hands, two feet, and a jaw, harnessed to a vast indefinite load that had to be dragged like a travois. My brain filled with useless visions of free-fall swims in the huge high-surface-tension water drop that is Circumluna's pride, of Elmo haranguing me on the grandeurs and glories of Texas, of my mother nursing me, of my father trying to explain to me what oceans were, and so on.

As my fingers touched at last the edge of the pool and longed to climb down in at once, a measure of sanity returned to me. I realized it would be a tricky business to get myself into the pool on my back, for if I floated on my face, I would have no way to get my nose and mouth out of the water.

Accordingly, although my consciousness was now wavering and every cell of my body screaming for moisture, I made myself crawl through a curve until the entire right side of my body was lying along the edge of the pool. Then I walked my left foot back of my right so my legs were again crossed.

Next I worked my right hand under my chin, clutching the edge of the pool with it, and walked my left hand as far ahead as I could and then down over the edge of the pool, where it found a convenient negative ledge.

All this while my eyes had been feasting on the water, as the thoughts of a lonely rocket pilot on his fuel. My right elbow, dipped in the stuff, knew chilly bliss. But there was a tiny admixture of apprehension. That water looked very deep. But I reminded myself that one floated as readily over

ten meters of water as over two—or over ten kilometers of
H_2O (incredible oceanic datum).

I strongly crooked the fingers of my left hand. My right
hand stood up under my chin. I opened my mouth wide
and my head tipped over toward the pool. At the same time
my left toes found the same negative ledge my left fingers
had, and they crooked too. My left hip rose.

As I teetered there, prolonging my agony a delicious moment and reminding myself of the precautions to take in
water, I decided I must have started hallucinating, for I saw
a long pink snake uncoil its tail downward from a top-story
window of the patio and its long pale-pink head emerge
and begin to sway.

But maybe that supercobra wasn't hallucination, for next
I saw Mayor Burleson sit up and stare at his feet. Then his
gaze slowly followed what I realized must be the blood
track I had left, until he was looking at me.

I took a deep breath and toppled myself over. I landed
with a splash on my back, precisely as I'd planned.

Cold shock almost knocked me senseless. Then, although
consciousness was still wavering and vision blurring, I began to be happy. Water is ersatz free fall, but good ersatz.
I let it into my mouth, little by little. Nectar. I swiftly
exhaled, remembering to do so through the nose, then took
another deep breath. I discovered that the blurring was
mostly water in my eyes.

I rolled away from the poolside as far as the leash of my
right arm let me, then in reaction rolled back. Through my
one eye above water I watched a Burleson reeling both
from alcohol and from my disordered vision. As he followed
my spoor to the poolside, his arms hung slackly, one still
holding the green bottle. His head was bent down until his
jowls were multiplied. He looked so much like a huge stupid
dog who had been taught to walk on his hind legs and to
guzzle, but nothing else, that I would have laughed except
I noted in time that my mouth and nose were both underwater.

Behind him, and even more out of focus, the hyper-serpent illusion or reality continued. Now the thicker section I had first taken for the serpent's head was midway to the ground. Perhaps it was something which the snake had swallowed in the top-story room.

Burleson kept getting bigger and funnier. He was near enough for me to note the owlish solemnity of his downward gaze.

Then he made a sloppy swinging grab at my right hand, missed, and almost fell in beside me. After teetering a long second on the brink—a mountain about to topple over sideways—he got his balance again. His first act was to take two more slugs from the green bottle. Then he aimed his gaze very carefully at my hand, spread the fingers of his own free hand for a second grab, and was funny no longer.

I did not want to be pulled from the pool only one-quarter restored. I did not want to be pulled from the pool, period. I did not want to fall again into the hands of Texans. The pool was not the best base of operations, but at least it was a base from which I might for a while be able to conduct independent negotiations.

Besides, I did not want to be near Burleson if he fell or dived into the pool. The wave he created might well swamp or overturn me. So as he grabbed again, I boldly pushed off from the pool's wall with a brisk backhand flick of my right hand. I intended to paddle myself with my fin-clenched fingers to the pool's center and there await developments.

The flick lifted my face from the water. I took another very deep breath.

It was well for me I did so, for the next thing that happened was that I began to sink. When I opened my eyes I was looking up through several centimeters of water—centimeters that rather rapidly became decimeters. I energetically flapped my finger fins downward. It slightly slowed, but did not halt, my descent.

Too late, it was crystal-clear what had happened to me.

With my preponderance of bone and almost total lack of fat, I massed considerably more than an equivalent volume of water and so was inevitably going down. I should have foreseen it, but who ever thinks of one's specific gravity, especially in free fall?

How I wished now that I had inherited my mother's pyknic tendencies and grown up a Fat, even though it would have almost certainly resulted in my becoming a comedian rather than a star of high tragedy. Mother would have floated like a butterball.

I flatter myself that I sank with a certain dignity, though I continued to flap my finger fins industriously and even made some tiny swimming motions with my ghost muscles, which worked a little now that gravity's clutch was slightly counterbalanced by my negative buoyancy. If I must die, let it be with a minimum of panic. Besides, the grip of gravity on a free-fall being tends to make him fatalistic—he is in the ubiquitous grip of a power greater far than himself. Soon, surely, I would be lying on the pool's bottom, nailed down almost as securely as I had been on the tessellated pavement above. Crawl then to the pool's side and climb out if there were cracks to climb by? I strongly doubted my oxygen supply would permit that, though I would make the attempt.

9 / In the Pool

Where the sea-beasts, ranged all round,
Feed in the ooze of their pasture-ground;
Where the sea-snakes coil and twine,
Dry their mail and bask in the brine;
Where great whales come sailing by,
Sail and sail, with unshut eye,
Round the world for ever and aye.

—"The Forsaken Merman," by Matthew Arnold

As I SANK, I idly noted a dozen or so scarlet threads rising from my chest. The broken glass had pocked me deeply indeed. Now was the time for barracudas, piranhas, and small sharks (but Texans would surely use big ones) to come nosing up to the threads and then snap me to chunks, bits, and ribbons in a tumultuous swirl of chaotic water—that is, if this pool were filled with such carnivores, as Terran suspense fiction had assured me was the custom of all evil millionaires, wealthy criminals, and politicos.

What actually happened was worse. I got the impression a white whale had dived into the pool or a medium-size white submarine been launched into it. The crash of its entry deafened me. Subsurface waves struck me. The water was vastly disordered. All the artistically curving scarlet threads vanished in a pink swish. Then a pale monster approached and glided under me. I awaited with minimal tranquillity the half-turn of the white shark and the great bite of its razor teeth. Considering my slenderness, I would doubtless be cut in two. In any case, it would all be over swiftly, the books agreed. I would emit one horrific groaning scream and—

What actually happened was that arms embraced me, I felt a female form long as my own against my back, while powerful kicks swiftly propelled me to the surface.

As I emerged, I blew explosively and gulped down great lungfuls of thick Terran air, which now seemed sweeter than the Sack's. One strong hand shifted to my armpit. The other cradled the back of my head. I faintly heard the kicks that were keeping us both afloat. My whole face and some of my chest were above water.

Then from behind me, in strangely muffled tones, Rachel Vachel said, "You okay, Captain Skull?"

"Yes," I replied, "but I can't hear you."

"Water in your ears. I'll fix that." Lips and a tongue expertly glued themselves to each of my ears in turn and sucked. Then, in a roar, "How's that?"

"Perfect, princess. You needn't shout," I replied. "And now, if it is possible, could you turn me over so that my chest and belly are not in direct sunlight?"

"Of course, but why?"

"So we can look into each other's eyes. There's another reason, but it's too complicated to explain."

By that time Rachel had me turned and was supporting me with a hand under my chin. Framed by plastered-down silvery hair, her face was more beautiful than I'd recalled. Her skull was well-formed—she had the makings of a good Thin. She was grinning, as if in the highest spirits.

Whatever her motives for rescuing me—generous, sneaky, or crazy—I suddenly felt so much gratitude and tender admiration that only poetry could express it. Accordingly I recited:

> Rachel, thy beauty is to me
> Like those Nicean barks of yore,
> That gently, o'er a perfumed sea,
> The weary, wayworn wanderer bore
> To his own native shore.

"By courtesy of Edgar Poe," I added.

"That's just plumb beautiful, Scully," she sighed, "even if this pool ain't perfumed."

"It is now, princess," I told her, looking deeply into her shining eyes.

"Oh, what a courtier!" she exclaimed. Then, chuckling, "So you think of me as a bark, Scully—a great big clumsy ocean-going vessel?"

"You are an oceangoing goddess," I told her. "While I am surely a most grateful, weary, wayworn wan—"

A great wave of weakness washed over me, almost blacking out my vision. I heard Rachel calling faintly, as if from a great distance, "Gloryosky! I forgot your pills. Is one of each color right?"

"Yes. Two browns," I managed to reply.

I felt her wet fingers place four pills on my tongue. I crushed them between my molars for swifter effect and downed them with a half-mouthful of pool.

When my vision cleared, she was still trying to close with one hand a small pink case tied around her neck by a pink ribbon. Her other hand was occupied supporting me. She got it shut, but not before I'd noted inside, besides the pills that she must have taken from my exo's cheekplate, a small, dialed box and a half-dozen or so mini-tapes.

Referring to the last, I asked politely as we bobbed up and down, "Some of your manuscripts, princess?"

"Yes," she replied, "includin' *Houston's Afire* and *Storm Over El Paso*. Scully, you're a skunk. Or at least you were last night, when you told Daddy about my lingerie drawers. He bust 'em all up, lookin' for subversive literature, and would have found the secret drawer for sure, except I was gettin' undressed so fast he had to scuttle out. He likes me to hand him out my clothes through a door open about six inches—before he locks it."

"But, princess," I told her gravely, "you did me, my father, and my family a great wrong when you revealed to your father the secret of the Lost Crazy-Russian Pitchblende

Mine and that I carried it on my person. Only a very odd
circumstance prevented your father from getting hold of
the map and claim when he searched and slashed up my
Sack suit."

"Scully, you're a numbskull!" she snapped at me. "Sorry
I got to tell you this, but that map-claim business is pure
dream. Bought from an Aleut who had it off a Cree Injun!
Why, that's the oldest swindle goin'. Scully, you got no more
chance of making money out of that mining claim than you
have of making time with La Cucaracha when I'm around.
Last night I brought it up just as a red herring to distract
Daddy and win back some favor with him. He'll believe
anything, long as it means more money for him. Scully, you
don't know the rudiments of high revolutionary intrigue."

"But, princess—" I began injuredly. Truly, I was shaken.

At that moment a shouting started at the poolside. Rachel
turned my face so that I too could see Burleson, hands on
knees yet still reeling a little, as he yelled over-shoulder
toward the gringo door.

"Hey, Governor! Come out if you can hear me. Come out
a-rushing. Your honorable daughter's swimming bare-naked
with that skin-and-bones revolutionary from outer space.
He's bare-naked too!"

I was impressed by the relish with which Burleson reported to Lamar his daughter's misbehavior.

"Sure you don't need a little mouth-to-mouth resuscita-
tion?" Rachel asked sportively. "You look peaked, you
know. It'd make Bilious Burly boil, besides drivin' Lushy
Lamar plumb loco if he gets here in time. Incidentally,
I'm not quite bare-naked, as those fat-asses insist on de-
scribin' the highly civilized state of total nudity. I'm wearing my flesh-toned mini-underwear, which is all the clothes
Daddy allowed me when he locked me up—unless you
count the profusion of unshocked pink sheets I knotted together for my escape."

"Bussing would be beautiful, but—" I began.

She was already off again with "You know, I think Daddy's got a great big sex-thing going for me, maybe unconscious, but maybe not. Else why this eternal lockin' in bedrooms and takin' away all the clothes except a tease-minimum? You know how he's always pickin' off his coat and pants lint that ain't there? I bet those are snowflakes from the blizzard of puritanic guilt that's forever buffetin' him!"

"Excellent armchair analysis, princess," I agreed. "But shouldn't we be doing something? Soon the houseboys will come running and then Rangers, I suppose, and between them they'll be able to figure out a way to capture us. Surely some of them besides yourself can swim? And is there not a cowboy waldo called a lasso? Have you your horse or swifter vehicle nearby? Then there may still be time for you to swim me to the shore away from Burleson and carry me —I am featherweight, you are strong—to that vehicle and——"

"Hush up and stop frettin', Scully," she ordered gaily. "Everything's under control and proceeding according to schedule. Now take the houseboys. Not a one of them turned up this morning. That great speech of yours last night sure started a bully ruckus. El Toro says you're guilty of premature activism and romantical individualism, but he's playing along. Jeepers, what I'd give for your actin' skill! But you'll teach me everything, darling, won't you? Why, there's rumors the remains of the late Austin's praetorian guard are holed up in Greasertown. Hunty-Wunt's having conniptions decidin' whether to rush, besiege, or atom-bomb. Hey, here come Daddy and Big Foot! Hiyah, Lushy Lamar! Mornin', Bilious Burly! Greetin's, Chincy Chase! Come on in, all of you, the water's fine. We're havin' *fun!*"

And with that she kissed me passionately until we had sunk at least three feet, whereupon with two powerful kicks she surfaced us again and I was able to honor that kiss with the gasp it deserved.

"You swim here at once, sugar, you hear me?" Lamar was raving, tearing his hair with one hand and pointing at us with the other. "It's a million bedroom-years I'm going to give you this time. And no clothes at all."

"Why, Daddy, I'd think you'd be happy you'd left me those two scraps of panties and bra," she called back sweetly. "For all you know, I may be wearin' 'em now. That is, if you're lucky. Tell me, Scully, have I got my pants on?"

As I groped for an answer that would be offensive to Lamar, yet still gallant, a large smooth metal hook settled around my neck. Rachel whipped it off barely in time. She shoved it away from us, then yanked it back. On the poolside, Sheriff Chase staggered and lost hold of the ten-foot pole on which the hook was mounted. It floated in the pool.

"Sugar, I'm begging you," Lamar called, on his knees now and wringing his hands. "Why, there hasn't been a like scandal since Jefferson Davis, looking for a place to smoke and purely by accident, walked in on Portia Calphurnia Lamar while she was taking a spit bath. Swim to your daddy, sugar."

Rachel called back, "Daddy, why don't you buy yourself a townhouse of teen-age sportin' gals? Come to terms with life, Governor."

"But that's not the same thing, sugar!"

During this interchange, three Rangers with laser rifles had come hurrying, as far as Texans ever do, out of the gringo door. Chase conferred with them. One retrieved the pole and started around the pool with it. Chase took out of his pocket one of those black squeeze cylinders Hunt had been playing with yesterday, and he inspected it narrowly. Simultaneously Burleson drew from a holster at his side a revolver of ancient aspect and goggled at it, somewhat wonderingly.

"Princess, we can't talk our way out of this, we must do something," I whispered urgently.

"Scully, I told you everything's on," she whispered loudly back, "but if it makes you feel any better—" She opened her

pink purse one-handed and clicked a lever on the tiny box
inside.

"Black Madonna calling Submarine. Come in, Submarine,"
she softly said to it, holding it close to her mouth and ear,
all three just above water. I heard but could not distinguish
the words of a reply. She continued, "Roger. Look here, me
and La Muerte are pool-center and we're going to be in
trouble in about thirty seconds. You'll be here in twenty-
five? Swell!"

Clicking it off and shutting her purse, she whispered,
"Antique crystal A.M. radio. Baffles the Rangers."

I did my best to feel encouraged. Did the pool connect
with a river or underground lake? It sounded difficult. Still,
the pool was deep. There was a big *bang* and something
very solid splatted the water a foot from my head. Blast
stung my skin. I saw Burleson leveling his smoking revolver
toward me, swinging it in arcs of about twenty degrees.

Rachel trod water strongly and swung me around so she
was between me and the gun. Meanwhile she yelped,
"Daddy, you gonna let him kill me? You want your lovin'
Rachel with holes in her, deader than the Laredo cowboy?"

Lamar sprang up and grappled with the Mayor, who
protested, "Just firing a shot across their bows, Governor,
maybe pick off the sky-greaser. No harm meant your precious one."

Chase shouted, "Come out, Miss Lamar, and tug La Cruz
with you. No back talk either—we've quit fooling. Boys,
get ready to boil the water around them."

The laser rifles were leveled to either side of us. Their
heat surely couldn't boil the whole pool. But maybe if the
beams were kept close enough—

Rachel put my hands behind her neck and then embraced
me. "Hold me tight, Scully," she said, treading water so that
I faced away from the patio. Perhaps she meant us to die
together. Little I could do.

The third Ranger was reaching the hook toward us. But

before I could warn Rachel, he jerked it away in a wide circle as he turned.

Weaving its way toward us among the cryptic towers was a menacing plume of brown dust. It grew larger and higher by seconds. I began to hear a roar.

"It's a twister! Run for your lives!" the Ranger cried, dropping the hook and pounding back around the pool.

Rachel turned us so that I was the one facing the patio. My hands were clasped together behind her neck. My chin rested on her shoulder. I closed my teeth on my wrist to make sure my head stayed up. Even if Rachel my beloved decided to sink us, I was going to stay up as long as possible.

The roaring was louder, closer. The two other Rangers and Lamar were shouldering each other through the gringo door, with Burleson a couple of groggy steps behind, while the third Ranger was about to pass him.

Chase, still at the poolside, was pointing something. Then it was as if an invisible hand and pen had very swiftly drawn a narrowing black line from him to us. Its end struck Rachel's back below my clasped hands and I felt her muscles go slack, even as leaked electricity tingled through me, almost making me unclasp my hands.

As we started to sink, because she was no longer treading water, and as Chase turned and lumbered after the others, the roar became deafening. The poolwide plume of dust hit the pool and became a vast plume of white spray.

I had time to suck in a big breath before it struck us. Amid blasting spray we were tugged upward a few centimeters, then shoved underwater by a great hand of wind.

Rachel's positive buoyancy more than counterbalanced my negative, but as we began to rise, we were again shoved under.

Coming up a second time, we made it. I blew through my nostrils, gasped through my wrist-obstructed mouth.

The tornado had halted over the patio, unable to decide whether to enter the house, climb over it, or back out. It was still shooting up spray from the end of the pool a few meters away.

"Scully, I'm paralyzed below the neck. Don't let go of me," Rachel gasped in my ear, her voice barely audible in the roaring.

"Don't worry about that, princess," I replied grimly, though my voice was much muffled by my wrist in my mouth. Let go of her? She was my float!

The tornado made decision three. Once more we were pushed under. When we came up for the third time, we were inside a weird, dim, tall igloo of spray. The tornado's eye, I told myself, doubtful if there were such a thing in Terran Nature.

The whole Nature theory lost ground when I saw, vanishing upward, my bent exoskeleton and slashed Sack suit, both in the grip of some metal claws on the end of a line.

My hands shifted their grip from each other to Rachel's hair, in which they knotted themselves. Unclasping my jaws, I let my head fall back.

Directly above, through what might be a large circular hole in spray-dashed transparent plastic, a fierce copper-hued face, made fiercer by lines of red and white paint and black topknot, was peering. Something snaked down and landed across my head and Rachel's. Unsmiling thin lips opened to command, "Grab on, palefaces! Must move now!"

What had fallen was a rope with knots every quarter meter. I clenched my teeth on it, then crawled one hand out of Rachel's hair to clench the rope with that too.

The rope straightened as it began to lift me from the water by head and hand. With the other hand I gripped Rachel's fortunately thick hair as strongly as I could.

As my body lifted from the water, I felt my neck stretching and hastily let loose my teeth. It had been a grand gesture, but I didn't want my spinal cord snapped. However, I told myself heroically, I would hang on with my hands to the rope and Rachel, to the point of shoulder dislocation and beyond.

My head flopped and I was looking down. As I felt my
shoulders begin to dislocate in stabs of pain, I saw Rachel
come to and grab the rope herself strongly—with both
hands and teeth also.

At that moment I had an utterly convincing premonition:
some day she and I would be a great aerial or even free-fall
team.

We were swiftly drawn through the hole and found ourselves sprawled in a vehicle that mostly wasn't there.

By that I mean it was constructed chiefly of a clear plastic
with the same refractive index as Terran atmosphere. Here
and there parts of it were visible—motors, a shaft, some rods,
and its crew of two.

They were the Amerind who had hoisted us and, sitting
at a medley of metal and plastic controls, Guchu.

He grinned at us but spoke no word.

Beyond the plastic enclosing us, brown dust was pouring
upward on all sides. Overhead, great swift-flashing invisible blades cut through it.

"It's a kack—CACC—Combo Air-Cushion and Copter,"
Rachel explained over the roar, crawling toward me.

Ruler-straight lightning bolts flashed through the dust,
turning it all dark red.

Guchu chortled. I felt the vehicle sharply tilt and rise. We
were free of the dust, though no more red lightning bolts
came.

Rachel cradled my aching neck and my head, turning the
latter so I could see how one of the big towers cut us off
from Lamar's ranch and the laser rifles of the Rangers.

Guchu said, flashing teeth, "We ride in the tall-boy rig
cover's shadow until we're out of range."

The Amerind said, "No dead Indian, no dead nigger, no
dead palefaces. Good."

I looked around with my eyes, somewhat listlessly. Even
sight of my poor exo and Sack suit didn't make me sad or
mad. The last hour had been a very full one.

The sophistication of the vehicle clashed with the air of

revolutionary simplicity and poverty I had encountered in the church and cemetery last night.

"If it's kack, why do you call it submarine?" I asked Rachel and yawned.

"Because it ain't one," she answered. She was dabbing antiseptics and fixing adhesive bandages on my chest. "'Nother red herring for the Rangers."

"And you're not Black Madonna, you're Mary Magdalene," I observed lazily.

"You hush up."

I noted, stamped in black letters on the plastic near me: ACIFICPAY ACKBLAY EPUBLICRAY. Slowly and with difficulty I translated that from pig Latin to: Pacific Black Republic.

Oh, well, I thought languidly, all revolutions are poorer than third political parties and must accept foreign financing and military aid.

Then I passed out, or simply went to sleep.

10 / Riding the Whirlwind

Ho for Texas,* land that restores us
When houses choke us, and great books bore us!

—"The Santa Fe Trail," by Vachel Lindsay

ONCE AGAIN I woke in the Sack, but this time my stay was shorter. Mother was cradling me in her plump arms against her pneumatic bosom. There was a rhythmic sharp tapping. Father must be throwing a set together a few hours before curtaintime. I pictured him slowly twisting in free fall, two plastic scantlings and a nail gripped in one hand, a nervous hammer in the other.

But then my nose was tickled by the acrid odor of hot metal. Was Father spot-welding again, against all safety regulations established by Circumluna for the Sack? Very likely—Father often broke regulations, but always for the sake of the theater and art, at least as he explained it. Then why the hammering, which really was in a more deliberate rhythm than Father's?

Why ask questions? I wasn't hurting. And I was where I wanted to be. Stay shut-eyed. Sleep.

Along with the tapping, I heard Father's panting breath. Rhythmic gasps. Anxiety stirred. Father mustn't work so hard. He would die. (One of my earliest secret fears was that Father would soon die, he looked so much like a skeleton. That was before I understood about Thins, Fats, and Muscles.)

The imagined scene altered, dropping back ten thousand years or more. We were a cave family at home. I could feel against my chin and cheek the coarse fur of the bear's hide

* Kansas in the original, but changed to Texas when the *de facto* annexation of Kansas by Texas was made public.

Mother wore. The hoarse breath was that of a dragon snuffing outside the cave. At a tiny hot fire, Father was forging the copper sword with which he would slay the dragon.

I opened my eyes. The last vision was closer to truth. I lay in a cave with stubby round spears of rock pointing down. I was softly cushioned against gravity, my head propped up. Longhaired fur covered me to my chin.

Across from me, an Indian sat behind a small walled fire, the heat of which I could feel. Wraithlike flames rose from the small red bed whenever I heard the snuffing. It was a bellows. Yes, he worked it by his knee.

Across the open furnace lay a femur of my exoskeleton, its cables removed. It glowed red in the middle, where the bend was. The bend was not as great as I recalled.

Pads shielding his palms, the Indian lay the femur across an anvil and began straightening the exobone further with taps of a tiny-headed sledge.

The femur was still attached to the rest of my exoskeleton. The other bends had all been straightened. The metal where they had been was discolored. The rib cage was gone. The shallow dents were still in my head basket.

The Indian was not the one who had been in the kack. This one's hair was silvery, his face a mass of wrinkles. Out of them, his black eyes watched me as he hammered. Nearby were piled my three cushion cases. That pleased me.

The red in my femur faded, but the bend was gone. The Indian pointed his sledge at me.

He said, "I have learned one thing, Death. Without your armor, you are very weak. I have always suspected that."

I smiled at him and nodded a forefinger. I did not think he would note the latter, but his eyes shifted to it. Perhaps my hand lay outside the buffalo robe covering me.

I also later learned that what pillowed me so softly, with some effect of free fall, were three eiderdown mattresses. I bless those gravity-conquering birds who think so much of their young that they line their nests with down plucked from their breasts.

I felt thirsty and hungry. As if the mere feeling were a cue, Rachel Vachel and La Cucaracha walked, smiling, into view, the hand of the former resting lightly on the shoulder of the latter. They both looked lovely in the red glow. Rachel had on her black Madonna garb, while La Cucaracha wore a flaming-red dress with belt and necklace of hammered-silver plates. She walked proudly. Rachel had to dodge stalactites with her head.

Without a word, Rachel drew down my buffalo robe and began to inspect my wounded chest, dripping on antiseptic here, renewing a bandage there, while La Cucaracha, using a corner of the furnace for stove, began to make a gruel of water and my protein food pellets.

After getting a sip of water, I told the Mexo-Tex girl I liked to chew the pellets dry. She allowed me to do so with a couple.

While the good food worked in me, I marveled lazily at the amity of the dear girls. Last time they had been battling for me like wolf against musk ox. Now they had made a truce. I wondered what that portended for me.

El Toro had entered and was standing before me, a hard grin on his swarthy face.

"How do you feel, comrade?" he asked.

"Very much better," I told him.

"*Bueno!*" he said with a nod like a gavel rapping a speaker's rostrum. "Very good indeed. You shall begin your work for the Revolution tomorrow with an appearance at Tulsa."

"It will take longer than that, comrade," I informed him in my harshest bass. I mustn't let these little Marxists think they owned me. I must take a strong line from the start. "Your metal-working comrades have done a passable job straightening my bones, as far as I can see. But I personally —with the Indian's help in holding and handling, of course

—must rewind my cables, adjust their tension, and test every motor, lead, and part."

"Not so!" he snapped at me and crooked a finger. There strode into view, yawning and rubbing sleep from his eyes, none other than Professor Fanninowicz. He bumped his head on a stalactite and cursed, "*Donnerwetter!*"

El Toro said proudly, "We had kidnapped him even before we rescued you from the pool. It is he who supervised the repairs to your skeleton. He worked through the night and into the afternoon. Three hours ago we permitted him to rest."

"Forced me to, you mean, you lazy and undisciplined subman!" Fanninowicz barked at him. He screwed a monocle into his right eye and, standing very erect after a quick glance overhead, surveyed us all contemptuously.

"Understand, please," he said curtly, "that I detest you all and your ignorant, sentimental revolution. When the Lone Star Republic, vessel of noblest fascism, arrests you, as is inevitable, I shall smile at your punishments and hope they will be of the harshest. If death, then only after torture!"

"Why, Fanny," Rachel said under her breath, in hurt tones.

Ignoring her, he aimed his glare at me. "And that goes for you too, you miserable mummer from the slums of space!"

Then he relaxed, lost height, and with a shrug that was surely only unconsciously Jewish, he smiling said to me, "However, I am hopelessly enamored of your peerless exoskeleton. It is monomania, an *idée fixe* against which even my sternest military compulsions and compunctions are powerless. Within twelve hours your exoskeleton will be in finer shape than when you received it from those Russo-American swine, the technicians of Circumluna."

I had a great many doubts and reservations about that, but I did not voice them. El Toro, Kookie, Rachel, and even the old Indian were simply too happily self-satisfied and too infatuated with their revolutionary cunning in having used Fanninowicz's monomania against him.

Next day we skittered for Tulsa, Oklahoma, Texas, in three kacks, taking different routes. We flew under and through low clouds shot with lightning, navigating in part by an echo device called radar, which was new to me, since there are neither swarms of water droplets nor starless times in space.

The kack's transparency made it seem as if we were swimming through a gray ocean. At any rate, the dank, dingy supersoup with its electrical seasoning was not to my taste. But it cheered my comrades because, they said, it disordered communications and hid us from Lone Star vulture planes.

El Toro told me, with mixed pride and envy, that Texas newsmen have dubbed me The Specter and that I have been declared Public Enemy Number One of the Republic. The Rangers have sworn to nail my hide to a barn door, which I hope is hypothetical, alongside those of Clyde and Bonnie, whoever they may be or have been. The search for us has become hot, El Toro affirmed, with both Hunt and Chase living up to their names.

"They going to burn you if they can, sky boy," Guchu assured me from the pilot's pad. "But have no fear. Death by fire is purifying."

Fanninowicz was not aboard our kack, which was a relief —the German is an insufferable combination of martinet (of me) and high priest (of my exo). But neither were Rachel and Kookie, which I found depressing and determined to remedy, if we lived that long.

I put in time talking with a grav-topped much bent Mex named Pedro Ramírez, who had been in a cyborged work gang for twenty years. He pulled his shirt off his knobby shoulder to show me the puckered scars where deep-probing tubes had once fed tranquilizers, energizers, and hormones from his yoke into artery and vein. He also insisted I inspect the curious callosities in his ears, made by the common plugs that had been housed there daily for two decades. Meantime he began softly to hum, I think without realizing it, a medley of monotonous tunes, and once I caught the curious English words:

> Every day, two hours times twelve,
> A million yokemen dig and delve.

But when I questioned him about the details of his gang work, he became excited and emotional. I easily quieted him with a few calm and confident suggestions.

I concluded that cyborging involves no direct control of the nervous system, but is merely a means of chemical and hypnotic supervision, the command plugs transmitting both an audio background of tranquilizing propaganda and also the orders of a Texan overseer observing the work site directly or by 3-D. Or the orders, El Toro told me, of a cyborged Mex strawboss, in turn overseen by a Texan, who can in this fashion control as many as a dozen work gangs.

It struck me as a vastly overcomplicated as well as degrading system for work more easily done by machines, or for that matter by uncyborged workers energized by coca leaves and tranquilized by marijuana. I decided the Texans favored it because it allowed them to keep the Mexicans uneducated and, probably more to the point, catered to the Texan conviction that Mexicans and other "primitives" are ineducable.

"And those pitiful *peones* don't even know the work they do, Esquel," El Toro topped my guesses. "They get powerful hypnotic commands, when the yoke is off, to forget the details and even nature of all labor they perform while cyborged."

"Hypersecurity, man," Guchu nodded. "Surer than cuttin' out the tongue and poppin' the eye. A blind mute can gesture and draw and maybe write, but nobody can tell what he's forgot."

I realized this was why my questions had disturbed Pedro

Ramírez. Nevertheless, after administering soothing suggestions, I asked if he had done work within the outsize oil-rig
towers.

"Never in *those*, Señor Espectro!" he assured me with a
shuddering, wide-eyed headshake. "No, never once!"

His denial struck me as too strong to be true—especially
along with the "dig and delve" drone—but I had no desire
to torment further in order to satisfy idle curiosity. So I
calmed him once more and shortly had him asleep, suggesting that he wake feeling well and happy. A leading actor
who is not a passable hypnotist is hardly worth his salt.

It occurred to me, as the trip grew long and I began to
ache in my exo, that it would be pleasant if there were
someone to hyp me asleep. Somehow I did not want to do a
self-hyp. I recalled wistfully the tender nursing I had got
from Rachel and La Cucaracha in the cave. I had loved
them as co-mothers then, nurses within gravity's womb. But
now I reminded myself, slapping the rib cage of my trusty
exo, that I loved them in quite a different fashion. The
thought heartened me greatly.

My rib cage was a new one, made of solid silver, weigh-
ing a few pounds more, but with a lovely dull shimmer. Its
luxury contrasted nicely with my martial head basket, the
dents in which had only imperfectly been beaten out.

But by the time we reached the central square of the
Tulsa greasertown, my mood was once more as low and
dark as the weather continued to be. The girls' brief greetings raised it a bit, but it immediately dropped to a new
low when El Toro whispered, "Just keep in mind, *camarada,*
that thirteen known informers have had their throats slit or
been otherwise taken care of, to safeguard tonight's gathering against interruption."

It seemed a dismally high price for a performance—
there'd been nothing about murder in my contract—and I
feared I'd be a flop. Up to my entrance, I kept seeing those
gaping gullets and also the pitiful bent-backs who had died
at Dallas, inflamed by my rantings, while the lightning of

electric whips and laser beams had been a frame for my thoughts.

But as soon as I faced my audience I was in a controlled revolutionary frenzy, sardonic and heartless as only Death can be. It's a perpetual miracle how a part takes hold and carries one, even when one actively dislikes the role.

I was afraid too that Fanninowicz had booby-trapped my exoskeleton, perhaps by time bomb, but it actually continued to operate more smoothly than ever. What strange and contradictory compulsions fire men!

At the end of my oration I was so worked up that I wanted to lead the mob into Tulsa's texastown to commit acts of violence. But locals did that and I took off with El Toro and the rest for the abandoned atomic shelter that would be our camp until we headed for Little Rock, Wichita, or Springfield, Missouri, as tactics dictated.

I wondered at an atomic shelter being deserted in a world that had endured one nuclear war and now seemed minimally peaceful, but El Toro explained to me that radioactives were everywhere in such short supply, due to their military and industrial use, that they would no more be used again as major weapons than the last gasoline would have been used for Molotov cocktails.

To my surprise, Fanninowicz haughtily confirmed El Toro's explanation, though with a curse for a world that had lost with Germany the industry and patience to mine and smelt low-grade uranium ores—and also with a final sardonic smile that lingered in my memory.

I pointed out that a small atomic bomb had been expended on Austin's praetorian guard.

"A few tacticals left, yes," El Toro agreed, "museum pieces, one might say. Texans are loco."

"Your figures on the radioactives shortage are right, Tor," Guchu said, "but you got the wrong analogy. Last gas wasn't used to run a motor, but to fry a black." He paused. "Or maybe a whitey. Who knows?"

He landed our kack in a drizzle where I saw only one darkness instead of earth. Then he turned toward me and said, "Real reason no earthling—except a few locos with bloated egos—would risk more fallout is that we all know we still got a little death ticking in our bones from the Big Poison War. Even you're getting a little of that death into you, Mister Death, every day you stay here. No, Tor, we got to have a confrontation. That's the trouble with you Mexes—always being gracious to people, to whitey even, and smoothing things out—combo, I guess, of the old hidalgo dream and your Indian ability to take anything that's handed to you and endure it, like your yokes, without striking back except for an occasional knife in the dark.

"No, we got to tell Mister Death here the truth. Such as the real reasons A-shelters are taboo. One, a lot of them got worse poisoned from fallout than the toplands—through groundwater and kinked ventilation systems, and because who hits low gets hit low back. Now don't get edgy about that, sky boy; any cobalt-ninety in this shelter has been ticking a hundred years. Two, whitey thinks the shelters have got hants in them and he's scared, though he won't admit it."

Ghosts I could laugh at, and did. Before we entered the shelter, I peered vainly for the moon. El Toro asked with a sympathy that surprised me whether I were homesick. I replied with minimal untruth that, no, I just wanted to know the date—I was uncertain how long I had been in the cave.

"It is the twenty-seventh of Alamo, Esquel," he told me. "Come down now."

I decided that the Texan calendar would have to do for me for my stay on Terra, or until I glimpsed Luna once more.

Ghosts did not seem so laughable when I was in the huge and shadowy shelter, where our camp was dwarfed and faint echoes returned from black unexplored corridors. But I saw no cracks or other bomb damage. Tulsa, I reminded myself, had lain inside the Texas Bunker. Dinner cheered me further and during it, while still stirred with aftershow excitement, I began with La Cucaracha a discussion of history which we carried into the curtained space I thought of as my star dressing room.

It turned out that she has a bright hard head on that exciting little athletic body—she pointed out rather bitterly that a Mexo-Tex female is the lowest of the low and must have ten times the brains of a man to get anywhere.

She insisted that most of the Texas history Elmo had fed me was pure Texas brag, though she did admit that back at the time of the annexation in 1845 Sam Houston had cowed Washington with the prediction that if Texas weren't admitted to the Union on generous terms—such as permission to divide into five states with ten senators whenever desired —then Texas would engulf all the west to the Pacific and assume leadership of the southern states when the inevitable break over slavery came.

"No, Esqueleto *amado*, in verity it was like this: the wealthy gringo junta that arranged the assassination of President Kennedy soon became the entire heart of the Texas Establishment. Thereafter things happened much as you've been told. The blacks, reckless and inspired as their Zulu and Madhi progenitors, carved out their countries to southeast and southwest during the disorders following the Atomic War. We forgotten Mexes, fiery but incurably fatalistic, indolent yet good workers and breeders, remained the undercats and grew into the new servile class."

I asked her what had happened to Elmo. She said that she had no idea, but that he was resourceful and shrewd under his blather and, whatever happened, would land on his feet. I agreed he had big ones. She admitted she had an affection for the man despite, or perhaps because of, his genially bullying ways. This led me to inquire indirectly whether she wasn't now lonely.

I was on the point of making time with her when, with

consummate disregard of privacy, Rachel Vachel wandered in. I expected another brouhaha, but the Black Madonna appeared not to note that Kookie and I were moving toward intimacies. Shortly the two girls departed, leaving me aroused and frustrated. I damned them heartily, summoned El Toro to help me out of my exo, refused to see Fanninowicz, downed a pill, and slept.

Our next revolutionary gathering was on Alamo twenty-ninth at Wichita, Kansas, Texas, a city much like Dallas or Tulsa, except I began to note scars of the Atomic War and also short Texans—poor whites and northerners not given the hormones.

El Toro kept me unpleasantly aware of the price being paid for my performances by telling me about the diversionary riots being staged in Little Rock and Colorado Springs to keep the Rangers' attention off Wichita. He also informed me that I am creating a panic across Texas. Not only is the Mex World in a fever of excitement at the coming of El Esqueleto, but the Tall World has got the jitters. There have been rumors and reports of the dread skeleton-man everywhere. I was simultaneously leading mobs in Denver and Corpus Christi. Twenty minutes later I was captured in Memphis. Meanwhile I was seen grinning horrendously down from a copter that buzzed the streets of El Paso. Et cetera.

I was flattered yet unimpressed. I asked El Toro how the revolution we've stirred up is going in the south. I got evasive answers. More dead bent-backs, I supposed.

I told myself not to think about that, but to remember I am Christopher Crockett La Cruz, touring Texas with the Revolutionary Ramblers on a physiologically limited engagement. No joke about that last—I was suffering from digestive disorders, while gravity became a deadly drag despite my exo and eiderdowns. I insisted on a warm bath at last, with a support net to keep me from sinking. Little relief. Could I be provided with a tub of heavy water? That might float me. I was laughed at, especially by Rachel, who said I had more expensive notions than Daddy.

Nevertheless she and I had a cozy chat together, which again turned toward history. In different ways we both became nostalgic about the vanished U.S.A., the industrial and scientific inspiration it gave the world, and its truly great men—Franklin, Jefferson, Houston, Poe, Lincoln, Edwin Booth, Ingersoll, David Griffith, Roosevelt Two (though she, like Elmo, thought him a figurehead), Dr. King, and so on.

It had been an ideal country for men with grand imaginations, for geographical and industrial pioneers, until they turned the grandeur to grandiosity and began to broadcast it over the newly discovered mass media. We grieved at that robust and shrewd land's fatal weakness for making right, then wrong decisions, and standing by the latter beyond all reason and with puritanic perversity. The Civil War, which freed the slaves, and the deals of the 1870's, which again crushed the blacks, re-creating tensions and problems that had to be solved with violence a hundred years later. The Great Experiment of prohibiting alcoholic beverages, which nurtured America's wealthy criminal class and allowed it to entrench itself. The later hysterical agitation against marijuana, with exactly the same results. (I was surprised to discover from Rachel how much, according to her thinking, Texas' sly legalization of weed, a Mex smoke to start with, helped lead Texas to her primacy among the states and also her domination of Latin Americans.) The First World War, followed by isolationism and repudiation of the League of Nations. The brief dream of a monopoly of atomic power, followed by unending nightmares. The Long Adventure in Indochina, with its tragic consequences for all Terra.

A nation nurtured on cowboy tales and the illusion of eternal righteousness, perpetual victory.

A nation that sought to create, simultaneously, in the

same people, a glutton's greed for food, comfort, and possessions—and a puritanic morality. Merciless competition—and docile cooperation. Timid safety-mindedness—and reckless self-sacrifice. A hard-boiled but docile young. Worship of success so long as it could be thought due to luck—and hatred of outstandingness granted by nature and/or hard work. Great scientists and scholars—and a contempt for same. The welfare state—and entrenched wealth. The brotherhood of man—and racial discrimination. In short, nul program. Order, counterorder, disorder. No wonder even Texas made more sense than that.

Rachel told me that Kookie's views of the Texas Establishment were much oversimplified, but admitted her father's power was derived ultimately from the Texan Cabal, which dominated American policies from the middle of the twentieth century.

She laughingly revealed she had no notion whatever as to whether she and her father were actually related by blood to the second president of the Lone Star Republic. Likely, Lamar had been a political name taken by one of her more recent ancestors during the bloody years after the Atomic War, when Texas conquered—for its own good!—most of a bomb-shattered and fallout-diseased U.S.A. and also Mexico, Central America, and Canada, finally establishing the atom-scarred Stikine and Mackenzie Mountains as the Russo-Texan boundary.

I pointed out to the Black Madonna that she and Captain Skull proved by their sentimentalizing over the U.S.A. that they were both hopeless romantics, addicted to lost causes. She liked that, and I was getting primal places with her when Kookie popped into my supposedly private room in the deserted country mental hospital, no longer approachable by wheeled vehicles, where our company was bivouacking.

Once again there was no fracas whatever, no observable hard feelings. Once again the girls tripped off together.

And once again I was left tense and uncatharsized. I decided to give up women. At least on Terra. And certainly for that night!

On Alamo thirtieth the weather stayed overcast. Likewise my spirits. We played Topeka. It was a rerun of Wichita. Outside of myself, the performance was strictly amateur. I rewrote the script, giving Kookie and Rachel brief appearances. Thumbs were turned down on my innovations by El Toro, Guchu, Father Francisco. Latins and Indians resent women getting the spotlight, they said. The committee was also shocked by my suggestion that I wear my blond wig for variety.

Later El Toro approached me privately about elocution lessons. I agreed to give him same, in strict secrecy—as far as his bull voice permitted. At least I might be able to get him to cut down on the muscle show.

I decided R. V. and La C. had entered into some private agreement about me. I played it very cool with them. No more tête-à-têtes. I couldn't stand another interruption.

For that matter, I would have found it difficult to be private with a woman if I had desired. Fanninowicz was forever at my heels, wanting to test my exo, check batteries, increase power, try out new wirings—his concern and new ideas were limitless. I felt like Frankenstein's monster pursued by Thomas Edison. I decided all Germans are maniacs.

Yet El Toro insisted I humor the Beady-eyed Bavarian as much as possible. And truly my exo was kept perfectly tuned.

But my physical condition was deteriorating, though I mentioned this to no one. No stiff upper lip, just didn't want to be fussed over. The Monocled Monster might have announced he is doctor of flesh-medicine also.

I kept reminding myself that my only real aim was (1) get to Yellowknife; (2) check and double-check on the Lost Crazy-Russian Pitchblende Mine, despite Rachel's damnably plausible discouragements; (3) put the bite on the com-

mittee and use my Circumlunan passport to hightail it for
the Sack on the first ship available.

Rachel asked me why worry about the mine, since it had
been clearly proved I don't have the claim with me, either
in my baggage or on my person. I wondered if I should tell
her the truth. Concluded: Definitely not!

At Kansas City, Kansas, Texas, on Spindletop first, El Toro
decided I needed a holiday. He took me and La Cucaracha
to a bullfight at the stadium of the former Wyandotte High
School. I was disguised by a big hat, big boots, padded suit
over my exo, and vast blond moustache over cheekplates.
El Toro and Kookie were my servants. We got by. My ability to pass as a Texan, at least under casual inspection,
struck me as something that might prove useful.

The bullfight was delightful. They used hormoned bulls,
huge and slow, true "cathedrals," while the matadors were
young Mexes, male and female, who dodged the bull acro-
batically and even did knee swings and giant swings on
horns. Like ancient Crete.

Kookie told me she had trained as a bullfighter, then
decided life as a "sociable secretary" provided greater financial satisfactions, and revolutionary work greater emotional ones, while acrobatics were useful in both activities.
This with a hearty wink. I remembered in time not to start
flirting with her. "'Play it cool, even cold,' is the motto of
La Muerte Alta," I told myself. What did I need with
women? Besides, if I held out, one of them would be sure
to give in.

Our revolutionary gathering that night was in the huge and
struggling greasertown along the Kansas River in Kansas
City, Missouri, Texas. The greatest stockyards in the world,
I was told, before it had taken a direct nuclear hit. Decades
later, when radioactivity had dropped to a tolerable level,
the Mexes had slowly built their way into it, partly forced
by local population pressure and partly spontaneously, with

the residual radioactivity providing some assurance that their masters would stay out, or at least cut their visits short.

I felt nervy from the start. Our stage was in front of a riverside warehouse with thick brick walls, which above the second floor had been melted into a hillocky glazed dome from which there still thrust the huge, twisted, rust-brown fingers of old steel beams.

Underfoot was a swept, randomly crackled, greenish and brownish tessellation of fused soil, its fissures filled with new dirt.

Around this rough nuclear plaza, in front of the shacks they dwelt in, our audience began to gather silently—intent sallow and brown faces with a large scattering of darker ones: "stay behind" blacks who were incurably rooted here or at any rate hadn't yet made it to Pacific Republic or Florida Democracy.

But it was hard to make out even faces. Our stage lighting was dim, despite the continuing overcast.

I was standing with the rest of the company in the dark inside the warehouse, back from its central doorway.

A few minutes before curtaintime there was a commotion as a gang of locals set up a wide-spaced lattice of narrow black rods in front of and over our stage, making it even smaller. No one could or would explain to me why, El Toro being away at the moment. It seemed theatrical insanity, further spoiling the audience's view of the actors and making them feel like beasts in a cage. At least I felt like one.

I fumed impotently, knowing that my comrades had little or no idea of what makes good theater. I scented trouble. I grew nervier. I wished the girls weren't there, but felt unable to talk to either of them.

And then a minute before my entrance, running over my opening lines in my head, I drew a blank. It was as if I had forgotten Spanish and English both, and probably Russian too.

Instead a wordless sight slid across my mind, wiping out

all other reality. I was in the same huge room. It was filled
with white light, so there was not a shadow. Files of beasts
lumbered into it. Men with unconcerned faces but spattered robes struck the horned heads with great mallets,
adroitly cut the sleek-furred throats (each man had his one
monotonous job), flayed off the hides, dismembered and
disemboweled the carcasses. My ears were filled with hoof-
clampings and great thuddings, with bestial grunts and
screams. My nostrils were likewise crammed with the stench
of frightened animals, their copious excrement, and the
floods of their rich, sweet blood. Other men with unconcerned faces constantly hosed the killing floor.

What startled me most was that the spurting, streaming,
flooding, omnipresent blood was not a darkish crimson, as I
had always thought of blood in quantity (something I had
never seen), but a phosphorescent carmine just off fuchsia,
suggestive of tropical blooms and lipstick and giddy body
paint.

Then I was being nudged in the side, not gently, and the
vision shot aside. La Cucaracha was reminding me that
my entrance cue had been spoken.

I strode on stage in a near trance, my entrance applause
a distant soft thudding no louder than the beat of blood in
my ears.

I had always tested negative for psi in the Sack. But now
I wondered how imagination alone could have created so
vivid a vision of a slaughterhouse.

Someone else than I said, "Yo soy la muerte," and for at
least the first five minutes I felt like a beetle lodged behind
the visor of an animated and vocal suit of armor.

Then, either the slaughterhouse vision lost its power or
else I grew big enough to take over the role of Death the
Universal.

The laughs I got were few and low, the cheers low too
but gutty. I think I never held an audience so well before.
In fact, I did too well. I must have hypnotized the lookouts
and my own comrades, for as I came to the finger-shaking

bit and "We must risk death and if necessary deal death," I believe I was the first one to hear the faint rushes of air and soft drones overhead, and glance cautiously up and, in one snapshot look, see poised above us six copters with antennae and coils and searchlights and other electronic items where landing gear should be.

Then, but not before my eyes were slits, the plaza was flooded with hot raw white light.

There was time for each member of the audience to spring up, to take one look or one step.

Then I felt the faintest tingling and numbing in my flesh.

At the same instant each member of the audience froze like a statue, paralyzed in posture and expression.

About a third of them, off balance at the moment, tumbled down, but without an iota of change in the look of the face or the contortion, however grotesque, of the body.

I shot a glance over-shoulder, noting that my actions were slowed down a trifle.

My comrades were moving about in slow motion, as if running through invisible water. Guchu was making toward me, where I stood stage-front. The others were headed for the warehouse doorway or already through it.

I looked back at the audience and, utterly fascinated, began to scan their faces one by one. Being an actor, expression is a mania with me. Now I found great confirmation for Leonardo's dictum that the grimaces of agony and ecstasy are almost indistinguishable, though I noted many an interesting trace of surprise, fear, and rage.

In their statuesque totality, the mob was a greater work of art than Murray's *Slaves of Gravity*, where 793 tiny figures are depicted struggling waist, shoulder, neck, or mouth deep from a curving surface of moon-marble, which might be a section of Luna herself.

It occurred to me that the crowd constituted a semi-accidental work of art that could have been titled, with apt ambiguity, *Field Slaves*, for now that I saw Rangers dropping from the copters on spinning shoulder vanes and also charging into the plaza afoot, all of them clad in oversuits of copper netting, I realized that the copters' electronic gear was projecting a paralysis field from which my comrades were protected in part by the copper or other metal cores in the black-painted bars around us, but I altogether by the secondard Faraday cage of my exoskeleton.

The Rangers, who also wore owl-eyed black gas masks, were a superb sight in themselves: black giants who were a tessellation of small ebon diamonds morticed with gold.

Guchu's upstretched fingers slowly clamped on my elbow and dragged on it.

"Come on, Scully," he gasped effortfully. "Make that effort, man. You can do it."

"Certainly," I agreed, turning swiftly. I was greatly irritated to be jerked from my supreme artistic reverie —*Death Contemplates His Victims*—but realized the black had a point: an emergency was certainly developing. So I forced myself to use the most courteous tones as I asked, "But do what?"

"Beat it through the warehouse, you dumb ofay," he exclaimed with such an attempt at vociferousness and speed —and rage at the readiness with which I moved—that he slumped on my arm and the last three words came on the in-gasp.

Since his rebuke was instantly provided with the multiple exclamation point of many objects clattering on the roof of our cage and several dropping through, I realized that Guchu had been altogether right and my attempt to be a crisis-observer wrong as always. (Yet it had been so fascinating!)

Instinctively we both took deep breaths. Then utter inky blackness exploded rather than flowed from the canisters, one of which had fallen at our feet.

I took one sight on the door into the warehouse. Then, since the erupting blackness prickled me through my Sack suit, I instantly closed tight my eyes, mouth, and nostrils, clamping the latter together with finger and thumb, while my other hand gripped Guchu as I made giant strides toward my target.

My face and hands prickled and stung, but not enough to incapacitate me.

Another object thudded in the dark somewhere near us and began to say self-importantly, "I am a sixty-second bomb. Fifty-nine. Fifty-eight. Fifty-seven. Fifty—"

"And I'm a ninety-year man, bomb, with decades to go!" Guchu answered the thing—and paid for his rash defiance with a horrendous coughing fit.

I continued to make tracks. Fortunately, my elocutionary activities have given me a lung capacity unusual in Circumluna, something which had also helped me in Governor (or would it now be President?) Lamar's patio pool.

When counting strides told me I was well inside the warehouse, I swabbed my eyelids with water from my cheekplate and risked another quick sighting.

We were almost out of the smoke. From a trap door five long strides, La Cucaracha waved us on, her eyes streaming, her other hand shutting her mouth and nose.

I made the trap door, my eyes stinging, and flickered a downward glance.

There was a round well five meters deep, with ladder rungs embedded in one side and with Father Francisco peering anxiously up from the bottom.

La Cucaracha scuttled down. I got Guchu's feet and hands on the rungs—he was blind and retching from the gas—and followed him as swiftly as I could.

Kookie called, "Close the trap!"

As I reached up, an incandescently scarlet laser beam missed my hand, spattered against and was also reflected downward from the trap's metal in-face. I felt heat between thigh and right knee, and that leg went limp. I heard Father Francisco gasp hissingly with pain.

I shut and bolted the trap, then made it down on arms

alone. Then I was hopping along a corridor I had to crouch in, supported to either side by Kookie and the *padre*.

There was an explosion that shook the floor.

Behind us Guchu gasped out, "Bomb weren't bluffin', anyhow. I *hate* a liar," and managed a croaking laugh.

I wondered if he knew what bomb he was talking about.

Around that time I discovered my right leg was useless because one of the femur cables had been melted through. The two ends dangled and jigged.

I also noted that the reflected laser beam had creased Father Francisco's arm. The wound would have bled, but the beam's heat had cauterized it.

Then I was being helped to crawl through a circular port. I found myself sprawled in semidark among my comrades in a flattened cylinder. Someone had closed the port and was locking it with a wheel.

Opposite the port was a window into darkness. Then a great white snout peered in with unwinking eyes and with long white feelers around its jaws.

The cylinder began to rock and to move in surges.

Shortly later I was told that we were in a river submarine—called "Airplane," of course, with consummate revolutionary duplicity—and that the white monster had been a mutated and haploid catfish.

We rode the currents of the Kansas and Missouri for weary hours without incident except for a few bottom-scrapings and glimpses of exotic river life. On his insistence, I told El Toro about the government of Circumluna. He expressed horror at what he dubbed "Sackabondage" and insisted I carry the revolution there. As soon as I had made him understand vacuum and decompression, he saw endless possibilities in bombs artfully placed. I let him elaborate his nonsense and rested my eyes on Rachel Vachel and La Cucaracha sleeping in each other's arms. I decided that, if I escaped alive from this mortal Terran brouhaha and were able to carry anything back to the Sack, it would be something very different from revolution—unless one considers all females conspirators and destructors by nature.

We landed at dawn at a swamp-circled hideout short of Missouri City. Fanninowicz was one of the few awake and on hand to observe our limping and dispirited arrival.

"Ho-ho!" he mocked. "I see you have had a brush with the Rangers! Next time—*kaaaaaah!*" And while making this nasty noise at the back of his tongue, he drew his thumb across his throat. "And as for you, you *schafskopf*, you bummer, you are no more fit to be trusted with your exoskeleton than a child with a computer!"

"That's how the Circumlunans teach their children math," I told him as I hopped along. "Splice my cable now, you Texo-Prussian paranoid!"

11 / In the Coal Mine

There are only two things in life you can be sure of:
Death and Texas.

—Old Texan proverb

"Infierno de los diablos!" El Toro cursed genially but seriously behind me in the silvery dark. "What are you doing up here, Esquel? Hunting for Texas owl-planes? I assure you, they will spot you first. Your exo will stand out in their radar like a metal tree."

I did not remove the borrowed binoculars from my orbits, but lowered their electronic gain best to observe the dark-and-glinting speck somewhere between my eyes and Luna's bright, crinkled border. When the almost point-tiny spangle had climbed a low mountainside and off the moon, I knew for certain it was Circumluna and the Sack in transit. I shifted my field to the stars around Luna. From the pale few I could see—so different from the multitude of the Sack's blazing nights—I recognized Taurus by the doubles around Aldebaran on one side of the moon and the Pleiades on the other. That meant that, for the Sack, Terra lay at the heaven's antipodes in Scorpio, beneath my feet.

El Toro pounded lightly with his fist against my leg, just above my knee motor. "I understand now, Esquel," he said. "It is the first night the weather has let you see the cold silver sun around which your little world revolves."

I nodded, but the point seemed to me that he couldn't possibly understand, not to any degree. For instance, my almost painful surge of relief at knowing the real date, not this grotesque Spindletop fourth, but the real date: sunth of Leo, terranth of Scorpio, lunth of Capricorn.

The scientific Circumlunans still measure time by Green-

wich, an invisible line a quarter million miles away earth-
ward and infinity away starward. But we Sackabonds
depend primarily on the times it takes sun, earth, and moon
to move across one of the twelve constellations of the zodiac
—sunth, terranth, and lunth. Our lunth is about half an earth-
hour, making our Sack-day about six earth-hours long, the
time it takes Circumluna-Sack to orbit the moon. Twelve
lunths make a Sack-day, ten Sack-days make a terranth,
twelve terranths make a sunth (earth's month), twelve
sunths make a starth, our Sack name for year. It's an impossible system if you try to make it precise, but okay and
highly aesthetic if you've grown up with it. Who needs minutes and seconds? Except in the clutches, and then you need
only speed. Besides, any good actor can count stage-seconds
perfectly in his head.

Or what could El Toro know about the momentary shivering illusion of free fall I felt as I permitted myself a final
glimpse of the dark sequin that was my home?

I lowered my binoculars and surveyed Terra's horizon
from the low hillock where I stood. Southward the silent
Ohio River, gleaming like a black nebula. Eastward the
blackened steel and masonry stumps of Evansville thrusting up through the undergrowth. Northward, prairie. West-
ward, the ruined works of the abandoned coal mine that
was our camp.

Rapping again above my knee, El Toro said, "Come on
now, Esquel. You've tempted the Texan bull long enough
and we have a job for you."

I looked down at his swarthy, handsome face. A wide grin
showed the pearls of his teeth. I envied him his chunky vigorous body, which stood its full four foot ten with ease
in the killing terragrav, while my eight foot six sagged in
its frame. I nodded and started down through the dusk,
taking short careful steps.

"You are tired, Esquel," he said. "Your exo stands straight,
but sometimes you hang from it—God pardon me—like the
Crucified One."

"I am neither a religious nor a secular hero, not even of the dubious revolutionary breed," I told him somewhat brusquely. "In fact, I spit on all such. I am just an actor working his way toward Spaceport Yellowknife. As for yokes, your cyborged countrymen must carry theirs, while mine carries me. Who is the better off? If you have to work out your somewhat grandiose sympathies—you really belong in grand opera!—light me a reefer."

I was sharp with him because my support bands truly were cutting me cruelly. The three days since Kansas City had marked and drained me. To a person unused even to one lunagrav, six play hob with the gut, packed into the belly like a length of limp pipe the Creator did not even bother to coil. Kansas City, Columbia, St. Louis, Carbondale— four revolutionary one-night stands without a layoff. Surely Terran actors of the nineteenth and early twentieth century must have been a hardy breed.

Columbia. My memories of our brush with the Rangers at KC had made me shake so that my exo rattled—until I made my entrance.

St. Louis. A gargantuan, half-lived-in graveyard, its skyscrapers a cemetery of melted behemothian tombs from the Atom War. But the biggest audience yet.

Carbondale. A whistle-stop, except for a host of cyborgs working in two of the gigantic tower-masked drilling rigs, from each of which a twisting trail of giant rock-laden trucks centipeded night and day, to build a wall somewhere north —Diana knows why! Or most likely she doesn't.

Along the path that zigzagged through undergrowth, El Toro and I felt our way to the ramp leading down into the shallow, worked-out coal mine. Ahead and below, a small, squat rectangle of light glowed. I sipped my stick, drinking deep of the evergreen smoke and holding it in my lungs, but although our footsteps began to syncopate, there was no soothing of pain.

El Toro said, "You draw apart from us, Esquel. You hug your hurt and loneliness. The girls in particular are distressed. I am sure that if you spoke a few gallant and sugary zeros into the ear of either—well, we have a saying that one night's sleep with is more restorative than a week's without. That is, if a man can imagine the latter."

I did not tell him of Rachel's and Kookie's trick of the one interrupting us whenever I was alone with the other, or of my determination to hold out against them both until one or the other surrendered unconditionally.

I said instead, harshly, "For me this is a business trip, not a romance, either with giddy, easily won females or the Bent-Back Revolution, which appears to be killing a hundred Mexes for every Tex. And acting, done in professional fashion, is the most tiring business."

I unintentionally kicked a bit of gravel that clattered down the slope. Instantly a near-blinding searchbeam shot up from the depths. Around it I made out the blurs of armed guards. I was both reassured and irked by this evidence of revolutionary preparedness.

El Toro observed, using a hand to shade his eyes from below, "It is odd to think that even Death should become weary."

"So my performances *are* falling off," I replied, quick to catch at any hint of criticism. "Soon, instead of firing your revolution, I shall be a cold rocket tube that coughs once and dies forever, reeking of hydrazine."

"No, no, no!" he protested, a little too much. "Why, only last night I was admiring your new *chiste*—I mean, gag—of pretending a duel with Ranger Hunt and President Lamar."

We'd had certain news that Governor Lamar had been made president of Texas in a hurry-up inauguration. Rachel Vachel had said this advancement of her daddy meant certain doom for the Lone Star Republic. I was doubtful; apart from this idiot involvement with his daughter and his compulsive lint-picking, Lamar had seemed to me a shrewd man and suave for a Texan.

El Toro went on eagerly, "The gag made my mind buzz. How would it be if we had two tall dummies representing *el presidente y el jefe?* Inside the empty clothes of each would be a nimble comrade moving the hated head on a pole. Besides providing extra realism, they would give the audience something to throw things at!"

"Not a bad idea," I told him, breaking it gently. From what I had seen of the marksmanship of most Mexes, they would be hitting me as often as the dummies. "*If* you can figure out a foolproof way for the men inside to see out uninterruptedly, so they don't fall off the stage. And *if* they'll follow my directions to the letter. And *if* you have foamed plastic or even papier-mâché to make the heads. And *if* you have a good caricaturist sculptor." I did not mention that I was an expert at the last.

"Enough ifs!" El Toro protested. "You always drown any-one else's ideas, especially if they involve you sharing the stage with another."

I looked down at El Toro. It was the first even mildly spiteful remark I had ever heard him make. Had he caught acting in only a week? But it is a most infectious profession, and with it go its vain and gossipy habits. Besides, a star must always expect jealousy.

"Not so," I told him mildly. "I have already suggested that the Señoritas Lamar and Morales——"

"And I have told you why that is impossible!" he shot back. "Women on the stage! Unheard of. Oh, in the cosmic or erotic perhaps, but this is serious revolutionary drama!"

"Serious revolutionary farce," I corrected. "Also, there is one fatal objection to your excellent idea. The dummies of Lamar and Hunt would have to wield swords back at me, else it would be only cruel slaughter."

"But my people enjoy cruel slaughter. Consider the bull-fight."

"The bull has horns," I reminded him.

"Nevertheless I could manage it. Observe!" he retorted, striking a position. "With my left hand I hold the headed pole upright, so," he continued with great earnestness. "With my upstretched right I manage my sword, which is lashed to the end of a pole, while my eyes peer through a large one-way transparent window in the middle of Lamar's robe. Hunt could be played by El Tácito," he added, mentioning a Mex who acted as my bodyguard, though tonight I had eluded him.

Someone laughed—Guchu, it was—and I was myself hard put to avoid grinning at the image of El Toro as the working mechanism of a giant puppet. We were now past the guards and searchlight, which had been turned off, and in a vast gallery of the mine, so low I had to duck a little, and dotted with massive crunch-ended posts of ancient wood supporting spooky megatons of solidity.

"You mentioned a job for me," I reminded El Toro.

The acting light died in his eyes. He pointed at two stringily muscular bent-backs, one old, one older, crouching by Guchu and regarding me with considerable apprehension.

He said, "Here are two who have worked in the great towers which you—and we too—want to know about. Perhaps you will try your hypnotic skills on them, as you did on Pedro Ramírez."

I moved toward them, curving my lips in a friendly smile. I noted, in the ears of both, the callosities of the cyborged. Their ragged clothing revealed many burn scars—some pale and stretched, others lumpy and twisting.

Death is not the ideal figure for a hypnotist, though he eventually summons each of us offstage with a mesmeric command. Few find his presence sympathetic or reassuring.

I got the old man under, but I was unable to get past the block on his memories of the work he did in the towers, except that he began barely audibly droning an unintelligible chant in the same rhythm as the two "dig and delve" lines I had got out of Pedro Ramírez. He kept it up faintly even when I told him to sleep.

Perhaps the older man, being closer to Death himself, was not so intimidated by me. Perhaps he even felt a certain curiosity. At any rate, he eyed me bravely, and when I questioned him about his work in the great towers, his mouth eagerly formed words.

But no sounds accompanied them, and none of us, including El Toro, could lip-read them.

I had broken the block for his upper speaking parts, but not for his vocal cords and lungs, perhaps because of a literal interpretation on the part of his unconscious mind of some prior hypnotic command such as "Keep silent." He could form words, because he wanted to, but he could not make a noise.

Then I had an inspiration. I quietly said to him, "When I say 'Go,' Federico, do the things you would do on a working day in one of the great towers. Perform each action fully, but move on to the next action when I say 'Next.' Begin at the doorway to the tower. Go!"

He got to his feet, his bent spine more noticeable now, the muscles of his torso and legs stiffening a little as if from the weight of the yoke, and he took three steps in a straight line.

"Next," I said as he was making the fourth step and incidentally nearing a post.

Federico made a quarter turn and stopped, gazing respectfully at emptiness. Then he straddled his legs, held out to either side his arms with hands hanging limply, and opened his mouth wide. It occurred to me that he might be submitting himself to a medical examination or more likely a search.

He turned in the direction he had first been going. Guchu guided him deftly past the post. We all followed. It was an eerie performance in the low-ceilinged, dim-lit forest of dead tree sections.

This time I said "Next" on his fifth step. He stopped and stood relaxedly, right hand lightly gripping something at shoulder level. At first I thought it a tool, then as he made no further movement, except to sag apathetically, I decided that it was a support by which he steadied himself.

Yet he *was* making other movements—tiny squirmings and hunchings, as if accommodating himself to other beings moving past and next to him.

Gradually his legs pressed together and his elbows close to his sides—the imaginary support was almost *at* his shoulder now. I saw him as one of a tight-packed crowd of beings. Texo-Mex cyborgs like himself, I presumed. I could almost hallucinate them, so strong was the illusion he created.

Without warning, he straightened up, his neck stretched, and his head was thrown back a little. At the same time he stood almost on tiptoe. And yet he seemed to exert no muscular effort to do all of this, or somehow the effort was cleverly masked. Truly the body's memory can do wonderful, perhaps miraculous things under hypnotic suggestion. It can create illusions.

I knew what the illusion was at once, for I know free fall when I see it. Inside the great tower his imagination had re-created, Federico was falling—and almost certainly with a group of others—in an elevator accelerating downward swiftly, probably almost at a terragrav, for the illusion was strong that he almost floated, right hand loosely linked around invisible grip.

I realized I did not know how long he had been falling and I was pleased to see an associate of El Toro, one Carlos Mendoza, holding a wristwatch between himself and Federico.

Suddenly Federico's feet were flat on the ground, his knees bent, the extensor muscles of his legs bulged. His free arm clapped across his guts, his other dragged heavily on the imaginary support. His jaws—his whole face—clenched together.

It was all over in not much more than a second, yet I think all of us winced with him at the strain of that illusionary deceleration.

"A mile and a quarter," Carlos Mendoza announced softly.

I looked a question at this *camarada* I hardly knew.

"That he fell," Mendoza replied. "Or his cage."

Meanwhile Federico was nonchalantly marching again. When I said "Next," he lightly gripped another support and sagged.

The whole pantomime of rapid descent and sudden deceleration was repeated. This time I remembered to stage-count. The fall took twenty seconds. That worked out to a distance of two kilometers, I calculated, dredging from the depths of my boring physics instruction the formula of distance equals one-half times six lunagravs (one decimeter) multiplied by time in seconds squared.

"Again a mile and a quarter," Mendoza whispered, agreeing well enough with my calculation.

Once more Federico marched, grasped, and fell for twenty seconds. This time his face and body broke out in sweat and he gasped for breath.

"It becomes hot three and three-quarters miles underground," Mendoza said tersely.

Or six kilometers, I thought, translating. I frankly felt frightened at the thought of penetrating so far into solidity. What it implied about the vast solid mass of Earth horrified me, as it would anyone knowing only life in free fall. At last the blank datum "Earth has a diameter of almost thirteen thousand kilometers" became terrifyingly real to me.

This time old Federico showed a new behavior. Crouching, he lowered his hands and lifted slowly one foot, then the other. Next his hands gripped something and moved slowly upward. Clearly he was drawing on a heavy suit of some sort. One could see his arms working into gloved sleeves. Next there was pantomimed zipping. Finally he lifted something invisible onto his head.

"It is like a space suit," I whispered.

His breathing changed. He inhaled through tinily puckered lips, exhaled through his nostrils.

"And the suit is refrigerated," Mendoza whispered beside me.

I caught his point. Old Federico had stopped sweating. The beads were evaporating.

I waited with interest. Now we would see the actions involved in his underground work and perhaps be able to interpret its nature.

He marched until I said "Next," then grasped an invisible handhold and again dropped two kilometers.

And again and again and again, taking him fourteen kilometers below the surface of the Earth! And each time he dropped, he seemed almost to float.

We all watched with intense, even horrified interest. Nearby the intent faces of El Toro, Guchu, Mendoza, El Tácito, and a couple more. I was sure each was pale under his shade of brown. Farther off, Rachel Vachel, La Cucaracha, and Fanninowicz with his guards. Only the German's expression jarred—he wore a sneer of incredulity and contempt.

I suppose that for an outsider my having the appearance of a tall and stooping Death might have added to the eldritch atmosphere.

The other old Mex, still in hypnotic sleep, continued his rhythmic drone. That was the only sound.

Environment added to the horror. That we should be in a dim-lit, oppressively low-ceilinged coal mine, its great close-set pillars marked by the strain of the weight they bore— all these things intensified the horror of the thought of a mine going already one hundred times as deep.

And yet it was all in the kingdom of the imagination! We half-dozen amateur actors (including one thoroughgoing professional) were witnessing a pantomime, based only on muscular and physiological memory, which created an illusion far more gripping than any of us could have managed —perhaps even I!

Federico repeated the drop eighteen more times—until by my calculation he was forty kilometers below Terra's surface, which agreed well enough with Mendoza's twenty-five miles.

"*Madre de Dios!*" the latter exclaimed softly. "That is the thickness given for earth's crust. He must be near the molten mantle."

At last Federico changed his act. Hoisting up a heavy something, he directed it downward between his feet. Bracing his forearms against his belly and hips, he began to shake in a taut violent way, so that his hard sandals beat a tattoo against the rock floor.

As if that sound had been a signal, the other old Mex's drone became louder and changed into execrably pronounced and accented English words, which it took me three or four repetitions wholly to understand.

> Every day, two hours times twelve,
> A million yokemen dig and delve.
> In your earplugs comes the boss's yell,
> "You'll keep on drilling 'til you get to Hell."
>> So drill, you yokemen, drill!
>> Drill, you cyborgs, drill!
> It's drill blacked out in heat and pain
> For your women and rum and maryjane!
>> And blast! And fire!

As I was listening, hypnotized myself, to the fifth repetition of that eerie chant, old Federico swayed, stopped shaking, paled, swayed again, and collapsed on the rock before any of us could catch him.

Perhaps the wierdest thing for me was that, as I swiftly moved to stoop beside him, I made a point of stepping over the drill that wasn't there.

We assured ourselves that Federico was suffering from no more than exhaustion. I brought both him and the chanting Mex out of their trances. We saw them comfortably at rest.

And then we talked.

"*Hombre!*" El Toro asked for us. "What can the Texans be wanting with mines twenty-five miles deep?"

"Gold and silver," El Tácito suggested romantically, for

once belying his name of The Silent One. "Diamonds big as kacks."

"They seem to be on the verge of creating artificial volcanoes," Mendoza said soberly. "But why, I ask, why?"

La Cucaracha said excitedly, "Texans already have big winds, big heats, big colds, tornadoes, floods, hurricanes, tidal waves. Now they want volcanoes and earthquakes too. *Everything* big."

I could agree with her on the last. The whole thing seemed like delirium. But then I had always felt horror at the thought of the innards of planets, the lair of gravity.

Rachel Vachel said, "I wish I'd spied on this more while I was with Daddy."

Guchu suggested, "Maybe they building a Doomsday Machine. Gonna stuff those deep holes with H-bombs. If they start losing to Russia or China, or the mood hits 'em, they blow up all Texas like one Alamo. Maybe blow up the world. 'Taking your enemies with you,' I think it's called."

El Toro extended a menacing arm at Fanninowicz. "You should know about them," he asserted. "What is their purpose?"

The German laughed harshly. "I do indeed. What you call the great towers merely house bigger drilling rigs, designed to probe for petroleum at depths of ten to twenty kilometers. Oil is being found in rock hitherto thought azoic. But this notion of great mines forty kilometers deep is nonsense. They would collapse from the pressures. And can you imagine anyone using a hand drill, even in a refrigerated suit, at temperatures of eighteen hundred to two thousand degrees Fahrenheit? Ridiculous! No, my dear sirs, you have let yourself be deceived by an amateur hypnotist and a subject who kept on repeating an action that impressed you. While your theorizations are all laughable."

I could tell from El Toro's expression that he was mightily tempted to use force on the exasperating Teuton, but persuaded from it because of the latter's usefulness in regard to my exoskeleton and other mechanical matters. Besides,

I believe we were all impressed by his logic. Germans are most convincing maniacs. There had already begun to seem something fabulous in the ideas Federico's behavior had generated.

My only thought was what an unaesthetic clot—worse than a Circumlunan!—the professor was, not to have appreciated the theatric grandeur of Federico's—and my—performance.

To tell the truth, I wasn't having many thoughts by then. I was too tired. In fact, I was more than tired. Supervising Federico's performance had taken me out of myself, but now I was feeling nothing but terragrav's horrible drag, as if I were perpetually in the agony of sudden deceleration Federico had portrayed at the end of each of his two-kilometer drops.

Rachel Vachel and La Cucaracha smiled at me side by side, inviting me to gossip with them, but threesome, not twosome. I was having none of that.

Signing to El Tácito, I walked to my quarters and was asleep before my head basket thudded softly into my pillow.

12 / Slum-storming

One thing I'll say for labour (the British Labor
Party); and that is, that it isn't as offensive as the
corresponding mutatory force which now threatens
culture in America. I refer to the force of *business* as
a dominating motive in life, and a persistent absorber
of the strongest creative energies of the American
people. This intensive commercialism is a force more
basically dangerous and anti-cultural than labour
ever has been, and threatens to build up an
arrogant fabric which it will be very hard to
overthrow or modify with civilized ideas.

—H. P. Lovecraft, 1929

THE NEXT TWO days I continued weary of body, heavy of
mind, empty of emotion. Old Federico's pantomime, in fact
the whole coal-mine episode, seemed more a haunting,
heavy-hued nightmare than a reality.

The Ohio Valley turned out to be a miserable region.
The general population has more short than tall Texans *and
some of the former are in the Revolution.* Poor whites. They
are refused the hormone because they don't make enough
money to support the extra poundage that goes with
greater height. They say they don't want the hormone.
Sour grapes in most cases, I think. Some of them are dwarfed
enough to go through Mex doors, though the law forbids that.
Most Mexes accept them as fellow revolutionaries, though
it frightens me to think how they must increase our security
risks.

The cities are as dwarfed as the people—ragged rings
around atom-glazed wastes on which new building has only
recently begun.

I have taken to writing another new script to fill in time.

Our show must somehow be improved. For instance, El Toro thinks he is learning acting from me, but is doing worse than when I began teaching him.

The first night we gave a rotten performance in Louisville. The second, a worse one in Cincinnati. Even I was lousy, both shouting and turning silent back on audience to get their attention. At the end they filed out silently. I doubt we sparked a single street-corner disturbance. I know who was at fault—me. But an actor cannot play a role like Death night after night without emotional fuel.

Accordingly I waited until Rachel and Rosa were together and then somewhat somberly invited them to my brick cabin in our quarters in a deserted motel beside a rusty-fenced freeway crossed by great gullies.

I waited until they were comfortably seated, had lit up, and were gazing at me curiously.

Then, ad-libbing all the way, for I had resolutely planned no set speech, I poured out my feelings to them.

I described the vast loneliness of a free-fall being on a gravity planet and in a strange culture. I explained the desolation of an actor playing a big role, especially an anti-human one such as Death. I revealed my petty foibles and childish self-pity as well as my idealisms.

In short, I spoke nothing but the truth. It was a great relief to me and it almost broke me up. But not quite. An actor remains an actor.

Next I praised them both lavishly telling them how I couldn't have made it without their imaginative help and comfort. I hinted at my further emotional and physiological needs. I ended by assuring them that I loved both of them greatly—and equally.

Only then did I remember that I had told them exactly the same thing in the church and that they had both called me crazy.

This time they were kinder. Perhaps. Rosa patted my knee and said, "Poor bones man. My heart is torn."

"Yeah, it's sure tough on you, Scully," Rachel agreed, patting my other knee. "But now let's get down to this bigamy thing you're trying to set up, if I read you right," she went on. "Which of us girls comes first?"

"Indeed yes," Rosa seconded, crossing her arms and beginning to tap the floor with the toe of her slipper.

"That is for you to decide," I answered, not loftily, but with great simplicity and sincerity. Then I crossed my arms.

"Sure you really don't like one of us more than the other?" Rachel asked. "And are trying to be kind to the loser?"

"Kind!" Rosa spat.

"No!" I said and then went on to explain how various forms of polygamy, from the linear to the complex marriage, are found in the Sack. Likewise for love affairs.

"Well, that may work up in the sky," Rachel responded when I paused for breath, "but down here we're not used to it."

"Indeed no!" Rosa agreed. "I have no intention whatever of becoming a 'sociable secretary' to you, *amado*. My heart is involved."

"Goes for me too, Scully dear," Rachel echoed with a sigh. "I'm too serious about you, see, to play around. Sure the balance don't teeter just a little bit more one way than the other?"

I did not trust myself to speak. I only shook my head.

"Well then, that's that," Rachel said. She looked at Rosa. "Shall I tell him, Miss Morales?"

"Yes, you tell him, Miss Lamar!"

"Well, Scully," Rachel began, leaning forward a little, elbows on knees, while Rosa sat up straight, "us girls figured you might conceivably take that insane attitude, and so we worked out our answer beforehand. Which is: you got to decide which one of us you want, and then speak out in the presence of both of us, so there's no chance for tricks."

"But don't you see what you're demanding of me?" I burst out. "You're asking me to insult one of you unforgivably!"

"That one'll be able to take it," Rachel replied serenely.

"You see, Scully darling, Miss Morales and I have come to understand each other on this tour, because of our mutual admiration of and attachment to you."

"*Sí, querido!*" Rosa put in almost excitedly. "Whatever happens, whichever one of us you choose, you have created a friendship between us which can never be broken. We, who were as cat and dog, are now as lamb and lamb. You can always pride yourself on that, *amado*."

"But don't you see that makes a threesome even more workable?" I demanded somewhat bewilderedly.

"No, dearest," Rachel said with great conviction.

Rosa said sharply, "Our undying friendship—you have that already. But as for love, it must be one or the other, never both!"

"Yeah, Scully, you got to make up your mind. It's the only way you'll ever have either of us."

Once more I could only trust myself to shake my head. This time I added an unrehearsed shudder—at the insanity of their behavior, at the torment to my own feelings, at the merciless perversity of the universe.

"Scully!" Rachel asked with sudden concern. "Have you really got that gravity sickness? We get to thinking of you as tireless and superior to all mortal ills, because you're the star and work by electricity. Haven't let your batteries run low?"

"I know what!" Rosa said with certainty. "The bees bonnet has been sleeping in his skeleton!"

"And what if I have?" I growled back at her. "We're revolutionaries. We've got to be ready for emergencies. Weapons close at hand. Skeleton—on!"

"You should have told us! We would have nursed you. We still will."

"Yeah, Scully, Rosa'n I'll be only too happy to help you off with your skeleton and tuck you in for the night, and help you on with it in the morning. And any other little thing you need. Worked fine back in the cave."

Maybe then I made my big mistake. If I had gone along

with their gag, one or the other would have been irresistibly tempted by my helplessness. Maybe.

But I had no intention of finger-crawling across any more patio floors. Even ones carpeted with ermine.

"I do not want either of you as a nurse," I decreed. "Or both of you, for that matter. My wants run in entirely different directions."

Rachel nodded sadly. "Well, I guess he's given us our walking papers, Rosa."

La Cucaracha agreed with an emphatic nod and with an upward look at a universe apparently as perversely incomprehensible as my own.

"But let's not make it so much like a funeral," Rachel said.

"No, to a bones man that would be far too cruel," Rosa agreed.

"Let's pass around a good-bye reefer," Rachel suggested. "Rosa?"

So, mostly in silence, we smoked a long stick of grass together, and then another. It was a gesture for which I was deeply grateful. It calmed my ruffled nerves and vanity. A little.

But, contrary to many stories, the mild drug does not result in libidinous orgies, except for those who greatly desire such. So when I had taken the last sip and pinched out the tiny butt of a third, the girls rose and I lifted a hand in somber farewell.

In the doorway they turned. Rachel said, "Scully, I'm sure I speak for both of us when I say that it's a rare privilege to work in the same company with a great actor such as you. We also think you're doing more for the Revolution than anyone since Pancho Villa and Zapata and César Chávez. We know the little things you're doing, too. The voice lessons you're giving El Toro, though we'll never mention them. The way you put up with Father Francisco and play along with Guchu and humor that maniac Fanninowicz. And—jokes about electric skeletons aside—the way you're plumb knocking yourself out to do everything you can for the show."

"But in that case surely—" I left the question unfinished while I looked at them in naked yearning.

They slowly shook their heads and softly closed the door.

It stayed closed.

It was still closed when the first glow of dawn glinted from cobwebs and dust grains on the windows.

The dawn glow also showed me my hideous visage in a mirror appropriately spotted brown with age.

I decided I was through with *all* women.

Perhaps forever.

Even Idris McIllwraith.

If she had loved me even a little, she would have come to me across the cold quarter-million miles, by flower-powered self-teleportation.

Things always change. And infallibly, thank Diana, they change for the better when they're at the worst. On the next day, Spindletop eighth, we gave a great show at Indianapolis. I could have taken ten curtain calls, but Death is humble, Death is the friend of every man, his comrade throughout life, reminding him to waste no moment but live to the full. And if man has any comrade at all when life is ended, that comrade is Death.

After our flop in Cincinnati, the committee had seen reason and given me a free hand with my new script and the cast, making me director.

Results: Father Francisco, wearing chest mike, was audible at last as he spoke his modernized, punchy prayers.

Guchu stayed in the spotlight and his psychedelic ravings all led to good revolutionary conclusions. He was an impressive figure, symbolically bringing to the Revolution the mighty support of Africa (his race) and Asia (his religion).

Rachel had at last a short, but effective part as Wife of Death, reminding me as I go off to work on Earth to take good care of my health, avoid chills, get enough to eat, and so on. She wore a skintight black suit with wide silver seams on the outside of her arms and legs to indicate bones. Other silver lines followed exactly her lower ribs, but went into whorls around her breasts. She had a narrow silver spine, girdle, and collarbones. Over this she wore a black cloak, while her platinum hair was tightly braided and coiled to suggest a helmet.

El Toro's oration was topped by a shorter but snappier one by Rosa. I knew that girl had talent! She wore a red Phrygian freedom cap, from under which her dark hair flowed; red boots; and a short red dress on which were scattered in black the Isis cross and a symbol I did not know: a circle with a three-armed Y in it.

Then, while El Toro sang the old version of "La Cucaracha," with its homely references to cockroaches, marijuana, and the Mexican revolutionary tradition, Rosa did a still snappier dance. Next: El Toro went into "La Muerte Alta," I returned to the stage with Rachel, and soon we had the whole audience standing and singing with us.

If our audience didn't rush out to riot, at least they departed in a happy and cocky mood, suffused with revolutionary enthusiasm, ready to assert themselves and use their wits, determined to take no crap from anyone.

Later El Toro, who has a good if untrained singing voice, asked me to give him lessons in grand opera. Why not?

Of course, I was careful to make Rosa's and Rachel's parts equal and keep my relationship with them coolly professional.

Father Francisco and El Toro rationalized the girls' being in the show by explaining to me that this far north there is a weakening of the Latin prejudices. True enough, there were as many short Texans and "stay-behind" blacks in the audience as Mexes.

There were reports by A.M. revolutionary radio of big Ranger raids in Columbus, Cleveland, Pittsburgh. We had dodged back west just in time.

Next night we had another smasheroo. It was in Chicago, a largely new, yet big city situated west of Chicago Bay, where devastation bombing let in the waters of Lake Michigan and where rust-boned, melted, still radioactive skyscrapers dream deep below.

Flying up to Chicago in our kack, I noted, in its transparent plastic, small stamped medallions, the print in which had been obliterated. I found one the file had missed and saw the familiar Cyrillic characters spelling out "Novy Moskva, C.C.C.P." For a moment I thought I was back in Circumluna, which remains stubbornly bilingual.

Guchu readily admitted the kack had been manufactured in Russia and only passed along by the Black Republic to the Revolution. "We're not up to those technologies, and neither is the Florida Democracy," he told me. "And we don't want to be. Outside of atoms to desalt our water and give us electricity, we operate by flower power. We don't have a big population. The unfit die young. What protects us from the Texans is the deserts and mountains, the free Injuns, and Afro-Russian aid, chiefly in atoms, which are getting hard to come by—the fissionable and fusionable ones, I mean."

Novy Moskva—New Moscow—is near Lake Baikal, he tells me. Siberia has become the Russian "Texas."

I was lying down at the time and also downwind of Guchu and the other three passengers, all Mexes, so far as the uncertain drafts inside the kack permitted.

I log as much horizontal time as I can. I am troubled by heart palpitations, splitting headaches, diarrhea, and varicose veins. Lying down distributes the gravity strain, which abets, I believe, all these symptoms. The last time I unzipped my tights from calf and ankle, I was sickened by the purple varicosities, which grew larger as I watched. Since then I have not opened my tights except minimally, for sanitary reasons, and even then I glimpse a varicosity of the superficial femoral vein.

To tell the truth, I have not been out of my carefully

mended Sack suit and also my exoskeleton—Rosa guessed right—since they raided us in Kansas City. So I have not had a complete bath for well over a week. So I stink and keep away from people, or at least downwind, when I can.

I also have taken to rum, with which El Tácito, my bodyguard, supplies me. I intentionally spill some of the rum on me, but I drink as much as I can carry too. It is a good analgesic as well as an acceptable male perfume.

I refuse to take off my exoskeleton partly from resentment —at the girls, Fanninowicz, all of them—but chiefly from sheer panic fear. I know the support bands are producing rashes and small hemorrhages, chiefly subcutaneous. But I cannot bear the thought of the helplessness I experienced in the patio. I am haunted by dreams of the Rangers finding me away from my lively titanium bones.

Or perhaps it is simpler. Perhaps I am just afraid of gravity, as men once were of "empty space."

I have also developed—from the soupy atmosphere, I should think—a deep, hacking cough, which I can barely control on stage. The rum helps that a little, too.

Thinking such thoughts as we took off from Chicago, I drifted into a horror dream. I was trapped amid the crushed and dying in a crumpled subway car in a collapsed tunnel in Old Chicago. I struggled helpless for an eternity. Then the boiling water rushed in and seared me awake. A dream? A gravity nightmare? I know nothing of subways, but I suppose I may have run across them in history study materials. But how could I see crumpled advertisements so clearly? Atomin, the Pain-Reliever that Penetrates Your Every Molecule. Coca-Cola. Kurb Kinky Kurls. Prepare Yourself for the Future with LaSalle Extension Courses. Double Your Pleasure, Double Your Fun, With Doublemint, Doublemint, Doublemint Gum.

Moonlight showed choppy whitecaps in black water below as we raced north across Chicago Bay.

Later I had chills and thought I was getting a fever. The explanation was much simpler, one I knew but had not kept in mind. On Terra it gets colder as one moves toward either pole.

After we played Milwaukee and Minneapolis, where we camped in an old hotel, it became clear that I must change to my winter clothes. I swore El Toro and El Tácito to secrecy and had them give me a bath. I did not permit them to remove my Sack suit until I was in the hot water, with thought that its pressure might work somewhat as that of the suit, controlling varicosities. Being out of my exo produced in me spasms of fear hard to conceal.

When they saw the shape I was in, El Toro exclaimed, "*Madre de Dios!*" El Tácito, true to his name, permitted himself only a grudgingly sympathetic grunt.

I directed my gentle but thorough soaping, rinsing, and drying. El Toro wanted to call in a doctor—and also Fanninowicz—but I reminded him of his oath. After my various surfaces had been powdered, salved antiseptically and analgesically, and most smoothly bandaged, they eased me into my cold-weather suit, which is black and very like the other, but thicker, and containing a spider web of heating elements working off my batteries. Also it has a hood snugly covering my skull, neck, and chin. Mask and gloves are available. The two Mexes helped me into my exoskeleton and I lay down to rest.

I thanked and dismissed them. But El Toro persuaded me to take a slug of rum, poured a glass for himself, and stayed behind.

"What do *you* think of our Revolution?" he asked me.

"I am earning my ticket to Amarillo Cuchillo," I replied, not at all inclined to bandy either platitudes or deep thoughts. I was relieved that I stank no more and that I felt less surface pain, but the bath had exhausted me.

He nodded. "There have been risings everywhere, even to the north. The news of El Esqueleto has gone ahead of us." Yet he did not sound enthusiastic.

"Many dead bent-backs?" I asked.

He grimaced.

"And in Texas, Texas, the Revolution has been crushed?"

He said, "Badly battered, though not extinct. It has not been conquered, but it has been countered. The Texans have pacified many of my people with shorter working hours for the cyborged, with more fiestas and bullfights, with free rum and Coca-Cola and with free reefers. But I asked you what *you* thought of our Revolution?"

I finally answered, "I believe it is necessary, but that does not mean I enjoy it."

"*Comprendo, camarada,*" he said and left me alone.

With Winnipeg, Texas, we arrived in an area where tall Texans are a tiny elite: managers, engineers, foremen, the police, the Rangers, and their wives and sometimes their children. The few short Texans are all embittered Canadians—they remember and use that name, though it is forbidden. The numerous Mexes are all cyborged workers—miners and farmhands and lumberjacks—shipped north with their cooks and women.

Our meeting—I can hardly call it a show—was held in a supposedly forgotten atomic shelter which the Mexes reached by a short tunnel from one of their compounds and which we entered by a longer tunnel, part of a disused drainage system. I had to go stooping, looking I suppose like a huge black bug. At the meeting there was little laughter. There was much hate. Midway there was a raid and all but one of us actors escaped because our entrance tunnel had not been known to the Rangers. I do not know what casualties our audience suffered.

Now our chief is Carlos Mendoza, whom I hardly know. And I am no longer giving grand-opera lessons. Next time I shall not be the first man to run—at least, such is my present boast. El Toro bought it.

Our next stop, on Spindletop seventeenth, was Victory, Texas, once Saskatoon, but renamed when the Rangers routed an Anglo-Russian army in the Battle of Saskatche-

wan. We held our meeting by a windbreak in the wheat-
fields. Here the Mexes live in a shack city. No need for
fenced compounds. Where could they run?

Tall Texan elite smaller, but tougher. No women or children. The deeply hated engineers and cyborg foremen. The
Rangers.

Almost no short Texans, but some Indians, who do not
cyborg well. They generally take their lives after their first
experience of the yoke.

Mendoza, who is something of a book man, told me that
one reason this area has remained uncolonized and unex-
ploited, except for wheat and wood and ores, is the growing
world shortage of high-grade radioactives. Earth's oil is almost gone, her remaining coal hard to come by, while the
Atomic War actually increased Terran man's dependency on
nuclear power. Even our kack, for example, is powered by
atomic batteries.

Fanninowicz heard Mendoza's little lecture and favored
him with a contemptuous and knowing grin. Typical German arrogance only?

Two days after Victory, we arrived at Fort Johnson, Al-
berta, Texas. Once Fort Murray. Much like Victory, except
timbering again replaces wheat-farming and the Indians are
more numerous. Here, I was told, is stationed a company of
Rangers with a red dress uniform, survival from the fabulous Canadian Mounties.

The only uniforms, however, that I saw—from a safe
distance, using electrobinoculars—were white fatigues. Toward evening I discovered the reason for them—camou-
flage. Snow fell and everything turned bright white.

Terra's weird natural phenomena still rouse in me a
sense of wonder, despite my punished body and wearying
mind. In the long silvery twilight, the flakes were like a
ghostly Milky Way falling past a wheeling spaceship.

I donned my gloves and mask. The latter, with its silver
arabesques, makes me look like Death the Witch Doctor.

Through the electrobinox I watched another of the huge towers in which cyborged Mexes do their mysterious work. I recalled Federico's pantomime and the "dig and delve" chant, and I found myself shivering at being near a forty-kilometer hole up which—my childish imagination insisted —the dragon of gravity might crawl and come to hunt me down, suck me from any hiding place, and crush me flat against him.

Not that I believed in such a hole. My mind shrank from the idea, and Fanninowicz's arguments had been telling. Still, it seemed unlikely that the Texans would be drilling for oil here, where Mendoza tells me the sedimentary layers are thin and the last glaciation has often exposed the underlying igneous rock: basalt, obsidian, feldspar, tufa, pumice, granite, pitchstone, and their hideous confreres.

But if not for oil, what?

Whatever work is done in the towers, I could see that it produced much heat. This one steamed amid the falling snow and remained stubbornly black, like a giant finger protruding from inner earth.

13 / The Gusher

When the Twentieth Century was only ten days old,
Texas ushered in with a black skyward sweep the
Age of Petroleum, the era of fast cars and the big
trucks that would lick the railroads, the mighty tanks
and jets that would dominate every subsequent war.
With a roar that was heard around the industrial
world, a tumult as mighty as Krakatoa's but
meaningful, at the sleepy town of Beaumont, near
the coast where De Soto's men had noted oil seepage
three hundred and thirty-eight years before, the
Discovery Well at Spindletop blew in. Within six
months, the price of Beaumont land had risen a
thousandfold. Oil was three cents a cask, water
five cents a cup. Within sixty years, one Texan in
eight was with an oil company, and one out of every
seven barrels of world-oil came from Texas.

—*Texas in Brief and Big,* Houston House, Chicago,
Texas

AFTER TWILIGHT HAD darkened into night, and we took off on
what I hoped would be the last lap of my Terran hegira,
our company was reduced to one kack and its occupants.
Besides Guchu and myself, there were Carlos Mendoza, El
Tácito, Father Francisco, Fanninowicz, and Rachel and
Rosa. The other two kacks were headed south, their ultimate destination Denver. Our tour was breaking up.

The snow had stopped falling. It lay in a blanket a half-
meter thick on the stunted evergreen forest below.

The night was very clear, but the twinkling stars were
dimmed by Luna riding low in the east and waxing again
toward full. I had spent almost a month on Terra. I looked
with tired longing at my mother satellite, tethering point of

the Sack and Circumluna, cosmically so near and yet so far.

Luna was not the only rival to the stars. Ahead, ghostly green flames burned up toward the zenith—the northern lights, another remarkable Terran phenomenon.

After about a half-hour, Rosa noted that the stars had a third rival, a purple glow on the southern horizon, directly astern. It was not so much a point of light as a small hemispherical shining.

It appeared to originate near or at Fort Johnson. We speculated unsatisfactorily as to what it might be. A fire? Some part of the search for us? Even an atomic bomb was suggested, though that was contradicted by the steadiness of the glow. Besides, no sound or shock wave caught up with us.

Fanninowicz contributed to this interchange a knowing sneer.

I said, "I wonder if the glow has anything to do with the drilling tower at Fort Johnson?"

The German's sneer wavered toward a scowl.

"Grand Emperor of Mechanics," I addressed him, "are you merely contemptuous of us? Or are you carrying a secret about the great towers?"

"Secrets!" he said, the sneer back in full. "I am forced to carry thousands in this company, simply because my mind holds a vast number of matters beyond your understanding. Especially in the intellectually inclined Teuton, the directional hormone produces taller minds as well as taller bodies. I feel no more contempt for you all than I do for chattering apes, I assure you."

I gave him up as a bad German job. I tucked away in my memory the point that the Texas growth hormone was directional, whatever that jargon might mean. Then I incuriously watched the purple glow until our steady northward flight put it under the horizon.

My earlier symptoms of gravity sickness had been replaced with a general lassitude that could not merge unaided into rest because of the pains of my deep bruises, rashes, and varicosities.

The other passengers went to sleep. With the aid of rum, I followed them there—and found only nightmares of cyborged fiery dragons pursuing me through red-hot tunnels that by degrees melted my titanium.

When I woke, unrefreshed, sunrise was reddening the eastern horizon. El Tácito had replaced Guchu at the controls.

The snow-roofed forest below had become dwarfier. The Land of Little Sticks, it is called.

The ground below was without any but the smallest hills. There was no sign of human occupation. Our largely transparent kack made the situation seem like a nothingness crossing a desolation. Except for my pains, I would have felt disembodied.

After we had breakfasted, each meagerly yet according to his taste, Rosa said, "May this one address you, Señor La Cruz?"

So it has come to señor, I thought. "Most certainly, Señorita Morales," I replied.

"How do you propose to depart into the sky after we reach Amarillo Cuchillo?"

"By way of the spaceport there," I told her. "If one of Circumluna's ships is not in, I will have to wait."

"Ah, yes, the spaceport," she answered with a dubious nod. "But how do you propose to wait in Amarillo Cuchillo, which is little more than a Texan working encampment?"

"I have counted on the help of the Revolution in this matter," I told her anxiously. "That was my understanding from our talks in Dallas."

"Ah, yes," Rosa replied. "But Dallas is Dallas, and also what is said in Dallas—while Amarillo Cuchillo is another thing. Carlos, what are our contacts there?"

"Among the Cree Indians," Mendoza replied. "They are wanderers, though some live in encampments outside the town. And of course among the cyborged, but such have no station or influence. As for town-dwellers, I know of none. Perhaps—" He broke off with a sharp headshake.

I guessed that he had been about to say, "Perhaps El Toro knew, but neglected to inform me." Another matter occurred to me.

"There is also the Lost Crazy-Russian Pitchblende Mine," I said. "Though I know some of you think it a fable," I added with a glance at Rachel. "Nevertheless, my sole reason for coming to Earth was to find it and lay claim to it if I can. To achieve the latter, I had hoped to make use of well-placed local revolutionaries as intermediaries. But even if there are nonesuch, I must still make a full effort. Perhaps in making the claim, I can use my Texan disguise, which worked well enough for me in the Kansas City Plaza de Toros."

Rachel interrupted with "But, Señor La Cruz, how will the matter of making the claim ever come up, since we know you don't have even the map with you?"

So she was señoring me too! "I have the map *here*," I told her icily, touching my head. "That was *one* thing about Terra I memorized in complete detail while still in the Sack. If the mine exists, I can find it."

"Yes, and you may have the claim in your head too, all perfectly memorized," Rachel rejoined. "But a claim in the head isn't a document. It isn't seals and signatures."

"I carry the claim *here*," I told her, laying my hand on my chest over my heart. "And as to how I propose to assert that claim—that is my business, Señorita Lamar!"

She shrank back a little with tipped shoulder, pretending to be withered. I could have kicked her! I caught Rosa quirking a grin. There was occupation for my other foot!

Mendoza said with mild argumentativeness, "But if you truly have the claim, I do not see the need either for map or mine hunt. A claim describes the exact location of a mine."

"This one does not," I asserted. Then before any or all could accuse me of insanity, I went on, "*However*, the original crazy Russian, who sold it to the Cree, who sold it to the Aleut, who sold it to my ancestor—that crazy Russian, whose name by the way was Nicholas Nimzovitch Nisard —he, before disappearing forever, deposited with the then Yellowknife Registry of Mining Claims, in an envelope bearing his signature, samples of the unique mixture of pitchblende, syenite, pitchstone, and granite from his mine. On the basis of those samples he was granted a provisional claim. If anyone can produce matching samples, plus a verifiable description of the mine's location, *plus* the provisional claim, then the claim becomes absolute."

"The Russian was crazy like a fox," Mendoza observed, nodding his head wisely. "He was afraid that the Registry, agent of capitalist government, might jump his claim."

I said, "So all I need now is your help in finding the mine. I know you carry radioactivity detectors as standard safety equipment, while this kack is the perfect vehicle in which to hunt for the landmarks of the mine: three large low outcroppings of rock forming the apexes of an equilateral triangle with sides a kilometer long. The outcroppings to north and south are of pale granite, but the one to the west is of darker hue—and there lies the pitchblende."

Mendoza nervously shook his head. "I fear I have not the authority to detach a revolutionary vehicle for such an individualistic enterprise."

"Is true," Rosa supported him. "The Revolution comes before all else."

Rachel said, "I think it's a mercy not to encourage Señor La Cruz in his delusions about this nonexistent mine."

Kicking, I thought, is much too good for those two abominable females. However, I found myself too weary and dispirited to indulge even in sadistic fantasies. I deserve all this, I thought. To put my trust in a gang of utterly selfish traitors such as constitutes any revolutionary committee—

Fanninowicz's cackle of sardonic mirth was the final stab to the deflating balloon of my ego, flattening it completely.

However, the cold laughter was followed by a warm chuckle. Guchu, whom I had thought to be asleep, had opened his bloodshot eyes and now lifted up on an orange-robed elbow.

"Aw, give the stupid square a square deal, I say. At first I agreed with you all—we'd used him and now was the time to dump him, along with Professor Fanninowicz. But then he told his story and, man, it was so crazy that my sympathies were aroused in spite of myself! Loco Russian to a Cree Injun to an Aleut to his bombed-out ancestor! Man, oh, man!" Again came the warm chuckle. "Not that we owe him anything as Señor La Cruz from the sky. First principle of being a black is that he can't ever owe an ofay anything. Ofays are a doomed breed and it's a kindness to help them along toward extinction—and that goes for you too, Miss Lamar. But taking La Cruz just as an actor—pure ham, but at least lively and hard-working—I think we owe him a little help hunting this crazy mine of his."

El Tácito looked back from the controls and nodded once.

Mendoza looked around, shrugged, and nodded too, albeit unwillingly.

I gazed at Guchu and opened my mouth to thank him.

But the words that came out were "Thank you for nothing, you bloodthirsty black, more besotted with your race than even Fanninowicz here! I imagine the first act of your so-called Pacific Republic was to slaughter every miserable white in California, giving priority to women and children."

Guchu's answering chuckle was as warm and rich as either of his earlier ones. I hadn't touched his ego, I hadn't got within a light-year of it.

"That's not true, Scully," he said. "Quite a few of them we made honorary blacks."

Not trusting myself to speak to him or so much as look at the girls, I crawled forward beside El Tácito.

"You heard what they said," I told him gruffly. "Please approach Amarillo Cuchillo on a south-north line, ten kilometers to the east. That is a trifle more than six miles."

Once again he nodded.

Except for changing the batteries of my exo, I spent the rest of the long day horizontal there, occasionally peering north—not hungrily, but with a definite, though very small appetite.

After a tiny eternity, the flat blue of Great Slave Lake edged reluctantly into view. To the west I could make out low forest; to the east, the barrens.

Then for a time land retreated in all directions. To me it was as if we were crossing one of those unimaginable oceans.

The sun was low when the barrens reappeared ahead.

Guchu took over the controls.

When the barrens had been below us for half an hour, the sun was setting. Its horizontal, deep-yellow light was just right to show me, a little to the west, three long shadows traveling east from the apexes of an equilateral triangle with sides about a kilometer long.

My teeth were chattering as I pointed out the miraculous sight to Guchu. I chiefly wanted him to confirm what I saw. It was impossible that I should find the mine so easily. There must be a catch somewhere.

If there was, Guchu didn't tell me. He just grunted appreciatively and swung the kack west and down.

The shadows of the two eastern outcroppings were about a half-kilometer long. But that of the western one, where the mine was, seemed to stretch east forever.

I snatched up binoculars. There was indeed a catch. The long shadow was cast by one of the now familiar huge towers.

My mind had been discovered and was being worked by the Texans.

Yet that didn't make sense. Surely the huge rigs scattered down across Texas at least as far as Dallas were not for mining surface deposits of pitchblende.

I focused more carefully and upped the magnification and electronic gain. Now I could see a great door standing open in the eastern side of the tower. Before it, figures tinier than ants were slowly milling about. I saw the hairline red needles of laser beams. A revolutionary rising?—I wondered, pulse quickening.

I scanned west of the tower. I saw nothing whatever besides the monotonous landscape of the barrens, until there came into view the narrow, dark-gold sheen of a river, dark short dashes of two bridges crossing it, and just beyond them the huddled low buildings and narrow streets of what must be Amarillo Cuchillo.

The tops of a few of the buildings still caught sunlight. Elsewhere, twilight was gathering.

Northeast of the tiny city I spotted an airfield with two huge Texan cargo jets and a narrow shaft, its upper quarter sun-gilded, which might well be the *Tsiolkovsky* or her sister ship, the *Goddard*.

I lowered the binoculars to rest my eyes. There was shadow around me. The kack had dropped out of sight of the sun.

Without warning, Amarillo Cuchillo became the center of a spider web of thread-thin, ruler-straight beams of light. Some of them, red, shot up toward infinity or lanced across the barrens.

Others, green, originated in the sky or in the northwest distance and ended around the city in incandescent points from which sparks fountained upward.

Some of the red beams ended similarly in points beyond Amarillo Cuchillo, two of them in the sky.

The kack rocked and a blinding green flare flashed across the thick plastic a foot above my head.

That convinced me that the Rangers had found us at last. Though why they had to shoot up the whole sky and landscape to down one miserable little ship of actors, I couldn't grasp. Sheer Texan exuberance, perhaps.

By the time I got my sight back, Guchu was landing the kack behind the southernmost of two eastern outcroppings.

Near at hand the rocky hillock looked almost impressive—a glacier-smoothed bump of granite ten meters high.

I could see the brown furrow that the green laser beam had melted in the plastic, not quite cutting through. The furrow was barely three decimeters wide, testifying to the photonic weapon's fantastic "choke" at a distance over ten miles.

There was a soft bump and my wrists were twisting. I realized that we had touched down and that Mendoza was trying to wrench the binoculars away from me.

I saw Rachel drop recklessly down from the kack's trap to the snowy carpet below. I too was seized by the desire to know what was going on. Jerking the binoculars away from Mendoza and upping my power, though not as much as I had for the duel, I followed her.

Offstage, the Revolutionary Ramblers are anything but a well-disciplined company.

The snow was barely ankle-deep. The wind of my movement instantly began to chill my face and hands. But I did not pause to put on gloves and mask, or even to turn up my suit's heat, until I was crouched beside Rachel on a rough granite ledge and peering over the hillock's top.

There were no more little red laser flashes from the foot of the tower, before the great door.

The earth's curvature now hid Amarillo Cuchillo, but the green and red laser beams continued their battle. I could no longer see the incandescent hits, though there were brief ghostly white glows here and there along the horizon's rim, and also long-lasting deep-orange glows that I took to come from flames. Several times too I saw brief glares and later heard the distant boom of explosions, but for the most part the battle was so silent that it seemed more like one more natural display—the northern lights reduced to a weird, bright geometry—rather than a human conflict.

Somewhere along the line I had decided that the laser display was not directed at us, that I and my fellow actor-revolutionaries had merely been struck one accidental blow and become witnesses of some much larger conflict. Though when one green ray flashed a half-kilometer overhead, I flinched.

I turned up my heating a notch, put on gloves and mask, and looked around me. Rachel was using my binoculars. Mendoza had found another pair and was peering through them. Rosa and Fanninowicz and Father Francisco had also come down. And El Tácito too, his pistols out, stolidly watching Fanninowicz and myself rather than the battle.

There were two battles, I remembered then. I snatched the glasses from Rachel with no more than a growled "I want them!" in answer to her challenging "I beg your pardon?"

I focused them carefully on the western tower a kilometer away, upped magnification and electronic gain to maximum, and gradually made out the details and gradually interpreted a sight that I am sure will never stop returning to me in nightmares.

The huge tower loomed darkly against the twilight sky. Facing me, two doors, thirty meters high and ten wide, stood open.

The inside of the tower showed a single great room. With one exception, the central space was empty. To either side a purplish glow showed me sections of great tall machines. One reminded me of one of those big gantries a rocket sometimes needs on a gravity satellite.

The reason it reminded me of a gantry was that I saw, standing in the center of the tower, a gleaming violet rocket taller than the door. It must be lit by invisible banks of floodlights, I thought. I fancied it quivered, as if it were anxious for the tower's roof to lift aside, so it could take off.

By Diana!—I thought—Texas is preparing a new conquest of space. I must warn Circumluna.

"Better be ready to come a-running, children," Guchu called from behind us. "The geiger shows a little activity from the direction of the purple tower. Nothing dangerous. As of now."

Then, *through* the rocket, I dimly made out more machines behind it. I realized, at first with relief, that the rocket was only a shaft of violet light shining up like a giant laser through a hole in the floor or ground and beating against the tower's ceiling, to be reflected as the purple glow.

The purple glow, fanning out through the door, showed me many bodies lying at random on the snow. Little bodies, the bodies of bent-backs. I think I saw stains beside some of them. At any rate, they did not move.

But there were many more Mexes moving about freely, seen blackly in silhouette. Some stood in groups. Others moved singly. When a group did move, there was a surge about it that I did not like. I do not know whether it reminded me of half-disciplined soldiers, or packs of animals, or what. I only know I did not like it.

Also, to one side of the door, there was what I took to be a small stack of big logs, bigger than the stems of any of the trees I had seen growing in the Land of Little Sticks.

If El Toro had been with us, he might have led us toward the tower. I only know that Carlos Mendoza did not, and that I had no desire to go there, and that I twice caught Father Francisco crossing himself.

My glasses kept going back in fascination to the violet pillar of light. I fancied that it pulsed and vibrated. It seemed almost a living thing. I marveled with a shudder at the Mexes moving freely in its glow, the crescent edges of their silhouetted heads like anodyzed aluminum or mercury vapor lashed by electrons.

I wondered about the source of the violet light. A huge vat of molten metal just below the floor? For there was heat there; the lengthening fan of dark ground before the door, where the snow had melted, showed that.

Or great filaments? Or a sea of thin vapor, conceivably mercury, electrically blasted into fluorescence?

Somehow I felt that the source was deeper than that. I pictured a great shaft going down, and down, and down, until I felt vertigo. Federico's shaft, but with all elevators removed and the change points smoothed out, until it was an uninterrupted forty-kilometer hole.

I lowered my glasses, blinking my smarting eyes and shaking my head to get rid of that illusion of dizziness.

I looked toward Amarillo Cuchillo. The lasers still lanced there, though I saw more greens than reds.

I was just handing my binoculars to Rachel when I heard Mendoza, whose own binoculars were still fixed on the purple tower, give a sibilant hiss.

Ignoring Rachel's angry protests, I snatched back the glasses and put them to my eyes.

I am sometimes sorry I did so, yet it is perhaps better that I saw, than she.

Eight Mexes were returning from the violet beam. A gang of eight others rushed with that unpleasant surge toward the log stack, which seemed slightly smaller than before, hoisted a log between them, surged with it to the center of the tower, and cast it into the violet light, where it was brightly and lividly visible for a moment before dropping into the hole whence the light came.

During that cinema-bright moment I saw that it was not a log, but a tall man with legs bound together and arms to his sides, a big man made bigger by the ropes swathing him from neck to ankles.

I watched that action repeated six times more, until the stack was gone. Although several attempts, which rocked me, were made to drag the binoculars away from me, I held on to them with the maximum strength of my hands and exoskeleton—held on to them and fought to keep them focused continually on the base of the violet column.

I do not think I wanted to watch. I believe I hated to. I know it tore me inside. One moment I felt like a snarling animal, next like a compassionate man, next like a maniac, next like a camera frozen in ice.

Yet I had to watch, I had to witness. I had each time to try, unsuccessfully yet desperately, to catch the expression on the face of the bound Texan falling into the brilliant hole.

Meanwhile I was hearing a faint shrill wailing that rose and fell irregularly. I told myself it was the wind rising. I told myself it was wolves. I told myself it was not the screaming of men, either in ultimate terror or murderous fury or the two mixed.

Buddhists have much to say about karmic burdens and duties, karmic works and acts, karmic moments when all of the moral past of a being, and perhaps future too, is laid bare, is nakedly seized and known. That perhaps comes closest to describing what I felt and why I had to feel it. Besides, was I not Death?

The glasses slipped from my hands, I don't know to whom. I stood there a long time, with head bowed. Or perhaps it only seemed a long time.

Then, among many unnoticed remarks, I heard someone, I do not recall who, say, "Yes, the cyborgs are all gone. The eight last threw something down the hole. Yes, a thing, not a man."

I looked up. The sky was dark. Toward Amarillo Cuchillo a few lasers still lanced, all green.

I heard someone—again I do not recall who; can it have been that in my peculiar state I was hearing not voices, but meanings? At any rate, I heard someone say matter-of-factly, "Well, the Russians have licked the Texans this time, that's for sure."

Until that moment, except for the brief period when I thought the Rangers were chasing us, I hadn't the faintest idea of who was fighting whom at the Battle of Amarillo Cuchillo.

And then I began to hear it—no, not the shrill wailing again, thank Mars!—though it was even fainter than that, to begin with. It was a sound that was lilting, and rhythmic, and deep, and—one had at last to recognize—both musical and human. It was coming out of the dark, across the white waste, from the direction of Amarillo Cuchillo, and it was slowly getting stronger.

For a long while I tried to convince myself it was an illusion, perhaps something generated deep in my mind to erase those dreadful screams, but then I realized that all those around me were motionless and listening too. And then I saw the first white form appear in the dark like a ghost, small at first, but growing taller.

I heard Guchu come up behind us and begin to whisper harshly, "You all better—"

I think he was going to say "—beat it back to the kack!" and then, seeing how far the situation had developed, changed his mind.

For he finished, "—hold damn still! Tácito, dig your gun in the professor's guts."

By that time all the marching men had appeared from the frosty murk. There were a scant dozen of them. They were in white fatigues and they carried their lasers at the slope, or hanging farther over-shoulder with muzzle down, or casually underarm. They all stood tall and now I could make out all the words of the march they were singing soft and low to a hauntingly familiar tune:

> From the hills of Guatemala
> To the frozen Arctic sea,
> Texas Rangers fight the battles
> In the name of liberty.
> We have kicked the Russki and Chinee
> Until his ass is sore.
> We're the Lone Star's guts and guns and fists,
> We're the Texas Ranger Corps.

At first I assumed they were headed for the tower, to hunt down the revolted cyborgs. Then, with a spasm of fear, I thought they were coming for us.

It turned out they were simply marching south between us, though much nearer to us than to the tower. They halted less than a hundred yards away. We all held dead-still indeed. With blown snow half coating us, we were hard to see. At least I hoped so.

In the lull of the wind, I heard a gruff voice say, "Wal, Custer done wuss," and another reply, "And so did Lyndon overseas, bless 'im," and a third comment, "Yup, the mysterious east weren't never meant for human man to meddle with."

I heard nothing else coming from the northwest, but the Rangers must have, for now they scattered and knelt in a long curve, their lasers pointing back along the line of their retreat.

What came out of the northwestern murk wasn't a band of pursuing Russians, but a big, long, white vehicle that moved silently across the snow, weaving like a snake.

It halted by the Rangers and I heard a hoarse voice command, "Jump aboard, boys. Haul your asses!"

They obeyed, though they didn't move as fast as the voice had demanded. Then the huge vehicle was slithering south.

I thought I heard again, very faintly, the two lines:

> Texas Rangers fight the battles
> In the name of liberty!

Perhaps I should have felt contemptuous, or at least sardonic. I didn't. Something deep inside me, which I had never suspected was there, was touched.

We had started back for the kack when the roaring began. It came first through the rock we trod, making it vibrate and shake. We staggered and reeled.

Then the roar became deafening as the purple tower blew up. First the violet beam grew much brighter and burst through the roof, shining toward the zenith as if exultantly bound for the stars. Then great gouts of bright purple molten stuff were mixed with it. Then the walls of the tower were driven outward. In a few moments, where the tower and great machines had been, there was only a cone of bright purple, viscous, semisolid lava, hugely squirming and swiftly growing taller.

The roaring died down, though the rock still vibrated underfoot.

Guchu yelled, "Back to the kack! The geiger's gone crazy!"

Fanninowicz broke away from the group and ran lumberingly up the hillock. El Tácito drew a bead on him. I forced down his pistol, saying *"Un momento! Por favor!"* and took out after the German. Rachel and Rosa followed me.

Fanninowicz stopped at the summit of the rocky hummock. He was bathed in bright purple light, while we who followed him stayed in the hummock's shadow.

Shaking his fist alternately at the purple pyramid and at us, he roared out, "Yes, the dirty Russians have won a battle, but now they will lose two, ten, a hundred! With his back to the wall, Hitler created the V-One and the V-Two! Now the Texans, sole heirs of the virile Germanic spirit, have won the means to throw back and conquer the jealous world! Faced by the shortage of radioactives, they have had the vision and daring and heavy technology to tap the pockets of radioactive magma under Earth's crust! Across their great land, at every likely spot, they have with admirable secrecy created the mohole mines! The Lost Crazy-Russian Mine was the clue that led to the new Spindletop! Everywhere the ultimate gushers are coming in, as at Fort Jackson last night, though you fools had not the wit to read the meaning of that glow! They will make Texas all-powerful!" And facing the glow with fist held high, he shouted, *"Sieg heil!"* and again, *"Sieg heil!"*

Perhaps I should have been touched by that too. I wasn't. All I could think was that Germans were maniacs and that the grandiose Texans were giving poor old atom-scarred Terra another horse-size dose of deadly radioactivity.

Meanwhile I had grabbed Fanninowicz's ankle and jerked. He came tumbling heavily down. Rachel and I each grabbed him by a shoulder and rushed him toward the kack. When he didn't move fast enough, Rosa kicked him viciously from behind.

As we scrambled aboard, Guchu yelled, "You dumb ofays are crazy-lucky I waited for you. Now hang on!"

The kack took off straight east, hugging the ground to get the most protection out of the hillock's low shadow. We traveled east many kilometers before we began the long circle north and west to find the tents of the Crees.

14 / Zhawlty Nawsh

Over and over the story, ending as he began:
"Make ye no truce with Adam-Zad—the Bear that
 walks like a Man!"
"When he stands up as pleading, in wavering,
 man-brute guise,
When he veils the hate and cunning of his little
 swinish eyes;
When he shows as seeking quarter, with paws like
 hands in prayer,
That is the time of peril—the time of the Truce
 of the Bear!"

—"The Truce of the Bear," by Rudyard Kipling
(1898)

FANNINOWICZ CONTINUED euphoric in the kack. He discoursed to us like a paranoically insane schoolteacher in his grandiose phase. He sprayed spittle like my father acting Macbeth and his voice often rose with an Iago's or Richard the Third's evil glee.

"It is a commonplace," he began, "that common men never perceive the wonders of science and technology until the rockets roar, until the nuclei give up their energy at interior solar heat, or until the rich thor-uranic lava spouts from a mohole. Now you have seen and the secret is out. So, attend me, children."

El Tácito made as if to club him with the butt of his rifle, but Mendoza shook his head.

"It has long been known, even to oafs like you," Fanninowicz continued without notice, "that Terra has a crust of solid rock as much as seventy kilometers thick. Below that is the mantle: three thousand kilometers of molten rock under increasingly vast pressure.

"Once it was thought that the mantle was slowly cooling and shrinking.

"But as early as the twentieth century, the preponderance of evidence indicated that the heat of the mantle was steadily maintained by cells of rich radioactives in it.

"These deep cells produced slow convection currents in the mantle, leading straight up to the crust, spreading sideways there and then descending. The Dutchman Veneg-Meinez first suggested that—which is to say that a German first developed the theory, for despite their reputation for peacefulness, the Dutch were the ancestors of the brave and long-mourned-for Boers, which proves the Dutch to have been subconscious Prussians.

"Up the slow convection currents rode the rich radioactive ores, bit by bit. They were the hottest and most expanded of all the materials in the current, since they were the source of its heat.

"Each current melted a dome in the solid crust above it. Some of the radioactives moved sideways with the current to its areas of descent hundreds of miles away. But others accumulated in an ever-richer pocket inside the dome.

"So pockets of molten radioactives are marked by mantle domes, somewhat as oil is associated with salt domes.

"The Texans——"

"I was waiting for them," Guchu muttered from the pilot's seat.

"Silence! By their ability to think big and to do big, the Texans provided the skill and unceasing industry to dig the roomy shafts."

"Lies!" Rosa interjected. "Our cyborged men provided that."

Fanninowicz continued unperturbed, "The lower courses of the shafts were lined with woven molecular-ribbon ferroceramics of great strength, through which the radioactives might gush upward, depositing on Earth's surface great cones of thor-uranic ores. The pharaohs built limestone pyramids in which they buried themselves with a little gold and a few soft gems. But the Texans have cajoled Nature into creating hundreds of radioactive pyramids, each worth hundreds of billions of dollars!"

"A few Texans got buried today in one of their hot pyramids," Guchu put in.

"While we Texo-Germans," Fanninowicz continued modestly but unshaken, "merely provided all the general theory and also the means to locate mantle domes."

"Which is?" Mendoza asked after a few seconds. He was still interested. Myself, I had become sickened by all this horrible talk of oceans of molten rock megameters deep. A planet is hell with a crust! Then it occurred to me that my nausea might be the first symptoms of a dose of radioactivity.

When Fanninowicz, prior to an elaborate yawn, brushed his hand through his short hair, I was pleased to see that none fell out.

"Oh," he said tantalizingly, "we have had some success with counts of antineutrinos coming through the earth at night from the sun. But chiefly we have located mantle domes by the same method the Great Fuehrer's naval command located battleships in the Atlantic—that is, by dowsing over maps of Texas! Ho-ho, I see I have startled you. I see you are prepared to sneer. Do so, if you wish. It will not alter the fact that we Germans are the ancient and original spiers-out of metals, the ultimate chemists, the chthonic race, the wise old kobolds, as the very names of the elements testify! Ha-ha!"

I did not listen to the discussion that followed, in which words like "cobalt" and "cuckoo" were bandied about. I was thinking that if only one dab of ferric ore were left in all Terra, a German would find it and forge from it an Iron Cross. My mind was also invaded by a compulsive, nightmarish vision in which a parade of Germans and Egyptians wound among vast, blue-litten pyramids, the hair of the marchers falling out on the way and their flesh shredding off and they slowly turning to shining blue skeletons topped by eerie animal heads and spiked gray helmets.

I was not aware the kack had landed until someone guided me from it, my exoskeleton jigging and shimmying from shiver jerks in my chilled ghost muscles. I dimly noted puckered, black-eyed, leathery faces framed in fur. I smelled old hides, unwashed live ones, burning fat, and cold machine oil. I glimpsed leather walls with shadows reeling across them. Then I felt coarse fur beneath me. I heard a faint shivery rattle and realized, just as I fell asleep, that it had come from my exo.

I spent the next two days in the encampment of the Crees, recuperating—which, to a man with gravity sickness on a gravity body, means no improvement at all, only a bitter hanging on to what little health he has, with growing irritability, fatigued restlessness, swift loss of reasonableness, and ballooning negativism.

There were a dozen tents masked by a strip of forest so thin and ragged that Amarillo Cuchillo and its airfield-spaceport could be glimpsed distantly through the stunted trees, with here and there small patrols of burly-looking Russians.

This nearness did not whet my hope. It only made me impatient.

Mendoza and the rest explained to me that I must stay hidden while they made contact and dickered with the Russians. My Texan height and generally strange appearance, they said, might arouse suspicion in the Russian military, who might not have been informed at all about the part I had played in the Bent-Back Revolt.

I argued at all this. Was I not El Esqueleto, I asked, and was he not known by now around the world? Even Rachel and Rosa could not win from me more than surly agreement to cooperate for the present.

The Crees were an interesting if somber folk. For instance, small jars of petroleum and chunks of coal were their money and also their gods, because they had learned that those black substances were the energy-filled residue of all animal and plant life. These they never burned, but used in trade and buried in small quantity with the dead, to "seed" them toward a similar immortality.

But the Crees did not interest me. They irked me with their atrocious English and worse Spanish and with their body odors, different from mine, though I suppose no worse. I did my best to ignore them.

As for staying hidden and sensibly horizontal, well, except when Russian patrols came near, I spent my days prowling about the camp with El Tácito in scowling attendance. I frequently stopped for glimpses of the silvery needle-prow of the *Tsiolkovsky* or the *Goddard* waiting at the spaceport to take me home—at any rate, that was why I felt it was there.

Meanwhile, I thought, I was wasting precious time that I could have put to use asserting my claim to the radioactive gusher, for, despite Fanninowicz's babble about dowsing and such, it seemed obvious that the Lost Crazy-Russian Pitchblende Mine had been the clue that had led the Texans to drill a mohole there.

My colleagues' suggestions that I forget about the mine, that I face the fact that Russia had never permitted the exploitation of her mineral wealth by foreigners, and that I consider myself damn lucky if they managed to procure me an exit visa and transport to Circumluna—all these reasonable suggestions I listened to with great hostility and a growing suspicion that they wanted me off Terra so they could seize my wealth.

Suggestions that I have patience—Mendoza's that I learn Cree, Rachel's that I take up bow and arrow, Guchu's that I drop acid—I only snarled at.

Perhaps by this time I had developed a mild chronic delirium from skin infections and fringe-adequate blood supply to the brain. But I doubt it. I think it was sheer bloated egotism on my part, slightly augmented by gravity disease. Here I was a great and heroic actor, and I was being treated like a bum.

At any rate, when Mendoza and Father Francisco went to dicker the first day and did not return, when Guchu and Rosa and Rachel—and even Fanninowicz!—took off on the second in the kack and didn't come back either or send word, I decided on action.

I engaged El Tácito in a game of gin rummy and then a bout of drinking same—I mean rum, not gin. When he was thoroughly soused, I put him to bed, took his lightning pistols, equipped my exoskeleton with my last fresh batteries, and waited for dawn.

At its first glimmer I emerged from our tent, menaced with my telescopic swords the Crees who would have stopped me, and walked straight to Amarillo Cuchillo.

Dawn was red when I reached the town and encountered a neat new sign with the ten Cyrillic characters spelling out "Zhawlty Nawsh." Like the Texans, the Russians had literally translated Yellowknife.

I also encountered my first pair of Russian soldiers.

I'll admit that their extreme burliness and even greater hairiness startled me at first. Ever since Tearful Suzy the space hostess had mentioned "them fearful furry Russians," I had assumed that all the references I heard to the hirsuteness of the Soviets were only one more ridiculous expression of that curse of Terran man, xenophobia.

Not so. The feet, hands, and faces—not to mention head, neck, and ears—of these two infantrymen were entirely covered by thick fur, which also bulked up their coarsely woven summer uniforms. Their nails too were thickened, somewhat in the direction of claws, but seemingly not enough to interfere with humanoid manipulations.

After the first shock, the effect was delightful. The human eye looks quite soulful when surrounded by fur, it has something of the effect of a dolphin's eye, while the fur itself modestly proclaims, "I am merely an animal, nothing special, comrade. There is nothing of the anthropocentric, supercilious, god-and-devil-creating witch doctor about *me.*"

They seemed easily to accept my strangeness too, after a moment's initial shock. Most cosmopolitan beasts, I thought.

And when one of the two responded to my *"Zdraste, tovarich"* with a softly guttural *"Spasebaw,"* and in answer to my question gave me the simple directions needed to reach the Registry of Mining Claims, I felt preposterously pleased, as if I were in a fairyland of talking animals.

Of course these were very different Russians from the generally hairless Slavic Thins, Fats, and Athletics of Circumluna, but in a way I liked them better—they seemed less supercilious, less morally conceited and puritanical.

One of the soldiers stayed at his post, the other companionably dropped in beside me, carrying his laser rifle in a relaxed, casual manner.

I pointed toward the distant silvery prow of the spaceship rising above the low buildings around us and asked, *"Goddard?"*

"Nyet," he replied.

"Tsiolkovsky?" I suggested.

"Da!" he confirmed in something of a growl, eyeing me for a moment severely before resuming his smiling, animal placidity.

We passed several bombed and laser-charred areas.

We met ten more furry soldier-pairs before we reached the Registry, and in each instance the first procedure was repeated, so that by the time I entered the dingy building I had an escort of what seemed to me charming and docile teddy bears, of average human height but more than human breadth. The facts that I was a good two feet taller than any of them and that none of them showed surprise at my height or exoskeleton doubtless added to my feeling of fairy-tale confidence.

It did not even bother me when the bear-soldiers pressed into the building before, beside, and behind me, and then remained in a half-circle around me as I introduced myself to a Kapitan Taimanov, a gloriously golden-furred Russian who appeared to be in charge of things at the Registry. I believed they were merely child-curious about me.

Taimanov waved me into a seat, called for vodka and caviar, and offered me a box from which I took a long thin cigarette. He snapped his furry fingers and a soldier leaped to light it. Somewhat to my disappointment, it was not weed, only tobacco; nevertheless I puffed it graciously.

Kapitan Taimanov was all smiles and courtesy. We chatted together lightly of Ivan the Terrible and Stalin, of Dostoevsky and Pasternak, of Moussorgsky and Khachaturian, of Alekhine and Keres. We almost started to play a game of chess. The only time his lip curled up from his formidable teeth was when a brown-pelted soldier ran his tongue around his furry mouth as I downed my sip and the captain his glass of vodka.

We complimented each other on our command of Russian, though his seemed to me a kind of pidgin compared to that I'd picked up in Circumluna.

Then he led the conversation around to myself.

For starters, I explained that I was a simple worker in the Communist underground in Texas and how I had played the part of Kawstee Chiluhvehk, or Bone Man—El Esqueleto —from Dallas to Fort Johnson, helping foment the Bent-Back Revolution, which had drawn Ranger units southward from Zhawlty Nawsh.

"Then I take it you are not one of ours?" he said. "I mean, those grown tall by deliberate misuse of the directional hormone in the laboratories and crèches of Lake Baikal, taught Texan, and sent to infiltrate that last evil stronghold of capitalism."

"No," I answered truthfully. "What is this about misuse of the directional hormone? I thought it was used solely by Texans to give them greater height."

He laughed and said, "I can see you are an innocent in some matters—that freakish thing, a native revolutionary." He paused a moment to frown, the short golden fur of his forehead furrowing. "Or else those at Baikal decided it was best to equip you with a completely false memory and identity. No matter. As for the directional hormone, we Russians employ it as Nature always intended—horizontally —so that we are stronger without additional strains on the heart, men able to cope with the surface gravity of Jupiter, if that should ever become necessary. It also acts upon our hair in a multiplicatory fashion, producing those pelts which make Siberian weather far easier to cope with and which also make summer nudity more aesthetic and cultural. Ah, my poor friend, you should see us sporting by the tens of thousands on the beaches around Baikal and the Black Sea!"

"Or around the nearest mud hole," I thought I heard a soldier mutter.

But Taimanov did not catch that. He was slowly and solemnly looking me up and down, concealing whatever pity or contempt he may have felt for my miserable figure— asthenic or cerebrotonic ultimate—in contrast with his own magnificent animal one. Finally he said most soulfully, a tear dropping from his left eye, "Poor tortured comrade, I can see without being told that you have spent many years in the prisons of Texas. It must have been there that you learned Russian, from some equally unfortunate and heroic captive. No, you do not have to explain, I know it all. They have accused us Russians of brainwashing our enemies by deprivation of food, sleep, and exercise, but what nation, except Texas, has applied carefully calculated starvation— and perhaps the rack!—to a point where a man is literally skin and bones, his muscles shriveled possibly beyond regeneration? Truly, the Soviets owe you much. But tell me this—what unsung genius of the Revolution provided you with that most clever powered framework which enables you to talk?"

"The Russians gave it to me," I answered, thinking further to win his favor—and actually lying not so much. At least half the technicians who had built my exo had been Circumlunan Russians.

"*Chawrtuh vuh ahduh!*" he cursed, half rising to his feet

and pounding on the table until the bottles jumped and it would have cracked, except it was four inches thick. "For fifty years the military has been asking the scientists for powered body armor for soldiers, and now at last we see it—secretly given away to a foreign agent by the state security apparatus! Your pardon, comrade, this is not your fault, but the practice makes me furious."

"You and your soldiers look to me so physically powerful," I put in placatingly, "that it would seem you would have no need of mechanical aids."

"True, we are as strong as Kodiak bears," he agreed. "But with powered body armor, we could leap rivers and single-handed encounter tanks and devastate cities. The atomic bomb would become a side arm. One soldier could liberate an entire Central American country. Grrr!"

The idea of bears able to leap rivers sounded to me about as desirable as spiders able to fly, though I did not voice the thought.

Meanwhile Taimanov was muttering, "Nothing too good for our foreign agents! Anything good enough for our soldiers! Grrr! But once more your pardon. Have more vodka. How else can I serve you?"

Emboldened by this encouragement and another large sip of vodka, I told him about my local mining claim. I pointed out that as an ardent revolutionary crippled for life, I perhaps deserved financial compensation.

He looked interested, said, "*Da?*" and inquired if I had documents to prove my claim.

Now was my big moment. I asked if he could provide me with the amenities of a powerful sunlamp and a razor or electric clippers.

Though mystified, he complied with my request. The electric clippers were especially fine and he confided in me that he cut his entire pelt close—*en brosch*—for the summer months.

Downing half of another vodka, I unlocked my rib cage at its center and folded it away to either side. Next I unzipped my winter suit from neck to crotch. The soldiers murmured approvingly at the amount of hair disclosed. I clipped it all off close and directed the large sunlamp at my ventral side.

"You are *that* cold, *tovarich?*" Taimanov expostulated. "Even the vodka has not warmed you? Perhaps a steam bath—"

I lifted my hand and pointed it toward my middle.

"Watch," I said.

The twelve pairs of fur-circled soulful eyes grew larger as tiny blue-gray marks began to appear on my torso. Soon the message there was completely developed.

Beginning high on my chest and traveling interminably downward, somewhat distorted by the scars of my patio crawl and by various rashes, but legible all the same, were line after line of slate-blue print and script, interspersed with signatures, X-marks, letterheads, and seals.

It was all upside down to me, but I knew it by heart.

For it was simply a facsimile of Nicholas Nimzovitch Nisard's provisional claim to his pitchblende mine, together with the three transfers of ownership and a Circumlunan confirmation.

My father hadn't entrusted me with the provisional claim, but, probably stealing the idea from some spy story, had had a facsimile of it tattooed on my chest and belly in a preparation of silver nitrate, so that it would be invisible until I exposed it to bright sunlight or a sunlamp, whereupon the hitherto invisible silver would precipitate out as a dark powder and the claim appear written on my skin, clearly and permanently.

I had certainly had a devil of a time keeping it undeveloped, especially in Lamar's patio. Now I felt fully repaid for my efforts.

I explained the gist of the document and its postscripts to Kapitan Taimanov.

He was amazed, as were his soldiers. He told me that I could undoubtedly obtain some large financial compensation, though it was not within his immediate power to grant it. General Kan would have to be consulted and possibly New Moscow. He poured me another vodka, offered me another cigarette, and came around his desk to examine the tattooing more closely.

I delicately sipped white fire and savored that burned essence of earthiness, tobacco.

Taimanov pointed a furry finger, horn-tipped, at the nethermost seal, a mandala quartering a cogwheel, tuning fork, beaker, and atom.

"What is that?" he inquired.

"The great seal of Circumluna," I explained, "confirming all the writing above to be authentic. You see, there is one further detail about myself which I have neglected to tell you: that in addition to my revolutionary status I am also a Circumlunan of the Sack, visiting Terra under the protection of—"

My words were lost in Taimanov's growl of fury and command. I realized that somehow success and vodka had made me careless.

Before I could so much as up the power of my exo, I was seized from all sides. A hard paw edge chopped expertly between my head basket and shoulder girdle, paralyzing me and, I thought, breaking my neck. Quite unnecessarily, another hand jabbed up under the front of my rib cage into my solar plexus, cutting off my breath.

Then Taimanov, his face the mask of an enraged bear, procured a pair of insulated wire cutters and snipped all the leads from my batteries to my servomotors.

I was hoisted up and rushed across the street to the old Amarillo Cuchillo jail, where my exo was removed and the two lightning pistols in my pouch waved in my face as proof that I was an assassin at least. I was shaken until I decided my neck wasn't broken, but would be shortly.

Next I found myself strapped down on a table, again quite unnecessarily, and being interrogated by a formidable black-furred Colonel Bolbochan, who smoked an atrocious fat cigar, about a Circumlunan plot to seize all Russia and, though he seemed to think this a matter of minor importance, the rest of Terra. He demanded to know how I had smuggled myself out of the *Tsiolkovsky*, what special instructions for sabotage and terrorism I had been given, and what devilish plans for further horrors the crew of the *Tsiol* had up their sleeves.

Apparently the ground-bear Russians were unable to assault the ship directly, though able to prevent its takeoff. It was a mystery to me.

In vain I insisted that I had left the *Tsiol* at Dallas and thereafter devoted myself to a rabble-rousing advantageous to Russia. In vain I assured him that the Circumlunan Russians were very nice people and constituted somewhat less than half of its population, and that they certainly had no designs against or much interest in Terran Russia. In vain I explained that I wasn't a true dweller in Circumluna, only an inhabitant of the subproletarian Sack, a harmless actor.

When after a short period I did not produce answers of the sort Bolbochan wanted, I was systematically beaten with rubber truncheons. The humiliation was immense and the pain most excruciating. I had feared I would be driven mad if again deprived of my exoskeleton on Terra, but that fear was quite swallowed up in the physical agonies I was suffering. The shock of the blows prevented me from inventing a story that might even temporarily have satisfied the colonel. It even stopped me from getting any profit from the philosophic notion that Death should make himself familiar with suffering, pain, and all other approaches toward . . . himself.

At one point I was asked to name my confederates: those still aboard the *Tsiol*, those who had sneaked aground with me, and also the still fouler beings—Terran collaborators with the Russo-Circumlunan devils.

The only thing that kept me silent then was the remaining tatter of rational thought that it wouldn't help me one bit to have Mendoza and Company rounded up and beaten like myself. Still, I would soon have confessed even that, to halt the torture, if Black Bolbochan's questions had not gone rocketing off into a farago about "moon monsters" that the satellitic Russians were planning to set loose in Siberia. Was I a moon monster?

He had embarked on an even wilder inquiry about "Mars beetles" capable of devouring all Terra's vegetation, when a grizzled General Kan came galloping in and raised his hand —to command, I supposed, new and more ingenious tortures.

But I never learned what they were, for at that moment a velvet-gloved inner blackness seized me and dragged me deep, deep down.

15 / Death, with Spiders

Here now in his triumph where all things falter,
Stretched out on the spoils that his own hand spread,
As a god self-slain on his own strange altar
Death lies dead.

—"A Forsaken Garden," by Algernon Charles
Swinburne

As I CAME back to consciousness—or rather, as consciousness came back to me, for I certainly didn't want it—I discovered that I was in my coffin and they were nailing it up.

The hammering awakened all of my old pains and a remarkable number of new ones. And the greatest of the new
ones was cold.

I figured that there must be about ten hammerers pounding away, and the nails by now as thick as pearls on a
string.

I knew I was still on Terra, because Gravity was in the
coffin with me. It struck me as peculiarly unfair that Gravity should operate even inside coffins. One would think that
at least death would bring release from the horrible force,
but it doesn't. Such are the merciless ways of Terra.

I commanded my eyes to open, so that I could look at the
absolute darkness around me. I knew it would be absolute
darkness, because no slightest glow came through my eyelids.

But my eyelids, which were heavy and thick with one of
the new pains, refused to part. One more proof that I was
dead indeed.

How I could still feel pain while dead was a problem
that I pigeonholed. I guess I didn't want to have to admit
that hell existed.

I attempted to reassess my situation philosophically. I

was in great cold, in absolute darkness, in great pain (pigeonhole that one!), and inside my coffin (and they were still pounding on it).

Well, one expects a coffin to be chilly and dark. It is also in the nature of coffins to be nailed up (though this one was taking a long time about it).

But, especially if one has any illusions whatever left about the courtesy of humanity, one expects a coffin to fit—to be, in my case, about ten by two by one and a half feet, inside dimensions. And, if humanity is especially considerate, to be comfortably lined, preferably with quilted silk.

My coffin had no lining and it definitely did not fit. In fact, from the way my body was contorted, I could tell that it was little more than four by four by four feet. My head, tilted up, lay in a bottom corner. My back was gravity-pressed against the coffin's hard bottom, which had a lattice of cracks in it, rather like the floor of President Lamar's patio. My legs rose sharply up and my feet were wedged into the upper corner of the box opposite my head.

Yes, my coffin was a mere box, an ignominious cube. And would they please stop pounding on it!

It next occurred to me that, as a hero of the Bent-Back Revolution, I should have been encoffined in high state, wearing my exoskeleton and with at least two gold medals, the other reading Socialist Actor Extraordinary.

But I clearly didn't have my exoskeleton. I was wearing only my winter suit and it was strangely loose on my torso, accounting in part for my frigid state.

I began to try to figure out what had happened to me prior to my encoffination. My first theory was that I had been thrown down the Crazy-Russian Mohole, landed in a bed of feathers a kilometer thick, and found myself in the Realm of the Dead, whose monitors had nailed me up in this cramping and shameful box as punishment for impersonating Death in the world above.

And were continuing to nail.

There were several things wrong with that theory. To

mention only one, the Crazy-Russian Mohole was filled from bottom to top with red-hot and blue-radioactive magma.

I tried to think of another theory, but the hammering wouldn't let me. Instead, it reignited my every pain.

It got louder and louder, less and less endurable.

It became a hammering not on my coffin, but on my head basket, then on my naked skull and face.

As I realized I had been wanting to do all along, I escaped by dying.

I instantly made a remarkable discovery. Whether one dies for a minute or a million million years, it seems no time at all to the one who dies.

For the next thing I knew, consciousness had come snuffling back to my body like the persistent beast it is. It sniffed me from head to toes, from feet to fingertips. Then it nuzzled my neck and leaped inside my skull and curled up there, wide-eyed, ears a-prick, and still sniffing.

I was in precisely the same situation as I had been before, except for one wonderful difference: the hammering had stopped. I still felt a wide spectrum of pains, but now I felt them silently. Whoever had been pounding my coffin had gone away.

Perhaps the pounding had been only in my head all along. Perhaps it had been the pounding of my heart frantically trying to make my ghost muscles work by oversupplying them with glucose and oxygen, and now at last sensibly shifted into neutral and only idling along.

I wondered if it was now pumping hard enough to keep alive my toes, which were so high above me. Oh well, better gangrene of the toes than gangrene of the brain, my consciousness informed me.

Where did I get that idea I was alive when I knew I was dead? Better suppress it. Cool it, consciousness!

I worked hard on keeping myself dead. I concentrated on stilling every part of myself, beginning with the toes. This worked very well on my muscles, since most of them were ghosts to begin with, nonfunctional in six lunagravs.

There was the bonus that as I stilled each area of my body, the pain stopped coming from it.

I worked at suppressing my thoughts too, especially an effort to remember what had happened to me.

I also held on to the sneaky point that if only I were patient, if only I remained passive while enough time passed—not very much—then I would surely be dead of freezing, dehydration, heart failure, starvation, or gangrene of the toes, in approximately that order.

I do believe I would have completed the operation successfully except for one very nasty circumstance.

Two large and sturdy spiders appeared on either side of me and began determinedly to explore the floor of my cubical coffin.

When I say "appeared," I do not mean I saw them. But I became aware of them. I felt them. However, I had started to get a glow in my eyes that seemed not so much the random shooting-off of rods and cones as light coming through my immovable lids. In fact, I was working to suppress that glow when the two spiders turned up.

It happens that I have an irrational dread of spiders, though there are few in the Sack and those chiefly in arachnidariums, where they get along as well in free fall as insects and all other tiny beasts to whom gravity or its absence are matters of small moment.

So that when these turned up in my coffin, I was pretty thoroughly terrorized.

A peculiarly horrible particular was that these spiders were cripples. Each had had three legs amputated, but the operations had been completely successful and they got around very well on their remaining five legs.

How I could know so much about the spiders without being able to see into their minds also troubled me. Not, as I have said, that I have any psi talents, or that spiders are known to be open to telepathy. Still, I was troubled.

Finally, the spiders seemed much too much interested in my wrists, persistently nuzzling them and even pushing and pulling them around. I waited each moment for the stab of a poison fang. Go on, spiders, get it over with, I found myself thinking—it will only be a sixth way of dying.

Then the two spiders approached my sides and began to crawl up onto my body, dragging my arms behind them.

It was at this point I realized that the spiders were my two hands.

Though it may seem strange to some, this was no great improvement. Lying helpless in the dark while one's two hands begin to operate completely on their own, schizo-phrenically, is almost as bad as spiders, believe me.

Pinching first my suit and then cruelly pinching the skin of my chest, which was to my surprise smooth and hairless, they crawled up side by side to my neck, where they parted, each making for an ear.

By Pluto, I thought, they are planning to strangle me!

Why the idea of being strangled, or even self-strangled, should have terrified me so, when I was exerting every atom of willpower to kill myself and/or keep myself dead, is pretty mysterious. Perhaps by now I was becoming luxury-minded and wanted to die in comfort, with ever diminishing pains.

But then I noticed that neither of my hands had left a thumb behind on my windpipe, as they would surely have done if their purpose had been strangulation and they had any sense at all.

I relaxed a bit and waited with some curiosity to see what they were up to.

You see, I was already crediting them with sense and purpose. They say a man is essentially two hands and a brain. I was pretty sure by now that my hands were coop-erating with a section or self of my brain below the con-scious level, which last level had been wanting only to die and/or stay dead—until this moment, when curiosity had begun to motivate it.

Meanwhile, my crawling hands had each gripped an ear-lobe very tightly with thumb and trigger finger. From this secure base, and with each digging little finger into cheek, they dug middle finger and ring finger into my upper and lower eyelids, and then spread.

This caused me even more pain than I expected, because it turned out that my eyelids were extremely badly swollen. Also, my eyeballs were unusually sensitive. I got the impression that this area of my face at least had undergone a severe allergic reaction, or else received repeated blows.

But no matter how hard I willed them to stop and despite the hoarse little screams that now began to issue from my dry throat, my fingers went cruelly and remorselessly about their business.

Bright gay light lanced into my eyes and tormented my retinas and the visual centers of my brain—a third and not to be underrated pain.

Finally tears came, and at first they were a pain too. For a while I saw only their glimmer and the yellow blurs of matter floating in them.

Gradually the pains diminished. My swollen lids became able to blink with my fingers' help and even assume most of the work of keeping themselves open. My tears washed the grainy, gluey stuff away, and I was able to see.

I was in a morticed stone cell with a door of bars and a small barred window. Its dimensions were those of the height of a Mexican door, so I assumed it had originally been built by Texans for bent-backs.

The light came through the window and another like it in the corridor beyond the door of bars. Cold wind came in too.

Through the nearer window I could see a high sign that carried, white on black, the ten Cyrillic characters spelling out "Zhawlty Nawsh."

So I was not in the hands of the Rangers, but the Russians.

Horrible memories began to rise.

I kept them submerged while I traveled my gaze down my body from my catercorner toes.

My black winter suit was open wide from my crotch to
my neck, revealing my hairless front covered by upside-
down lines of legal writing.

I remembered everything—in particular, every last stupidity.

It only made me want to die all over again.

But even as I felt that, I noted that my fingers had left
my eyes, which stayed open a fair slit without manual aid
and were crawling down my torso toward my crotch, where
I was intuitively sure they intended to start zipping me up.

This indication that the survival urge was once again in
control had the effect of steadying if not cheering me. While
my hands worked, I began the unpleasant business of as-
sessing my situation.

Fortunately in such a case one need not begin by facing
the worst, but can work up to it by easy stages. For instance, the first healthy reaction to a feeling of extreme
guilt is the attempt to shift as much of that guilt as possible
to other people.

So it was not unnatural that my first thoughts were about
my father, not angry so much as gently pitying thoughts,
very sentimental.

The poor old boob, I thought, running his theater in
space, not knowing a damn thing about Terra, but dream-
ing his idiot dream about the mining claim that would one
day make us all rich.

Did it occur to him that the claim was only provisional,
that the country in which it was registered had changed
hands at least once and now two times, that the Terrans
have millions of laws to stop boobs like himself from asserting their rights and claiming cash due them, and that without exception the Terrans are a planet of swindlers and
roughnecks, intent only on money and power and ready on
the slightest provocation to substitute violence for legal
procedure? Oh, no!

And then he had got the superidiot idea of sending me,

his only son, down to terrible Terra to cash in on the mining claim.

He did get the Longhairs to build me a remarkable exoskeleton. I granted him that. But did he otherwise enlist their aid in his project? At least they knew a hell of a lot more about Terra than he did.

No and double no! Instead he supplied me with a cloak, cane swords, and an idiotically secret document.

And I, superboob that I was, had accepted this ridiculous role, even gloried in it. For a whole terrible month on Terra, I had not lived, I had *acted* my way through everything.

First I had been tempted by a mysterious role in a Texan palace revolution.

Next I had eagerly plunged into the role of Death, leader of a grotesque adobe-hut revolution.

Finally I had been unable to resist putting on a brief show of surprises for some talking bears—an ultimate in wrong-way animal acts.

Had even my love for Rosa and Rachel been anything but theater? Probably not. Everybody is always telling us actors that because we feel or seem to feel so much in the theater, we can't feel anything in real life.

Well then, face it, Scully, I told myself. For you, the great themes of Love and Death can be nothing but melodrama. You're playing a small role in a vast thriller with an unknown finish.

Except that your role, bar last-minute rescues, seems just about ready to finish in death in an unheated Russian prison cell.

So start playing that role and quit bawling!

At that moment I heard a familiar voice roaring in the corridor. The language was Russian, but the import was pure Texan.

"Quit fussing at me, you furry little fools! I want to see Comrade La Cruz instanter. As consular agent of Texas in Zhawlty Nawsh, I got the right. Besides, can't you get the fur out of your eyes long enough to recognize General Kan's seal and signature? If you keep hindering me, I'll report you to him. I'll report you to Number One in New Moscow. I'll hold up on those chess sets from the Black Republic. I'll even stop that shipment of firewater and fish eggs I got coming in from Quebec! There, that's more like it now."

Then a great familiar bulk filled the barred, Mexican-short doorway.

"Wal, partner," the bulk said, "you sure have got yourself in the goldurnedest, most miserablest, hopelessest fix since Sam Houston got his army backed against the San Jacinto River just before the like-named battle."

I never would have thought that a time would ever come when the person I was most happy to see of all the *hombres* in the ripsnortin', melodramatic universe was Elmo Oilfield Earp.

16 / Fixing

After the burial-parties leave
And the baffled kites have fled;
The wise hyenas come out at eve
To take account of our dead.

—Rudyard Kipling

BY THE NEXT day, twenty-fourth Spindletop, Elmo had got me, in quite rapid succession, the following comforts: soup, a mattress, a battery to heat my winter suit, a larger cell, and—at last!—my exoskeleton. The Russians had removed its swords and all batteries but two, so that it operated at about quarter power. Sometimes I felt I was carrying it around, rather than it me. And when I plugged in my suit heater, it stopped moving altogether. Still, it was wonderful wearing it again.

At first I had been so happy to see Elmo that it had not occurred to me to wonder how he came to be there.

Later, thinking it over, I realized he must have been planning everything from our first meeting at Spaceport Dallas, possibly even earlier. I did not ask him straight out if he is a Russian secret agent, and he certainly did not volunteer that information.

The war is over, he tells me. Russia says she is planning no further advances, Texas no reprisals, and a truce has been agreed to. Elmo's story is that he is a loyal Texan who just happened to be in the neighborhood when Texas sorely needed a consular agent in Zhawlty Nawsh. Just happened to be! But perhaps I had best pretend to believe this tall tale. As the big rascal says, "Scully, most people in this imperfect world are so set on what they got to have, come hell or high water, and on what they won't take under no

circumstances, that there just got to be a few fixers around
—broad-minded *hombres* willing to sacrifice their personal
integrity, or even on rare occasions their sacred honor, just
to get life moving again, or keep it barely turning over like
a wore-out engine."

He confirmed my belated suspicion that all the rank-and-
file Russians and most of the officer and bureaucrat class
firmly believe that the Russians of Circumluna are the ultimate devils, the super-Trotskyites, worse than Chinese,
Texans, or the blackest-dyed fascists or inkiest blacks.
Well, why shouldn't they, after a century of propaganda
attributing every evil from meteorite showers to anti-Soviet
dreams to the malignant intervention of intellectual Russians in the sky?

But, Elmo says, the Russian inner elite, her real rulers,
have come to realize that their country desperately needs
certain items that only Circumluna can furnish them: fine
instruments, computer circuits, new higher maths. They
are seeking a rapprochement with Circumluna that will
permit trade without scandalizing or driving into revolt the
rank and file.

General Kan, I gather, is the sole local member of the
elite. He has been able to prevent attacks on the *Tsiolkovsky*,
but he must keep her crew in quarantine to satisfy military
prejudice. He also was the one who halted my torture, though
not daring to go so far as to command special care for me.
That had to be left to Elmo the Fixer, so he could be blamed
if necessary.

We had beet borsch for dinner.

Next day Elmo procured me the unheard-of amenity of a
hot bath. I was unwilling until I learned El Tácito and
Mendoza would give it to me, in guise of Elmo's greaser
servants. I was considerably refreshed, though my varicosities, etc., had worsened dismally. I quit prison-pacing—slow
motion in my under-batteried exo—got a maximum of horizontal.

Tas slipped me twin notes from Rosa and Rachel. Both hoping for my swift recovery and wishing me good fortune. Both signed, "Affectionately." I wondered if either or both of them would come to the moon with me. By their ultimatum to me, I would have to choose between them. It would be a very hard choice. I decided to play the scenes as they came.

That evening Elmo brought such good news I could hardly believe it. It set my imagination racing. Through General Kan, he has learned that the Russian inner elite is considering a deal whereby I, as hero of the Bent-Back Revolution, would be presented with a "reward" of materials needed by Circumluna. Later, still as hero, not Circumlunan or Sackabond, I would make "Party contribution" of stuff Russia needs from Circumluna.

As part of the deal, I would also have formally to give up my family's claim to the Lost Crazy-Cree (new name) Pitchblende Mine. I asked him, "Why so much fuss by pirates over paper proprieties?" He replied, "Scully, you don't understand these Russians. If their fur were as all tied up as their nerves are inside them, they'd be kinky as blacks. They're not relaxed like Texans. They don't think broad and easy about moral and legal issues. When they pull a fast one, they want every detail that reflects a bit of good on them pinned down tight."

I then asked him worriedly that if the "gift" to me were automatically supposed to go to the Circumlunans, would I also be able to use it to get from the Circumlunans the concessions I wanted for the La Cruz Theater and all Sackabonds. He told me, "Look, Scully, you hang on to that gift and you bargain with it until you get what you want. I guarantee you the Longhairs will play ball. I'm sorry to say it, Scully, but I sometimes think you weren't born with the business sense of a squirrel—what am I saying, squirrel, I mean lemming."

On reconsideration, this made me wonder if Elmo weren't in on the whole deal to bring me down to Terra—the building of my exoskeleton, even Father's idiot notion . . . I didn't know where to stop.

Next day, Spindletop twenty-sixth, there was a hideous development. Elmo brought news that the Russians were demanding the facsimile mining claim, removed from my chest, before they would play ball. They insisted on their "pound of flesh," were bad as Shylock. They promised to make a repair skin graft on me, but that would take more weeks, months on Terra with chances of survival very slim. Elmo said, "Don't worry, Scully, I'll argue my best with them, though they're stubborner critters than President Austin was, bless him, the pighead. When a bear decides to claw you, it's hard to change his mind by appealing to his logic and common sense."

That night we got soup with tatters of meat in it, but I couldn't touch it.

To get my mind off the horrible possibility of being flayed, I gave it the tough task of figuring out which of the two girls to ask to marry me. After long listings of their good and bad qualities, my feelings, etc., I decided on Rosa Morales. The chief point was that, under all fieriness, she has basic Latin submissiveness, while Rachel would try to run me. I was not happy about my decision, but determined to stick to it.

Elmo also reported that Fanninowicz had formally defected to the Russians. When and if he recovers from the dose of radioactivity he got at the gusher, he will go to Novy Tech as full professor of engineering and design power armor for Russian soldiers, borrowing many details from my exoskeleton, I'm sure. It figures. If all Terra felt peaceful except one destruction-bent farmboy, a German would build him a slingshot.

On Spindletop twenty-seventh, the Russians were still after my hide. Yet life must go on, no matter what horrors loom, so when Rosa visited me in jail, I proposed marriage to her. She kept me in suspense for a long time, made me really argue.

Clincher was when I told her she would be top free-fall dancing girl and star acrobat in La Cruz Theater. I added, "Besides—but don't tell anyone this—I have always had a terrific yen for short girls."

She yielded then and immediately demanded we summon "the Honorable Miss Lamar," and tell her about my decision in Rosa's presence.

Here I drew the line and also blew my top. I insisted that while still on Terra I simply could not bear to hurt Rachel, who had done so many things for me, even saved my life. She could be told after Rosa and I were off Earth, but not now. Rosa told me the marriage deal was off. We argued and argued.

We finally hit on a compromise. With Rosa looking on and fighting over each word, wanting to make it harsher, I wrote Rachel a letter breaking the news gently, but telling her in no uncertain terms I was marrying Rosa and leaving the tall Texan forever, sorry about that. We then gave the letter to Elmo, to be delivered to Rachel immediately after *Tsiol*'s blast-off.

I also extracted from Rosa her promise—hand on imaginary Bible, heart crossed—that she would not tell Rachel, by word or indirection, about her victory.

I told Elmo I would be taking him up on that "wife" reservation on *Tsiol*. He grinned and made a ring of thumb and middle finger, to assure me it was as good as done.

Afterwards I felt miserable, but reminded myself I had taken the only sensible course. After all, every woman in the universe is basically monogamous and accepts other arrangements—polygamy, even polyandry, etc.—when they are the only game in town.

Secretly I knew I would grieve forever for Rachel. Yet I consoled myself with the knowledge that I had done the wise thing.

Besides, there is always Idris McIllwraith.

Twenty-eighth Spindletop was a day for rejoicing. The Russians agreed to content themselves with photographs of my ventral side, plus quitclaim signed and sworn to by me, provided Father sends down original claim by first rocket. I patted myself on chest with *great* feelings of relief. Departure was planned for the next day.

All my happiness was completely dashed when Rachel paid me an unexpected visit in jail. From zenith to nadir in one easy jump. She was wearing her Black Madonna rig, damn her, minus pistols, of course, and looking very chipper.

Her chipperness faded, but she kept a brave smile as she said, "Captain Skull, I wish to tender you my sincerest congratulations and wish you a long life of bliss."

"Thanks, but what do you mean?" I asked, automatically sparring for time. "That I won't lose my front skin? Yes, I'll be happy about that the rest of my life. I don't know about blissful."

"You know what I mean," she said softly. "You and Rosa. From the first time I saw you together, I knew you were meant for each other. That's why I lit into her so fierce. Even then I realized I was just a clumsy old Texas gal, meant to be a poetry-writin' and little-theater old maid, and nothin' else. But don't you grieve, Scully, don't you give me a thought, except maybe to remember just for a moment on dark nights in space that there was once a platinum-haired girl in black on a silver horse, who loved you a little."

"What do you mean, me and Rosa?" I asked. Dammit, Rosa had promised me she wouldn't tell. "And who is supposed to have loved me a little, you or your horse?"

"You know what I mean, Scully," she said and then added in a shaky whisper, "Marryin' up. Gettin' hitched."

"Did Rosa tell you that?" I demanded furiously, my voice shaking. Dammit, a promise is a promise.

"Oh, no, she didn't tell me in so many words," Rachel assured me. "But I knew she'd been visiting you and nobody could have misread the meaning of the brightness in her eyes. Besides that, she danced all over the tent." Then the Black Madonna drew herself up. "As for my horse, Scully, if he ever meets you again, I hope he kicks your face in!"

At that moment I became, in absolutely cold blood, an utter cad. I said, "Listen to me, Rachel, Rosa lied to you, or at any rate, she did everything in her power to create a false impression. When she visited me yesterday here, she asked me to marry her and I turned her down. Oh, I was as nice about it as I could be—you and I both know she's a good little trouper—but in essence I turned her down. You're the only woman I ever loved in my life, princess, and you know it. Captain Skull's heart is yours—to tromp on or toss aside, if that's your pleasure—but yours forever!"

Despite my eloquence, it took me a remarkably long time to win her. She was especially suspicious about me having turned Rosa down. Feeling myself every second a vicious hypocrite and complete villain, I had to invent proof after proof until she consented to believe me. And then there still remained all the work of persuading Rachel to marry me. I finally managed it only by promising her she'd be star tragedienne of the La Cruz Theater and that we'd produce both *Houston's Afire* and *Storm Over El Paso*. (Would they be fringe-acceptable? Oh well, we have play-doctors. I'm one myself.)

I also had to add, "Besides—but don't tell anyone this—I have always had a terrific yen for tall girls."

"How'd you find that out?" she demanded. "What other tall females has your fickle heart been fixed on, Scully darlin'?"

Great Jupiter! I had to talk fast and watch my every word not to bring in the name of Idris McIllwraith.

But in the end she did accept me.

And then—oh, my aching mind—we had to repeat every detail Rosa had insisted on, down to Rachel's supervising me while I wrote the letter of sad rejection to Rosa and we sealed it and handed it over to Elmo for delivery after the

Tsiol's blast-off. My nerves were zinging for fear he'd give the show away, but he didn't.

After Rachel had gone, however, he did tell me, "Scully, I must say I think you're a natural-born hero of the punishment-seeking sort. Wives are a combination of gadfly, rattlesnake, and colt or cow. I ain't ever had the unwisdom, and maybe nerve too, to take on even one. And here you are putting yourself in the ring with two—and not on Terra either, where at least there's space to disappear into, but up in the Sack, where I gather things are a bit cozy. Oh well, every man to his own insanity. I suppose you'll be wanting another 'wife' ticket on the *Tsiol*. Guess I can wangle it, if you'll agree to give the Russki photographers a free hand with you the next couple days."

"Can't be 'wife,'" I told him. "*Tsiol's* crew is all Russki, and Russian Circumlunans are all most conventionally moral, at least as far as us Sackabonds are concerned. A bigamous actor is just what they're waiting for. Had better be 'sister,' I guess. At least our heights agree."

"'Sister' it'll be. But how you going to justify that to Rachel? Or Kookie either?"

"My problem. And one more favor, *amigo*. On take-off day, please see to it that each of them is privately summoned to *Tsiol* at different times, and that they're at least strapped down—and preferably given spacesickness, et cetera, injections—before they know the other's aboard."

"Do my best, old hoss, though it'd be a mercy to you if I botched it."

Soon as he was gone, I flopped and stayed horizontal twelve hours. The session with Rachel had really finished me. And tomorrow, photographers! I wondered if Russki ones are such wearisome clots as Sack "artists of the camera." What artistry is there in pushing the button of a machine that sausage-slices visual reality?

Also, of course, guilts, fears, and apprehensions tore me. Even in the Sack, bigamy must be by freest consent of all parties concerned.

Oh well, man is by nature polygamous, or at least aspires to be so, and women must make the best of it. For they *are* the best, or else I, to name one, wouldn't want any one of them—let alone two.

The Russki photographers finished with me on the last of Spindletop—and they came closer to finishing me, too, than even my marathon wooing of Rachel. They also proved much worse than Sack snapshooters, throwing me around and posing me as if I were a sack of flour, demanding the impossible of me physically, especially in motion shots, grudging me occasional minutes in which to eat, eliminate, and pass out, just as if there were no labor laws whatsoever in the Homeland of Socialism. (Guess there still aren't.)

They wore out all my batteries, so I would have had to be carried abroad the *Tsiolkovsky*, except that General Kan made a surly quartermaster hunt me up replacements from those used in C.C.C.P. power weapons. He also restored me my telescopic swords, because cameramen wanted process shots of me pinking Austin, Lamar, Hunt, Chase, Burleson, and a whole detachment of fake Rangers. From now on I am a gone goose in the Lone Star Republic. No one there will believe I was anything but a knowing Russian agent from the moment I landed in Dallas.

The photogs also made use of me to the very end, for the last shots had to be of me boarding *Tsiolkovsky* amid a crowd of cheering Mexes and Cree Indians, who had gotten themselves a commissar now and were finding life a little more strenuous, what with the rigors of Russian overlordship being added to the rigors of nature in this new slice of Hither Siberia.

But somehow I managed to endure the worst the photogs could dish out and still stay erect on my exolegs. If all those pix don't sell me—and indirectly Circumluna—to the Russki rank and file, I don't know what can.

During those last shots I managed to say my warm goodbyes to Guchu, El Tácito, Carlos Mendoza, and Father Francisco, who blessed me surreptitiously and told me he has discovered he has a mission to convert the Crees, but not to mention it.

Guchu said, "Back to the Acificpay Chosen for me. Every time I consort with you ofays, I find you're crazier squares than before. Drop out, man, and turn off."

Old Tas grunted a sardonic, "*Vaya con* La Muerte, El Esqueleto." I countered, "Before I 'go with Death,' he'll have to fight me to the finish." He shrugged. "What other way?"

Mendoza shook my hand. "For El Toro too," he said. We squeezed hard.

Elmo contacted me at the end, though he was careful to keep out of the pictures and our conversation out of earshot. He explained, "A fixer's got to keep out of humanity's eye and forgo the plaudits of the public, no matter how much his ego'd be soothed by a little notoriety. Yeah, the gals are both aboard, God help you, just as you asked for them to be. Here's a pack of reefers and a jug of tequila to soothe your nerves—they're gonna need it. Now you screw the most you can, you hear me, out of those Longhairs for your 'gift.' Nobody looks after a man but a man. Remember you got no head for money, but lucky impulses, and you'll never go far wrong. Incidentally—but keep this under your head basket—don't expect Texas to take her defeat lying down. Russia's got one mohole mine, but Lone Star's got two hundred."

"Which side are you really on, Elmo?" I asked him impulsively.

"Mine," he grinned at me. "Leastways, that's all anybody's ever going to get me to admit to when I'm honest-talking."

Going aboard *Tsiolkovsky* was like returning to Circumluna, except for the continuing curse of gravity. Everything was clean, except me. All the people were calm and intelligent, even if slightly condescending. I saw the "gift" carefully stowed, then followed my learned doctor-stewardess to my water mattress in a small alcove curtained to either side. I flopped gratefully.

"You will remove your prosthetic," she informed me in purest classic Russian.

"*Nyet*," I informed her.

She shrugged. "I shall strap you down."

Another "*Nyet*" from me. "There are handholds," I added.

Another shrug from her. "Injections?"

"*Da*," I agreed. She made them, sniffing at me a little.

When she was gone, I opened the curtains on either side. To my left and right, on similar mattresses, but strapped down, were Rachel Vachel and La Cucaracha. Each smiled at me dreamily. Then they saw each other.

"Why, you dirty, double-crossin', bigamy-bent Bluebeard," Rachel gasped.

"Beard black," I informed her coolly. "Bigamy is the mildest of marital variations in the Sack."

"Liar! Blasphemer! Betrayer of virgins!" Kookie spat at me from the other side. "I warn you, you black worm, never trust me with a sharp knife. I shall employ it to separate you from your organs of generation!"

"I'll hold him down," Rachel told her.

"Beloveds," I said serenely, "in Cincinnati one of you said, 'It may be different in the sky.' Believe me, it will be. Meanwhile, let us look on this simply as another theatrical tour, indefinitely extended."

"My anger is destroying my mind!" Rosa wailed.

"Scully, Ah'm fit to be tied," Rachel said.

"You are tied," I reminded her.

The stewardess returned. "Raise ship in one minute. Now minus fifty-eight seconds. A disturbance here?"

"Indeed yes!" Rosa cried. "I am this villain's wife and I wish to get off this filthy ship at once!"

"Ah'm his wife," Rachel contradicted her. "And Ah'm the one wants to debark."

I moved my forefingers in little circles at my temples.

The stewardess looked at a card in her hand. "It says

'sister' here." Unsmiling, she waved a finger at me once. "You folk of the Sack give Circumluna a most unfortunate reputation. You are not *kulturny*. But what is one to expect of actors? Minus forty-three." She departed.

At that moment the p.a. system most opportunely struck up with "The Saber Dance" from Khachaturian's *Gayne*, almost drowning out the girls' outraged babblings. I lightly touched a finger to either ear. I could feel the drugs taking hold. But I resisted them through the shock of blast-off and the dreadful minutes of eighteen lunagravs until breenschlusz.

Then, even as I was passing out, I felt the delicious release from bondage. My ghost muscles stirred. My exoskeleton became an encumbrance. I was back in my only proper environment.

17 / A Hundred Years Later

Far away the Rachel-Jane
Sings amid a hedge of thorns:—
"Love and life,
Eternal youth—
Sweet, sweet, sweet, sweet."

—"The Santa Fe Trail," by Vachel Lindsay

My GREAT-GREAT-GRANDSON has just returned from a trip downstairs. For sentimental reasons I wished him to wear my exoskeleton, but the Longhairs have invented an anti-grav suit that is little more than silvery overalls. So Good Old Titanium remained in his transparent museum ovoid.

Times change. But only a little. The La Cruz Theater-in-the-Sphere goes on from hit to hit and flop to flop. Longhair synthograv (inevitable mate to antigrav) makes entrances and exits easier. Thought projectors give new dramas enriched subjective content.

Father and Mother retired, are thinking of spending last years in new transparent-translucent all-plastic satellite, the Ship, building 180 degrees away in same orbit as Circumluna. A quarter of Ship's population will be Circumlunan colonists, the rest Terran refugees.

My wives still bicker with me and each other, but mostly we get on famously. It is years since they confessed to me that way back in Dallas they had decided to come with me to the Sack as bigamous wives. They had just wanted to get out of me the best deal they could.

Long ago we produced *Houston's Afire*. It has become a stock item in our repertoire. Next week we premiere *Storm Over El Paso*.

Rachel Vachel quite rapidly transformed into an exquisite

Thin and, besides her tragic acting, poetry, and playwriting, began to alternate strip routines with Idris McIllwraith. With such activities and the passing years, President Lamar's daughter has developed a more relaxed morality, which is natural in a Texan, come to think of it. But I do not know about her affairs, if any. I never spy on my wives and expect, though I do not always get, the same courtesy from them.

La Cucaracha remains completely unchanged, a natural Athletic, a demanding wife, and a shrew cat for jealousy. She is the Sack's unequaled aerobatrix and now that we have synthograv, entertains with classic flamenco dances.

Fifty years ago, partly to assert my independence, I had a mad love affair with Idris McIllwraith, which for two weeks was the talk of the Sack and Circumluna's shame. It ended when Rosa sliced me twice, fortunately only across the chest. She was fined—for nicking bubble with wild slash and almost depressurizing Sack compartment.

Poor Idris. Twenty years ago Rachel developed a serious heart degeneration—it is not safe to go Thin after childhood. But then Idris was explosively brained by a tiny meteorite—first time such a thing happened—and Rachel received her aged but hale heart as transplant. She sometimes asks, "How's it make you feel, Scully, to have your old girl friend's heart beating inside me?" How to answer that one?

Aside from Idris we are all going strong. Circumlunan biologists have developed the Texo-Russian directional hormone and are applying it neither vertically nor horizontally, but temporally, so that a man is taller in time. In any case, who ever dies in free fall? At first and even second appearance, it is a most harsh environment, yet I believe life and man were meant for it. Life itself appeared and had its first great flowering in a kind of free fall, the sea. As life shifted some of its companies to land, the battle against gravity continued—the insects by their lightness and wings, the bird also. Even our immediate and happy-go-lucky tree-dwelling forebears had their own small idea about the achievement of free fall. Now with our nullgrav existence and technological antigrav, we are perhaps really going somewhere. At any rate, it can be a good life.

For almost a century Russian "gifts" squared Sack's account with Circumluna. But then, due in part to great military reverses, a new spasm of Marxist fundamentalism and of hate for Sky-Russians developed in C.C.C.P. "Gifts" cut off quick. Circumlunans, used to them, blamed us Sackabonds. It was chiefly to find a new source of Terran funds that Christopher Crockett La Cruz V went downstairs.

He tells a strange story. Greatly aided by mohole radioactives, Texas mounted war after war against Russia and China. At the same time, unbridled and paranoidally grandiose use of hormone was creating generations of Texans ten and twelve feet high. These sometimes had brilliant minds, but were tragically short-lived—height's and mass's strain on heart and whole system, plus effects of mounting radioactivity of air, ground, sea, all else.

Texas had an army deep in Mongolia, when its general, a nineteen-year-old, thirteen-foot military genius of the Alexander-breed succumbed to early heart disease. At the same time, the Seventh Bent-Back Revolution was successful. Within a year all tall Texans were dead, unless there is truth in the report of small Texan colonies in Australia and Antarctica. They had gone the way of the dinosaurs and Peking Man—size developed at the expense of more important survival traits—too big for their ego and their dreams.

What was left of Texas became the curious nation of Anarquia Mehico—if a self-styled "anarchy" may be called a nation. Its boundary with Russia is approximately the ancient one between the old United States and Canada. The furry ones have become more and more arctic, uninterested in temperate-zone conquests. Besides, all the land to the south is badly contaminated by radioactivity from the moholes.

Anarquia is a curious and fairly promising nation, I gather, though it must devote much of its thought and energy to purifying its poisoned air, soil, water, people, and germ plasm. The combination of Latin, Indian, and short Texan (honorary Mex) seems not a bad one. Tall Texas left much salvageable industry, while the Mexes, gaining ground with each revolution, became a more prudent and industrious race.

At any rate, the La Cruz Theater and the Sack have found new funds there to help to pay their rent to Circumluna. The donor was the Mendoza-Earp Foundation for Serendipitous Studies, founded by the Carlos and the Elmer Oilfield whom I once knew.

Carlos lived to a great age for a Terran, dying only a quarter century ago, while Elmo disappeared in Africa some fifty years before that, during a mysterious "fixing" mission for the Pacific Black Republic. He left Mendoza, by illegal channels of course, a considerable fortune.

Recalling how he both sucked me in and took care of me, remembering his tall tales and belly realizm, but above all else his irreverent good humor, I like to think of him still going on with his "fixing," somewhere.